THE COMING OF THE "TALL MEN"

The ship came to a dead stop and hovered. A door slid open in its belly and a dozen figures dropped out. . . .

Cale stared, horrified. Even as he watched, the figures seemed to sprout wings and float toward earth, firing arbuses as they came.

He knew who they were. Here, on this planet, they were clad in trench coats and fedora hats, their temple pieces disguised as sunglasses. On other planets they would wear other things, but their intent was always the same: to kill.

These were the *ga'lim*, the "Tall Men." They operated in secret, in the dark places of the government where Cale and his father did not like to look. That they were here meant only one thing: The Dragit did not intend for anyone assembled to escape. . . .

INVASION AMERICA:
ON THE RUN

• • • • • •

Christie Golden

DreamWorks

ROC
Published by the Penguin Group
Penguin Putnam Inc., 375 Hudson Street,
New York, New York 10014, U.S.A.
Penguin Books Ltd, 27 Wrights Lane,
London W8 5TZ, England
Penguin Books Australia Ltd, Ringwood,
Victoria, Australia
Penguin Books Canada Ltd, 10 Alcorn Avenue,
Toronto, Ontario, Canada M4V 3B2
Penguin Books (N.Z.) Ltd, 182–190 Wairau Road,
Auckland 10, New Zealand

Penguin Books Ltd, Registered Offices:
Harmondsworth, Middlesex, England

First published by Roc, an imprint of Dutton NAL,
a member of Penguin Putnam Inc.

First Printing, November, 1998
10 9 8 7 6 5 4 3 2 1

 REGISTERED TRADEMARK—MARCA REGISTRADA

Printed in the United States of America

BOOKS ARE AVAILABLE AT QUANTITY DISCOUNTS WHEN USED TO PROMOTE
PRODUCTS OR SERVICES. FOR INFORMATION PLEASE WRITE TO PREMIUM
MARKETING DIVISION, PENGUIN PUTNAM INC., 375 HUDSON STREET, NEW
YORK, NEW YORK 10014.

This book is dedicated
to Michael,
my *Kia-thamaa*

ACKNOWLEDGMENTS

This book could not have been written without the help of several people. I'd like to thank Steven Spielberg, who created *Invasion America* in the first place; Harve Bennett, for his unstinting faith in and enthusiasm for my work; my "wise" readers, Michael Georges and Robert Amerman, for spotting plot holes before they got too big; my editor, Laura Anne Gilman, and agent, Lucienne Diver, for providing me with a project that proved to be nothing but sheer delight; Malcolm Simpson, M.D., an old and dear friend, who helped ensure that Dr. Rainsinger knew what he was talking about; the members of the Navajo nation; and John Hallack and Joseph F. Buchanan from the University of Utah, who helped me better understand the university and its computer system circa 1981. Any errors in this text are entirely my own.

Though some of the locales are real, they are, of course, filtered through the author's imagination. Many, such as Broken Rock and Turquoise Mesa, are entirely fictional, as are all the characters. Again, thank you all. May you walk in beauty.

PROLOGUE

• • •

September 1976
Mount Elgon, Uganda

The African rain forest had a song.

No pleasant melody this; it was a wild song, its musicians the innumerable creatures who lived here, and the wind and rain themselves. Thunder boomed in the distance and the air was heavy, hot, and wet. The white doctor, recently arrived from the United States, used an already saturated handkerchief to wipe his face. He heard the noise of the rain forest, but not its song.

The dark, sweat-beaded face of the man in front of him was implacable and inscrutable. "I don't sell sick monkeys," he repeated for the hundredth time. The thunder boomed again, closer this time. The wind stirred the sides of the tent, hastily erected against the elements for this clandestine meeting.

The doctor closed his eyes, summoning patience. "Look. I've told you before—I'm not from the World Heath Organization, I'm not from the Centers for Disease Control, I'm not from *any* official organization at all. I represent private interests. Believe me, I know enough to have you arrested already. I hardly need sick monkeys as proof."

The man's brown eyes narrowed. "You don't make

any sense." His English was perfect, rolling off his tongue with the musical intonation of the Bantu that was his first language. "Suppose I did sell sick monkeys. Why would you want them? Labs, they like healthy monkeys. Not sick. I get you plenty of healthy monkeys. Good for testing. Good for business."

A sudden flash, then a deafening crack. The doctor winced. The wind picked up, and the rain began to come down in earnest, pounding on the tent and adding its own percussion to the song of the rain forest.

"We want to study the illnesses themselves," lied the doctor.

The man laughed heartily, showing white teeth. "You crazy."

"Perhaps," agreed the doctor. "But this is what my client wants."

"I tell you again, I don't sell sick monkeys."

A vein began to throb at the doctor's temple. His patience was evaporating. "Listen to me," he said, dropping his voice to a growl and leaning forward. "WHO is planning to send an investigation team to Uganda within a couple of weeks. They've traced the shipment of infected monkeys to you—just as my client has."

He felt a keen rush of enjoyment as the man's eyes widened. "Shipping sick monkeys accidentally—well, it happens. But if WHO found out about this island of yours—"

"Only a few, I swear it!" the man cried. "Only when the shipments are short—and some of the monkeys, they might not even be sick, you know?"

"Take me to the island. Let me get a sampling of monkeys, and WHO need never know about this. Okay?"

The man nodded. For a long moment, there was silence. The doctor savored the victory, then made a note of the rain. It was heavy now. It always rained in the afternoon in the shadow of Mount Elgon. But soon enough, the rain would stop, and he would be on the last leg of the journey.

The man before him was utterly cowed. His eyes were downcast, and he was no doubt contemplating the ramifications of the WHO team discovering his illness-infested island in Lake Victoria.

The doctor leaned back, smiled, and took a pack of cards from his pocket. Thunder boomed; lightning flashed. They were going to be here a while.

"You play poker?" he asked.

CHAPTER ONE

● ● ●

April 12, 1981
In orbit about the planet Earth

Jaran K'Lara thought himself the luckiest person in the entire universe.

Excitement and pride swelled inside him as he stood, shoulder to shoulder with the rest of his crewmates, his bright, slightly slanted eyes glued to the huge viewscreen. For this brief moment, all but the most essential activities aboard the ship had slowed to a halt. The crew had gathered in the enormous, open room that served as everything from conference center to dance floor to theater for the royal passengers—a place the crew was not usually permitted. The reason: to be witnesses to history.

For seven generations, the house of K'Lara had attended the Ooshas of Tyrus and their families aboard the Royal Yacht. Jaran's father had been the personal attendant to the previous Oosha, the ruler whose foresight had led to this moment. Jaran was young yet to aspire to a comparable position. But then again, the new Cale-Oosha, Ruler of Tyrus, was young himself— a mere twenty-one. Perhaps it would not be long before Jaran rose from steward to attendant. It was something for which to hope, to dream.

And dreams never seemed more likely to be realized than now, this moment, when Jaran and the rest of the crew of the Royal Yacht watched the hopes and dreams of the late Oosha unfolding under the loving auspices of his son.

The people of Earth—*Erdlufi*—bore a strong resemblance to Tyrusians. Their temples weren't as deep, and their eyes didn't have the characteristic Tyrusian depth and slanted angles, but other than that, they could pass for Tyrusian. The reverse had certainly held true. Tyrusians had been on Earth for nearly thirty years, covertly planning for this moment—open, public contact. Jaran, of course, wasn't privy to any details—it was hardly a steward's affair—but he knew what the rest of Tyrus knew: plans were being made that would consummate in trade negotiations. Tyrus was an old planet, and like all old things, old planets eventually die. It needed Earth's resources, and could trade Tyrusian technology for what it required to the benefit of all involved.

And now the young Cale-Oosha, handsome, intelligent, a perfect diplomat, was with his uncle, the Dragit, preparing to lead the discussions. Like many other pivotal events in Tyrusian history, this one would be chronicled. Jaran and his crewmates were privileged in being able to watch events unfold as they happened. A huge cheer had gone up when the smaller vessel carrying the Oosha, his uncle, and his guardsmen had left the Royal Yacht; another, even bigger cheer had filled the room when that vessel touched Earth soil and their Oosha stepped out.

"The *Erdlufi* women are in for a treat," said a voice at Jaran's shoulder. He glanced down, grinning, at Shalli Ysai, who smiled back at him and winked.

"Don't get your hopes up, Shalli," teased Jaran. "Cale can't marry anyone not of noble blood, you know."

"Didn't say I wanted to marry him," replied Shalli, "just that he's pleasant to look at."

Cale had now descended the light-rung ladder and had stepped onto the Earth's surface. The camera focused in on his handsome face, and Jaran thought he caught the sparkle of unshed tears. His own throat suddenly closed up with emotion.

Noble Cale, he thought, overwhelmed by a rush of fierce loyalty, *may I serve you as well as my ancestors have served your family. Blessings be with you!*

Suddenly the Oosha ducked, and those crowded together aboard the ship saw various *Erdlufi* aircraft approach. The loud, abrasive chopping sound the machine produced was what had startled the Oosha. Jaran grimaced as he regarded the squat aircraft with its primitive propellers.

"Ugly, aren't they?"

Beside him, Shalli, who was one of the ship's technicians, murmured her agreement, a shadow of disgust on her lovely face. "They could certainly stand to benefit from our technology," she said.

Now Cale-Oosha was conducting an inspection of the troops. He didn't seem to like what he saw. Every man returned the Oosha's traditional Tyrusian greeting by dilating his pupil and revealing the doppled field inside. Jaran realized it at the same time Cale did—all the men were Tyrusians.

"Not a single human among them," said Jaran's friend Gevic. The assistant cook had maneuvered his way up from the back to stand beside his friends. Taller and broader than the slightly built Jaran and the dark-haired, slim Shalli, getting through the crowd had been a simple task for him. He and Jaran exchanged glances. "I thought there was supposed to be a delegation to greet the Oosha."

"So did I," replied Jaran. "Wonder what's going on?"

Clearly, Cale didn't know either. He planted his fists on his hips and turned to the Dragit. "I came to see Earthlings, Uncle, and you show me a parade of Tyrusian officers! Where are the people I came to see? Where *are* they?"

The Dragit appeared completely at ease. "I can explain, Your Majesty." He turned, and gestured imperiously.

A gasp rippled through the assembled crowd as a section of paved earth opened up. A large, shiny metal cylinder emerged and opened. An elevator into the earth.

"Yosh," said Gevic.

Jaran didn't say anything. He couldn't drag his eyes away from the screen. An underground city—why? For a moment, unease fluttered inside him. He pushed it away. The Dragit no doubt had his reasons. His men had been on Earth, they knew the situation. Jaran—and Cale—did not.

Still, he shifted his weight, the light feeling of elation he had experienced earlier growing into something heavier with each moment that passed.

"Commander Rafe's putting on his temple piece," said Shalli. Her voice was soft, pitched for Jaran's ears only. Sure enough, Commander Rafe, the leader of the royal guards, had put on the small piece of equipment that permitted him to focus his mental abilities. Jaran's fingers automatically went to his own temple piece. Everyone wore them on the ship; they were standard-issue equipment.

Still . . .

Now Jaran noticed that the young ruler was wearing the Exotar—the metallic glove that had been the mark of Ooshas through eight hundred generations. The young Oosha wasn't impressed with ceremony. Jaran had never even seen him wear the Exotar before. It made sense, though, that he would wear the badge of his kingship to such vital meetings. Didn't it?

"Why underground?" said Gevic. "I thought the *Erdlufi* cities were located on the surface, like ours are."

Jaran shook his head. He didn't speak—he was straining to catch the conversation going on between Cale and the Dragit. They were standing in a huge, cavernous room. Primitive screens blipped on the walls, and a holographic globe of the planet turned slowly on a broad base that was easily ten feet. They were not alone. Rafe, the guardsmen, several of the Dragit's military officers, and a whole slew of the men who had greeted the Oosha upon his arrival were also in attendance.

The Dragit was speaking now. ". . . exploration of this planet, it became clear that the behavior of these so-called 'humans' constituted a potential threat."

"A threat?" repeated Cale, surprise in his voice. "I never heard that. What kind of behavior are you talking about? Why was my father not told about all this?"

The Dragit turned toward his nephew. "Your Majesty," he said, "your father was a good man. However, quite frankly, he was not the strong leader we expect you to be. He never grasped the obligation we have as a superior culture. Think of it as our destiny."

The room on the Yacht had fallen utterly silent. No one was making comments or exchanging quips anymore. Everyone was staring at the screen, caught up in the tension of the moment.

"My father was a strong believer in negotiation." Cale, his voice clear and laced with righteous anger. "Surely, a conference with their Gro would have—"

"It doesn't work that way, Your Majesty," retorted the Dragit. "There *is* no Gro of Earth. This is a planet divided. There's no sense of unity, of working toward common goals for the betterment of all. Each side possesses weapons of mass destruction. The only thing these leaders will respect is a superior force. We must build such a force—and use it in the future."

"I can't believe I'm hearing this!" cried Cale. *Neither can I!* thought Jaran, his heart thudding painfully in his chest. "Build a superior force and use it? You're talking about conquest!"

"Not conquest. Pacification. The infrastructure is in place. All we require is your blessing. Will you give it to us, Majesty, and let us conquer this fertile planet in your name?" The Dragit's voice was soft, but it had an edge.

"One of the principles my father held dear was that the rights of others are sacred," replied Cale, his voice equally soft, equally dangerous. "He taught me that."

"Your father," replied the Dragit implacably, "is dead."

"He would never have approved of this plan!"

"Ah, but he is gone. You are here, and this choice is yours."

Jaran realized he was trembling. *Cale . . .*

"No," replied the Oosha, as Jaran had hoped—and feared—he would. "I forbid it."

The Dragit frowned. "Then, Majesty, we must forever disagree."

Even as Jaran registered what had just happened, his mind reeling, he felt the cold press of an arbus in his back.

He gasped, and the metal dug deeper. Out of the corner of his eye, he could see that he was not alone. Everyone who had stood, raptly watching the screen, now either had a weapon pointed at him or her—or else was the one wielding the weapon. Cries of alarm went up. Some struggled. From overhead, Jaran heard the clatter of boots on the overhanging balcony that circled the room. He didn't dare crane his neck to see.

Jaran, sweating, closed his eyes and cursed himself silently. Treason. He'd seen it coming, had denied it even as it unfolded right in front of him. The hands of the traitor behind him moved over his body, searching for any hidden weapons. Jaran, a lowly steward, carried none. Satisfied, the man reached up to Jaran's face, plucked off his temple piece, and pocketed it.

The viewscreen went dark, even as Rafe flung himself in front of the young Oosha. Apparently, they weren't to be shown the assassination itself.

A voice boomed throughout the ship. Sick, Jaran recognized it as that of the captain.

"A revolution is taking place on the surface of the planet Earth. The unenlightened reign of Cale-Oosha has been replaced by that of his uncle, the Dragit, also of the royal line. Those loyal to the Dragit will be rewarded; those who foolishly ally themselves with the late Cale shall suffer his fate. You have two cycles to make your decisions."

"Hands on your head," snapped the man at Jaran's back. Swallowing hard, Jaran complied. "Good. Now, move." And the man punctuated the order with a prod from the arbus. Wordlessly, Jaran stepped forward. Beside him, he saw Shalli and Gevic also being herded toward the back of the room, along with the rest of the frightened men and women who crewed the vessel.

No, not the rest of them. Only some. Others were turning, laughing, clapping their weapon-wielding friends on the back and leaving freely. Many of these Jaran had considered friends. He felt suddenly hollow inside, weak with a rush of fear. How deep did it go, this treachery?

"I'll follow the Dragit!" came a cry from the far end of the room. "Me too!" A whole chorus rose up as, fearful for their lives, men and women who had once pledged loyalty to Cale-Oosha now cast aside those deep vows as if they meant nothing. They were led off, still with their hands on their heads and weapons pointed at them; no doubt to be interrogated as to the sincerity of their conversions.

Some seventy were left, Jaran, Shalli, and Gevic among them. The doors slammed shut. Above them, on the walkways where once Cale-Oosha and his guests had sipped fine Tyrusian liquors and discussed art and politics, the armed guards Jaran had heard enter began a steady patrol.

"I can't believe this is happening!" Shalli reached out for Jaran, and he put his arm around her shoulders. She trembled against him. Black humor made him smile. He'd adored Shalli for a long time, but she'd never indicated that she returned his affections. And now, she was in his arms. Great timing.

"Sons of Manglers," growled Gevic. His hands clenched. "I should have known, I should have—"

"There was no way we could have," replied Jaran, wearily. "If they could surprise the Oosha and his Royal Guard, then how were ordinary people supposed to know?"

"What do we do now?" asked Shalli. Gevic, too, was looking questioningly at Jaran.

"That depends. Who's going to follow the Dragit?" asked Jaran. He thought he knew his friends, but he had to be sure.

Shalli's black brows drew together in a dreadful frown. A stream of curses issued from her lips, and she finished with "before *I* cast in *my* lot with that sorry son of a—"

"The late Oosha spared my father's life," said Gevic simply. "You know that." Jaran did know the story. Years ago, Gevic's father, young and desperately poor, had stolen to feed his family—and been pardoned by a sympathetic Oosha, who had given him employment aboard the Royal Yacht. Like Jaran, Gevic was part of a generational bond of servitude to the true Oosha.

"Then we've got to get out of here," replied Jaran simply. "Somehow."

Gevic looked around, and Jaran saw what he saw: most of the crew aboard the Royal Yacht followed the usurper, and probably had been aware of the planned coup for some time. The few who remained loyal to the true Oosha had been skillfully herded into a single room to watch the "ceremony" unfolding on the planet. At the time, Jaran had thought it a privilege. Now, he knew it was nothing more than the simplest of traps for the most gullible.

He was only a steward, from a line of stewards. Gevic worked in the galley. The only one among the three friends who could be of use in this situation was Shalli, a technician. But could—

And then, Jaran permitted himself a smile. Shalli withdrew from his embrace and, subtly, lowered her arms and shook them slightly. He saw a temple piece emerge from up her sleeve to drop into her palm. Long, dirty, clever mechanic's fingers closed around the precious item. Shalli met Jaran's gaze, smiled a little herself, and winked. His admiration for her increased. What a cool head she had, even now, when she—like he—was scared to death.

He looked around with renewed hope, assessing the situation. There were twenty to thirty prisoners enclosed in the lower area. Above them patrolled six guards, all armed and all watching the prisoners closely. Everyone aboard the yacht had had basic training in hand-to-hand combat and was familiar with a variety of weapons—even stewards, galley cooks, and mechanics. They had to be. Suppose the Royal Yacht was boarded by hostile forces?

Like his own men, thought Jaran glumly. He shook his head as if to dispel physically the thought. All might not yet be lost. Cale might have effected an escape, somehow—might be down on the planet, alone, maybe injured, in need of help.

One thing Jaran knew for certain. He'd never join the ranks of the traitors. He would go to his death before turning his back on the rightful heir to Tyrus, and he knew his friends shared his commitment.

"Shall we start asking the others if—" began Gevic.

"No," replied Jaran. "Some of them could be the Dragit's men, pretending to be loyalists in an effort to stop any escape plans before they start."

"Zak-tuk! I hadn't thought about that," replied Gevic, paling.

"I trust you two," said Jaran solemnly. "I trust you with my life. Now. Shalli, you've got a temple piece. Do you think you can take out one of the guards with it?"

"No. My powers aren't that strong. Either of you—" She broke off as the other two shook their heads. Suddenly an idea occurred to Jaran.

"We can pool our thoughts—triple our strength," he said excitedly.

"I don't know" said Gevic skeptically. "Thought-combination isn't always reliable. Sometimes it back-fires."

"Do we have any other options?" retorted the young steward. Gevic grinned, shook his head, and tossed a lock of hair out of his broad, friendly face.

Shalli took Jaran's hand and pressed the temple piece into it, folding his fingers closed. "Here. Your skills are the strongest of the three of us." As unobtrusively as he could, Jaran slipped the temple piece into place and held out a hand to Shalli. She twined a warm hand into his. Gevic took the other one, his meaty, stubby fingers awkwardly closing around Jaran's soft, uncalloused ones.

Jaran took a deep breath, said a quick prayer, and began to concentrate.

In his mind's eye, he saw one of the guards—a fellow steward who worked in the laundry. Jaran imagined him in as much detail as he could, down to the scar above the man's lip, the thinning hair, the somewhat mussed uniform. He saw his enemy staring down at the milling crowd of loyalists, visualized the gun he held, noting how he held it, cradled against his shoulder.

Sweat dappled Jaran's brow. *Not . . . yet. . . .*

He changed his focus, thought about his two friends to either side, felt their hands, strong and supportive,

clasped in his own. He imagined their mental energy
pouring into him, until he was like a bottle filled with
liquid, filled to the top, overflowing with power—
NOW!

His eyes flew wide and he focused on the guard's
arbus. Obeying the silent mental command, the
weapon leaped as if pulled from the startled grasp of
the guard. It sailed through the air to land in Gevic's
outstretched hand. At the same moment, the guard
hurtled over the railing to fall, screaming, to the floor
below. Shalli was on him at once. Quickly she ripped
off the man's temple piece, slipped it onto her own
brow, and continued searching the injured man for
further weapons. She found two small, lethal *har-nors*
and gave the dartlike weapons to Jaran. Then she was
roughly pushed aside by others in the crowd, others
who were angry and wanted to get their hands on
the guard.

The fall of the guard had sparked a frenzy of activ-
ity among the prisoners. There were perfunctory cries
of warning and then Jaran heard the sounds of shots
being fired randomly into the crowd.

Wildly he glanced upward. He focused on the man
firing and then this man's weapon, too, flipped out of
his hands. There was a roar of pleasure and a sudden
scramble among the prisoners for the weapon. Then
energy fire screamed upward, catching the guard full
in the chest. He stumbled backward, dead, felled by
his own weapon.

Jaran grabbed Gevic and Shalli. "Come on!" He
had to scream to be heard over the noise. "The escape pods!"

His first, foolish hope had been somehow to recap-
ture the ship, but he'd quickly realized that the roots
of this "revolution" went far too deep for that. The
best they could hope for was to get to the escape pods
and head for Earth, the blue planet, and hope that

they weren't blasted out of the sky before they made it.

Gevic paused and fired upward, striking the railing near one of the guards. It melted under the heat of the energy blast and the guard, startled, stepped backward.

Jaran caught his friend's arm. "Don't waste your fire! The door—Blast it!"

Gevic nodded his understanding and in one smooth motion swiveled the arbus around and began firing at the massive doors. Others had rallied after Jaran's example. The room had become a roiling sea of violence and arbus fire. Gevic, his broad face grim and intent, fired blast after blast into the doors, while Jaran took careful aim, concentrated, and hurled one of the *har-nors*. It landed solidly in the throat of one of the guards, who was dead before his body even hit the ground.

All at once, Jaran began to shake. His stomach soured. *I just killed a man.*

"Jaran!" Shalli seized his arm and shook him out of his horror-induced daze. "Gevic's blown a hole in the door! Come on!"

Swallowing hard, Jaran began to run with the rest of the crowd. He was vaguely reminded of a herd of *liishi,* who in earlier times turned the plains of Tyrus white as they stampeded for miles when startled by predators. *Liishi* were almost extinct now, along with much of Tyrus's wildlife—much of Tyrus—and now the Dragit had gone and ruined all chance of negotiation with the *Erdlufi—*

He felt the heat of the melted metal door as he shoved his way through. Once outside in the corridor, he looked wildly around. Shalli and Gevic struggled to make their own way out, and, even as he watched, Shalli went down, trampled underfoot. She screamed as her abdomen came into contact with the superheated metal. Over the smells of fear and sweat, Jaran now scented the odor of burned flesh.

At once he dived in after her, heedless of the press of the frightened crowd. He found her arms, pulled, and then she was on her feet and stumbling out. Her face was absolutely white. Even her lips were gray with pain.

"This way!" It was Gevic, gripping his weapon and firing a bolt of energy down the corridor to clear it. Half-holding Shalli, who was frighteningly silent, Jaran stumbled behind his friend.

They were almost there.

The press of the crowd eased as the prisoners fled in all directions. Jaran heard the echoes of arbus fire farther down the corridor and knew the besieged guards had called for reinforcements. He only hoped the way was clear to the escape pods.

Others ran beside them, bumping into them and jostling the injured Shalli so that Jaran feared she would lose consciousness. Even as he watched, her legs gave way and her eyes rolled back into her head. The burn of the melted doorway had fused her flight suit to her skin in one large welt of black, and he fought back nausea. He couldn't imagine the pain she must be enduring. Quickly, he swept her up into his arms—*zak,* she was little—and followed Gevic.

There were forty-some escape pods. Each could house up to twenty people in an emergency, fifteen comfortably. Already some had filled up and were en route to Earth.

He glanced out one of the portals and froze in horror. The escapes were not going unnoticed. Red energy blasts, under direction from the usurper's men, struck one of the little pods and it shattered into pieces. He turned away before he could see the bodies. Even if they got to the escape pods, there was no guarantee that they'd make it to Earth. But it was their only chance.

Then the guards were there, too, and even as Jaran hastened up with the limp body of Shalli in his arms, he saw Gevic open fire.

The fire from the weapons was reflected in the black-and-blue metal structure of the normally rather dark corridor, and the sound echoed. Jaran, mindful of Shalli, pressed back into an alcove around the curve of a corridor and caught his breath in ragged gasps.

What could he do? How could he help? His own mental powers, even augmented with the temple piece, wouldn't stand against an onslaught of the Dragit's armed men. He forced himself to calm down, made a conscious effort to slow his racing heart.

Think, Jaran. Think. . . .

He went over the structure of the escape pod bay and tried to imagine what it looked like now. Bodies of his friends probably littered the metal floor and—

. . . stay focused, don't think about that. . . .

—the Dragit's men were most likely engaged in two tasks: killing the loyalists and halting the escapes of the ones they didn't kill. Which meant they were busy firing and shutting down the escape-pod mechanisms by—

Jaran's purple-blue eyes flew open wide. That was it.

He edged forward now, still carefully cradling Shalli, and peered around the corner.

Sure enough, twelve men were firing into the crowd while several others were busy at the controls. Even as Jaran watched, a shiny metal door slid down with an inexorable, reverberating *thunk.* An instant later, Jaran, his eyes flickering toward a portal, caught sight of an empty pod being jettisoned into space.

The walls were part of a standard safety mechanism. All crew personnel were familiar with its operation. If the Yacht were ever to be boarded by hostiles, the primary concern would be the safe evacuation of the royal passengers. The wall slammed down before the pod disengaged, to prevent its being boarded by intruders. The Dragit's men were operating the emergency doors and then firing the empty pods for easy retrieval at a more convenient time. Seven pods had been so jettisoned, and within a few moments all of them would be.

The single entrance to the entire bay was also controlled by a protective wall. Jaran narrowed his eyes and focused his gaze on the mechanism. He licked his lips and tried not to be distracted by the death and pain all about him. He found the button with his mind and with all his will demanded: *Shut down!*

At once, despite the frantic efforts of the enemy to countermand the mental order, the huge metal doorway that blocked access to the bay from all other parts of the ship slammed down. Two of the Dragit's men were caught and crushed. Jaran didn't even spare them a thought. They'd chosen to ally with a traitor; they'd paid the price.

Shouts and whoops of shocked joy filled the room. Jaran couldn't spare time to rejoice with the others—he could hear, already, the booming sounds behind the door that meant that soon the Dragit's men would find a way through.

"Let's get going!" he cried, and dived for the nearest pod. Gevic was right behind him, clutching his arm where an arbus blast had burned it. Others crowded in until finally Jaran had to yell, "Go to the next one! There are more! We've got too many in here!"

But frightened people do not often listen well to logical instructions, and these people were terrified. Reluctantly, Jaran reached and keyed in the command for the door to iris shut. The last thing he saw before the lock clicked closed was a young woman's tear-streaked face.

"Don't worry," soothed Gevic to the rest of those in the pod. "There are at least half the pods left. Everyone'll make it out all right." Now, he saw Shalli, and concern flooded his homely face. "What happened? Arbus blast?"

He reached out his arms to take the young woman and Jaran gently handed over his precious burden. "Get the medikit," he told Gevic. "She fell on the melted door. Got a bad burn, I don't know how bad."

The rest of the makeshift "crew" of the pod were talking, and people were milling about. Jaran stood up and waved his hands for silence.

"Listen, everyone. I'm glad you all made it, but we're going to have to get out of here immediately if we're going to get out at all. Everyone must sit down, or this thing won't operate."

"Where are we going?" cried one man.

"Can we get back to Tyrus?"

"What about Earth—what about the Oosha?"

"Sit *down* or we're not going anywhere!" yelled Jaran, starting to get angry now. The edge of his voice cut through the hysteria, and, one by one, people sat down. At once, a force field shimmered around each of them. It would protect them from whatever jostling the pod might encounter on its way to—

Where? Jaran seated himself by the controls and realized he didn't know how to pilot the pod. He sensed that he had, unconsciously, assumed command. He'd gotten his friends to the escape pod, he'd saved the rest, and now he had his own little crew who turned pale, hopeful faces to him. Maybe someone else here knew how to pilot this thing, but he knew that every second counted right now. The Dragit's men might blast through at any time and halt all of them—for good.

He took a deep breath and hit "Autopilot."

The pod launched itself into the darkness of space and hurtled toward the nearest safe landing place— Earth. It would navigate itself safely and find a habitable place to land somewhere on this alien planet.

Jaran began to shake with reaction. They'd escaped, yes—but to what? What awaited them on Earth?

Cale-Oosha, Jaran thought despairingly, *I hope they failed. I hope you're alive down there. I hope you're safe.*

And then a bolt of glowing red fire struck the pod.

CHAPTER
TWO

● ● ●

April 12, 1981
Charles Air Force Base
The Utah Desert

"Cub looks a lot like his father," said Milo Kaslik as he, Sergeant Ashley Stephens, Lieutenant Sean Anthony, and the medtech they jokingly called "Doc" watched the viewscreens.

"He sure does," said Doc. He finished the last of his sandwich and washed it down with a swig of the hot, black Earth drink called "coffee."

The four Tyrusians had been stationed at Charles Air Force Base for the last six years. They had been selected because of their resemblance to the *Erdlufi* and had regarded the assignment as one long holiday despite the intense workload. The sky here was blue, the air clean, the food exotic but edible, the natives friendly. Earth was a nice place, and all four of the friends were looking forward to the day when they could "come clean" with the natives. Tyrusians could help the humans, and their planet could help Tyrus. Everyone would win. It would be a delight to be, as the *Erdlufi* put it, "The good guys."

Now was the moment they'd been waiting for, and although none of their shifts was scheduled for duty, they'd dragged themselves out of their cots and were glued to the screen. No one wanted to miss a minute of this.

"The Oosha's so *young*," lamented Kaslik. Doc, Ashley, and Sean exchanged winks and chuckled freely at Kaslik's expense.

"Aw, everybody's young to you, Old Man," said Sean, grinning.

"Hey, wait a minute," said Ashley. She was seated, staring at the monitor. "Something's going on."

Doc, Sean, and Kaslik pressed in. The discussions between the Oosha and his uncle had shifted into an argument.

"What's—" began Doc.

Ashley frowned. "Quiet! I can't hear."

The Dragit was smiling. "When Cale's father died, as the eldest surviving relative, I led the Hundred Days of Mourning." He glanced over at Cale. "And I shall do the same for him."

Ashley gasped and clapped a hand to her mouth. "Oh no," whispered Doc. Kaslik had gone pale. Sean, eyes wide, worked his mouth, but nothing came out.

Frozen, eyes riveted to the screen, they watched the coup unfold. The tragically young Oosha, shocked beyond the ability even to react, stood gaping while Commander Rafe flung himself onto his ruler. They both hit the floor hard, and arbus fire barely missed them.

"They're gonna kill the Oosha," whispered Doc.

Screams issued from the speakers; screams, and the sounds of arbuses firing. Cale rallied, used the Exotar to deflect a shot that would certainly have killed Commander Rafe.

Doc hardly blinked. His lips moved and he repeated the words: *They're gonna kill the Oosha.* The coffee mug fell from limp fingers to shatter on the floor.

The crash snapped them out of their daze. Wildly, Ashley glanced around. They were alone in the room.

"Did you three know about this?" asked Doc. Kaslik, Sean, and Ashley all shook their heads.

"It sounds like it was, uh, a backup plan or something," stammered Sean. "I mean—they gave him a choice."

"Some damn choice," growled Doc. "Kill a planetful of innocent folks or be killed yourself."

"We've got to make the same choice, gentlemen," said Ashley, her normally husky, low voice now even rougher with emotion. She glanced up at them. "What's it going to be?"

It was the ultimate moment of decision. For a long moment, the four eyed each other suspiciously. Finally Doc swore, reached for his own arbus, slammed it down on the table, and threw up his hands in disgust. "Shoot me if you want," he said, "But I sure as hell didn't sign on for this Earth duty to be an Ooshakiller."

Ashley stared at him, then her full lips curved in a slow smile. "Me neither."

Kaslik looked ill. "But—they'll execute us!"

Ashley's slow, soft smile spread. "Only if they catch us, Kaslik. Only if they catch us."

Sean was the only one who had not yet cast his lot in with them. Doc turned to the young man, put a hand on his shoulder. "Son?" he said. "You with us?"

Sean turned miserable eyes on his friend. "I—I can't. I'm sorry." Then, in a soft voice, "I'm scared, Doc. Ashley says they'll have to find us—but damn it, you know they will! We know how thorough we Tyrusians can be." The last comment was laced with bitterness. He took out his arbus and handed it to his friend.

"Sean, I ain't about to kill a friend if I ain't gonna kill an Oosha," snapped Doc.

Sean laughed, shakily. "I know, Doc. But hit me on the back of the head with that thing real hard, will you?"

"Sean—" Ashley rose with sinuous grace. "Are you sure?"

"Sure I'm sure. Knock me out, and that way I've got a reason for not stopping the three of you." His feeble grin faded. "Good luck. And don't worry—I won't betray you."

"We know you won't, Sean," said Ashley, holding his gaze with hers. The last Sean Anthony saw of his three best friends was Ashley's blue-purple eyes, sorrowful and sincere in her beautiful face, as the arbus came crashing down on his skull.

The little Oosha had escaped, but not for long.

The Dragit waited impatiently, secure in his War Room, getting frantic reports from various sources. Cale was in a trangula. No, Cale had been spotted in the biolab. No, wait, he was elsewhere—he had made it to the ship—

Finally, the Dragit himself, while punching buttons that called up different camera angles across the base, spotted the brat fleeing with the ever-annoying Commander Rafe across the open field. They were sprinting for the small vessel in which they had first arrived on Earth, hoping to commandeer it.

"Camera fifty-six, Konrad," he said into the microphone beside the screen.

"Roger that," replied Colonel Konrad. "We'll get him, sir."

As the Dragit watched, eyes narrowing, floodlights snapped on above ground. Cale and Rafe stumbled, Cale flinging up his eyes to shield them from the harsh, white light. The earth between the fleeing ruler and potential safety suddenly gaped open and Manglers—Manglers who had been kept hungry and ill-tempered for precisely this moment—were released.

The one thing the late Oosha did right, mused the Dragit, *was authorize the gengineering project on Kaon.* Naturally, though, he'd been too soft-hearted and had later recanted, calling the products of the program "obscene" and "monstrous." The Oosha had canceled the project. Government funding of the program was stopped immediately, and the entire thing was supposedly dismantled. The Dragit's own personal funds had ensured that the gengineering experimentation had continued, covertly. The Dragit nodded, pleased, seeing the creatures produced by his wealth earn their keep.

They had a long, scientific name, these creatures who had no parents, but everyone simply called them "Manglers." To the Dragit, peering at the screen at the ruler he had just overthrown, the ugly, unnatural beasts were a beautiful sight. Growling, ducking monstrously large heads crammed full of teeth, they scuttled on impossibly angled legs toward their royal dinner.

Predictably, it was the loathed Commander Rafe who snapped out of his shock first and began firing at the Manglers. "Fire all you will, Rafe," muttered the Dragit under his breath. "There are so many more to come."

Rafe pointed, shouting something, and Cale took off running. At that moment, the Dragit saw that Konrad had emerged from the cylindrical entry shaft and begun firing.

"Good, Konrad. You'd better not let him escape," said the Dragit to himself. Suddenly his eyes went wide. "What . . . who. . . ?"

Cale was heading for the northeast gate, which was effectively blocked by a powerful force field. On the other side of the invisible field, pacing and looking agitated, was a young woman. Cale went down, struck by Konrad's fire, but somehow got to his feet again.

The Dragit felt blood rush to his face. Cale lurching forward, despite what must be agonizing pain . . . Cale reaching up, cutting through the field with that cursed Exotar of his, the Exotar that by all rights should be sitting on the Dragit's own hand . . . Cale stumbling through, helped by the unexpected and most unwelcome *Erdlufa*. . . .

Cale . . . Cale . . . *Cale* . . .

The title of Oosha should have been his. He'd have known what to do with it, how to manage his planet far better than his idiot brother had done. And now the crown of Tyrus sat upon the unlined brow of this whelp of a boy, this baby Cale—

He'd eluded them. Furious, the Dragit thumbed on the microphone. "Konrad! You fool, the Oosha has escaped!"

"He won't get far, Dragit." Konrad's voice crackled over the microphone in an attempted reassurance. "We're monitoring the situation. I'm pleased to report that Commander Rafe is dead. Please turn your monitor to Camera Twelve and observe."

Somewhat mollified, the Dragit did so. He began to smile. Camera Twelve showed only a huge inferno of a destroyed fuel tank and the crisped bodies of Manglers. No Tyrusian could have lived through *that*.

One thorn in my side eliminated; one more to go, he thought, and the thought gave him pleasure. Cale had passed beyond the eyes of the base's cameras. If the Dragit wished to watch the boy's demise with his own eyes, he'd have to go topside.

Colonel Konrad said nothing when the silent shape of the Dragit appeared beside him, but he began to sweat just a little more.

Everything had gone according to plan, except they hadn't counted on the Oosha's damned luck. Konrad stared through the binoculars, focusing on the Jeep with Cale and his mysterious female rescuer.

"They're on the third bend of the road," he said to his adjutant. "Send in the chopper. I want them dead at any cost."

"Aye, sir!" replied the young man, and hastened to

carry out his orders, relaying the message. Only a few seconds later Konrad was rewarded with the sight of one of his helicopters rising toward the Jeep. From this distance, he couldn't hear the sound of the bullets, but through the night-vision binoculars he could see them. They hit their target, and the glass windshield of the Jeep shattered.

It had to have killed the foolish girl and her royal passenger. Had to. And Konrad's hopes were confirmed as he watched the Jeep spin wildly out of control, crash through the guardrail, strike a boulder, and bounce upward. Unfortunately, the vehicle crashed into the helicopter responsible for its driver's death, and Konrad regretted that. The man had been an excellent chopper pilot and a fine soldier, but he had died for the good of his planet, after all.

Even from where Konrad stood, the huge fireball that resulted was clearly visible with the naked eye. Konrad, lowering his binoculars, took a deep breath. He struggled to maintain an air of solemnity when in fact he felt like whooping with joy. The last, most difficult problem had just been solved.

"Groho Zanek," said Konrad soberly. He turned, a half smile on his lips, and bowed slightly as he faced the Dragit. His eyes flashed with excitement. *"Zhvee nogo Groho."* The King is dead. Long live the King.

The Dragit grinned.

Upon reflection, mused the Dragit as he sat at a celebratory dinner aboard the Royal Yacht with the engineers of his victory, the entire coup d'etat had gone as smoothly as he could have hoped. It had lasted only a little over an hour. The meal consisted of Earth delicacies—flavors, he thought with an inward chuckle, he'd better get used to. He spooned chicken soup into his mouth and savored it while the final outcome of the coup was summarized.

The young man who had been assigned to give the

updates was amusingly nervous and stood so straight that the Dragit was mildly fearful for the boy's back muscles. He stared straight ahead, not daring to meet his new ruler's gaze, and barked his report.

"The vessel in which Cale-Oosha was transported to Earth is crewed entirely by your own men, *sir!* There was never a chance that he could have taken the ship even had he reached it, *sir!* The Manglers dispatched everyone who attempted to cross the field, *sir!*"

This was getting annoying. The Dragit spooned up the last bit of soup and turned toward the young man. Silent as shadows, servers clad in the Dragit's colors stepped forward to remove the empty bowl.

"Private, I appreciate your enthusiasm. However, I am not across the room, I am well within earshot, and your report will take less time if you cease ending every sentence with 'sir.' "

The youth flushed. "Understood, s—understood."

"Continue." The main entree was served, and the Dragit dived with gusto into something called "steak."

"We have recovered the bodies of all the royal guards save that of Commander Rafe, s—and witnesses spotted him at the site where several Manglers were incinerated."

The Dragit shot a glance at Konrad. "His body ought to be there too, Colonel."

"The bone density of a Mangler is much greater than a Tyrusian's," replied Konrad calmly. "What would burn Tyrusian bone might not destroy Mangler bones. Commander Rafe is ashes, Dragit, and ashes cannot harm you."

Satisfied, the Dragit nodded and waved that the young private continue. This "steak" was delicious. He sampled the "mashed potatoes" and found them also excellent.

"As for the Oosha himself, his vehicle was utterly destroyed. He is dead as well."

The Dragit couldn't resist a smile. He felt like smiling every time anyone said those happy words, "the Oosha is dead."

"The Royal Yacht is secured, and all aboard are loyal to you, great Dragit," continued the private. The Dragit wondered if the boy wasn't going to start swapping "great Dragit" for "sir." He hoped not.

The choice of words made him pause in mid-chew. "You said, secured. Does that mean security was ever an issue?" He regarded Konrad, arching an eyebrow.

"You yourself advised me to be careful when replacing yacht personnel," replied Konrad, sipping his wine. "Cale knew many of the crew individually, and you told me that—"

"Yes, yes, I remember what I said," interrupted the Dragit. "I know that there were still many aboard who knew nothing of the coup and who were loyal to the Oosha—the *late* Oosha. What I'm asking is, did this pose any kind of a security risk?"

The room suddenly fell silent. The lump of steak and mashed potatoes sat heavily in the Dragit's stomach, and he slowly put down his fork. He turned his gaze to the hapless young private, and said, softly, silkily, "Well?"

The boy swallowed hard. "Killing the messenger" was one tradition common to both Earth's and Tyrus's histories, and he was no doubt recalling that little fact. Nonetheless, he continued.

"The loyalists were surprised and contained. However"—and he swallowed again—"however, there was a breach in security and the prisoners managed to escape. Several made their way to the escape pods, and some of these did actually utilize the pods for their intended purposes."

"They *escaped?*" The Dragit slammed his fist down on the table in fury, and the silverware jumped. "How in the name of—Konrad! What kind of incompetents are you foisting off on me?"

Konrad flushed with anger. "Sir," he growled, "all of my men were here at the base. Those men were under your command and—"

"You recommended the names!" roared the Dragit, giving full rein to his anger. "You helped me select them! I hold you accountable, Colonel, make no mistake!"

The Colonel's lips thinned, and he glanced away. "Acknowledged."

At the far end of the table, flanked by "airmen" of various ranks, there was one man who had remained silent through the whole exchange. He was clad not in uniform, but in a less-ornate version of the Dragit's own clothes. He was tall and thin, almost spidery, and his slanted eyes and deep temples distinctly proclaimed his Tyrusian heritage. Those eyes had followed every nuance of expression on every face, and the sharp ears had missed nothing. Now, the man at the far end of the table allowed himself a slight smile at the colonel's discomfiture.

"Continue," snarled the Dragit to the private.

"Twelve pods were jettisoned. Of those twelve, two were destroyed outright and three more severely damaged. The rest, we believe, did manage to make it safely to Earth despite our best efforts."

"Seven," growled the Dragit. "Seven made it safely to Earth. Well, I'd call that a *security risk,* wouldn't you, Colonel Incompetent?"

"Dragit," replied Konrad, his eyes hard and angry, "a handful of Tyrusian loyalists scattered across this planet isn't going to pose any kind of a risk. They will probably die, or be killed, and at any rate they're stranded here. There's no Oosha left for them to rally around. If they do survive, they will simply learn to blend in with the human population and disappear."

"Oh, but there is an Oosha, after a fashion," replied the Dragit. "He's a martyr now, and martyrs never truly die. If there's anyone on this planet who is not my man, then he's a risk."

"Sir, with all due respect, you're being paranoid."

At that, the Dragit threw back his head and laughed. No one else at the table joined him. Finally, the mirth fading, he trained his gaze on Konrad.

"Am I? For over forty-seven cycles of our planet's turning, I have watched my back. I have set traps, I have made plans, I have eliminated every obstacle to this moment carefully and with the utmost patience. I have never underestimated anyone or anything, and it has always worked to my benefit. Paranoid? Perhaps. But I am here, and I have eliminated my enemies, and I will continue to do so. Do I make myself clear?"

The man at the end of the table had stopped eating now. His bright eyes, a brilliant shade of purple, flickered from the Dragit's face to the colonel's.

The Dragit and Konrad stared at one another. A muscle near Konrad's eye began to twitch. He pressed his lips together until they were almost white. Finally, he said between clenched teeth, "Very clear. Dragit."

"Excellent." The Dragit glanced at the young man. "Are you finished, private?"

The boy hesitated, and the Dragit didn't miss the slight nod that Konrad gave him. "Aye, sir."

"I think not," said the Dragit lightly. "I think there's something else. Colonel, would you care to enlighten me?"

Konrad swore an Earth oath under his breath. He threw his napkin on the table and rose abruptly, the chair scraping against the floor.

"All right, there is more. It's not a threat, but I'm certain you're bound to perceive it as one. Approximately fifty of my men deserted this evening. Seems they didn't have the stomach to murder their ruler. We have caught, interrogated, and executed ten of them, but the rest remain at large. If I may be excused,

I'll go to my quarters at the base and prepare a paper for you to read in the morning. Sir."

For a moment, the Dragit was so angry that he wondered if he might be choking. He wanted to kill Konrad. Kill him, right now, drag him onto the porcelain-and-silver-decked table and bang his head against the heavy mahogany until his face was pulp.

But that would serve him little. Konrad had helped him win the first leg of his victory. He needed the man's expertise, his—how did the *Erdlufi* phrase it—"know how." He swallowed the anger much as he might have swallowed a bite of steak and forced a smile.

"I look forward to your report, Colonel. Dismissed."

With a quick, angry nod, the colonel turned on his heel and stalked out of the room—the very room, mused the Dragit, where the loyalists to the Oosha had been corralled.

The room from which they had escaped.

Slowly, the Dragit turned to look toward the man at the far end of the table. Their eyes met, and the man nodded.

Saris Krai, valet, attendant, and sometime assassin for his master the Dragit, didn't even need to be told what to do. It had become obvious earlier, once the news about the escaped loyalists had become public knowledge. Couple that with Konrad's own men deserting, and Saris knew with a deep sense of satisfaction that his own, unique talents would be required.

Saris and the man who now went by the human name of Colonel Konrad had known—and hated—one another for many years. There had been an unspoken competition between them for the esteem of the Dragit. When once, Saris had failed the Dragit on an espionage mission, Konrad had moved in and completed the job in a more forceful, but nonetheless effective, manner. Saris had exacted retaliation of his own at a later date. Back and forth the two servants of the same master had gone, each currying the Dragit's favor in his own fashion.

Now, the colonel was in deep disgrace. Now, Saris could move in and take care of the Dragit's worries. He knew his task without being told; he was to eliminate all possible security risks.

Like ship jumpers and deserters.

An easy, and pleasant, job.

Saris's thin tongue crept out to lick his lips, but it was not to savor the admittedly delicious Earth food. It was in anticipation of the delights of the hunt to come.

CHAPTER THREE

• • •

April 12, 1981
The Utah desert

Eighteen-year-old Rita Carter felt almost dizzy as she stumbled out into the night, and wondered if her legs would buckle.

Thus far—and the night wasn't over—she'd made it through getting lost in the desert, witnessing the landing of an alien ship, saving the life of the ruler of another planet, and fighting a monster Cale called a "Mangler."

But it was the kiss that had undone her.

Her lips tingled from the gentle, sweet press of his; she felt warmth still, though the desert night was cold and she was no longer in the protective circle of his arms. But he was beside her. Now his hand curled, warm and strong, about her fingers, and in the grip were universes of unspoken but nonetheless vowed promises: *I will not leave you. I shall not fail you.*

She'd fight a dozen Manglers for that.

Rita glanced out at the night sky, saw the billions of stars twinkling above her, and fancied that they shared her sudden, unlooked-for joy. *Thank you,* she thought with a rush of emotion. *Thank you for sending me Cale-Oosha.*

"Cale—"

The voice belonged to Commander Rafe, who Cale had described to her as "my teacher, my protector, the thorn in my side . . . Friend, I guess, is the best word."

Friend to Cale he might be, and Rita didn't doubt it, but a sudden chill penetrated her giddy warmth at the tone of his voice. He stood awaiting his ruler outside the cave, and the fey combination of moonlight and shadow made his large, powerful frame seem almost ominous to Rita.

Beside her, Cale straightened. "Yes, Rafe?"

"You had perhaps best say good-bye to your rescuer now." Again, a coldness, an edge to the words. Rafe was not going to like what Cale had to say.

"Rafe, Rita has honored us by deciding to accompany us."

"Cale—come here a moment."

"Whatever you have to say to me, my old friend," and Cale's voice was still soft and filled with affection, "you may say in front of Rita."

Rafe took in a deep breath, let it out in a puff, and folded his arms. "All right. Rita—from the bottom of my heart, I thank you for the life of my Oosha. We are assuredly in your debt. However—"

There's always a however, thought Rita. A sudden rush of irritation drove out the last bits of her dreamy pleasure. Gently but firmly she disentangled her hand from Cale's. He understood and stepped back.

"However, what?" she demanded, sticking her chin out.

He hesitated, uncomfortable now that he was confronting her directly. *Get used to it, Rafe,* she thought. *I can fight my own battles.*

"However, this is a very dangerous situation," said Rafe, recovering. "You know what Cale-Oosha is up against. There are men—men in high-ranking positions in your own military—who want him, and anyone associated with him, dead."

"Why?"

"It's a long story."

Rita smiled with false sweetness. "Hey—we've got time. In fact, we've got a hell of a lot of time. Now that I've driven my Jeep into a helicopter we're without transportation. Do you know how long it's going to take for us to get back to Salt Lake City? Oh, forgive me—you don't know where or even what Salt Lake City is, do you? Tell me, Rafe, what's the game plan? What are you and Cale going to do now? How are you going to survive?"

She'd moved forward now and was actually making the big warrior back up a step or two. "I—"

"You are in so much trouble."

"I am aware of that! And why, pray tell, are you so eager to become involved?" Rafe shot back.

"I'm already involved. What makes you think they won't come after me even if you two take off?" replied Rita.

"Zak," gasped Cale. He moved in to stand beside Rita, touched her shoulder gently, then dropped his hand. "I had not thought of that. Rafe, we know how to fight my enemies. She doesn't. She knows how to live on this Earth. We don't."

"Gee, sounds like we ought to team up," said Rita, her voice dripping sarcasm. "Tell you what—I help you guys out, and you watch my back, okay?"

Cale smiled. "Oh-Kay," he said. Rafe was silent. They'd outargued him this time, but Rita was certain that this would not be the last time she and he would clash.

She took a deep breath, held it, then exhaled. "All right. Let's load up what we can and—hey." She pointed at their flight suits. "I don't suppose you have anything on underneath those?"

They shook their heads.

"Then hitchhiking is definitely out. We're going to have to walk back. Hope you guys are in good shape." She turned and entered the cave. Cale and Rafe waited to be told what to do. Rita went through her provisions and was able to pull together some food, drinking water, blankets, a small pup tent, and some other necessary items. There was only the one back-pack, which she rather maliciously loaded with the heaviest items and wordlessly handed to Rafe, but she bundled the blankets and tent up into packs. A quick check to make sure she had matches, and then she nodded, satisfied.

"Let's go."

It was over seventy miles back to Salt Lake City and the tiny apartment Rita rented off of Second Avenue. Seventy miles of, first, rough terrain and, second, a long stretch of highway. Interstate 80, to be precise.

She had a plan, but first, they had to make it back to civilization. Both Rafe and Cale looked more than fit enough to keep up with her, and so they proved to be.

They walked for several hours, until dawn, Rita asking questions the whole way. Rafe was silent most of the time, looking back over his shoulder as if expecting pursuit. Cale, though, eagerly answered her questions.

They came from a planet called Tyrus. At one point, Cale paused, searched the sky, and found a small white star. "There it is," he said with a catch in his breath. "That is the star Tyrus circles, our—our sun."

Tyrus, though, was dying. Some of it was the natural progress of a planet—after a few billion years, most planets gave up the ghost. That much Rita knew. But, Cale told her sadly, "much of what is killing my world, we have caused. Our cities are protected by sheltering domes. Within, all is well. But outside, we cannot even breathe without aid. Tyrus has very little left to give. So, some thirty or forty of your years ago, we began to search off-world for places to live, or peoples to trade with."

"Thirty or forty . . ." Rita did the math. She wasn't big into UFOs or aliens, but she knew a little. "That was at the end of our Second World War."

Cale nodded. "Yes! You had learned how to harness the power of the atom. We had been monitoring you. It was at that point that we deemed you technically proficient enough to hold negotiations with."

"Cool," said Rita. "So, why didn't you land a spaceship on the White House lawn and start talking?"

Cale tilted his head, puzzled. "White House?"

"Where the President lives."

"President?"

She glanced up at him. "The leader of my country?"

"Country?"

"Wow, major culture clash here. I'll explain later."

"My father wanted to talk. He wanted to begin immediate negotiations, but—" Cale suddenly broke off.

"But what?" pressed Rita. Cale remained silent.

"But the Dragit, Cale's uncle, talked him out of it," said Rafe, speaking up unexpectedly. "And now we know why."

"Rita." Cale stopped suddenly. He took her chin gently in his hand, turned her face up so that he could see her expression in the moonlight. His own face was shadowed, but even so, she could see that his forehead was furrowed with concern. "You must believe me on this. I came to talk only. I had understood that a conference with your Gro—your Earth's king—had been arranged. Any plan for invasion, I had never heard of before tonight—and when it was presented to me, I forbade it. You do believe me? I could not bear it if you thought I came to conquer your people!"

His touch was feather-light, his voice pleading for her understanding. "Of course I believe you," she replied. "I saw what they were trying to do to you— and to Rafe. They're the ones with an army, not you, and—"

She stumbled. The full horror of the situation suddenly smote her, and her gut clenched. Cale was there, a strong hand beneath her elbow, supporting her. "Rita? Are you well?"

"An Army," she breathed, looking up at him. "An Army. My Army, the Army of the United States! I have to sit down." She put the action to the word as her knees buckled.

Cale was there, wordlessly handing Rita a canteen. A ghost of a smile flitted across her lips. A few hours earlier, he hadn't even known what a canteen was. She accepted it, screwed off the cap, and took a few swallows. The water crept past the sudden lump in her throat, and when she glanced up at Cale and Rafe her eyes were stinging with tears.

Betrayal. She'd felt sympathy for Cale, upon learning how he had been betrayed by his uncle. But now she knew the pain of that particular cut herself. The Tyrusians, over the last thirty-five years, had infiltrated the military of the United States of America. They had claimed an entire base for their awful purpose. How deep did it go? How high up, how far-reaching, how many people did the tendrils of Tyrusian ambition twine about?

Betrayal. Her country's military had betrayed her. And she wept bitterly at the knowledge, with the strange, adult sensation that her innocence had been brutally torn from her this night. Cale slipped an arm about her and let her sob in silence, and not even Rafe chided her.

April 13, 1981
A motel on I-80

Rita's plan was simple, and it worked well. Once they had made it down to the interstate, she checked the three of them into a motel and called the one friend she had in the world, Carrie Dalton. Carrie was a poli-sci major, and for a wild moment Rita badly wanted to put Cale, Rafe, and Carrie in a room together and watch the show as they tried to explain each other's political systems, but she stifled the impulse.

More important than Carrie's choice of major was the fact that Carrie actually had a car on campus. Rita concocted a dramatic yet plausible story about the Jeep veering out of control and going off a cliff, and Carrie agreed to come pick her up. Before she left to wait for Carrie out in front of the motel, Rita turned to Cale and Rafe.

"Stay put. I'll be back as soon as I can."

Three hours later, considerably poorer and driving Carrie's car, Rita returned to the motel. She carried several plastic bags and dropped them unceremoniously on the carpet.

"Here. I had to guess at your sizes, so they may be a little large. Next time, you guys get to tackle the mall yourselves."

Hesitantly, Rafe and Cale picked up the bags and peered inside. Rita had bought them clothing—shirts, jeans, and sneakers. She was amused that she had to give them quick instructions about how to don the clothes. Then, to her horror, Rafe and Cale reached behind them and began to unfasten the flight suits.

"No!" she yelped. They stared at her, confused. She pointed to the bathroom. "In there. You guys can't change in front of me."

"Why not?" asked Cale innocently.

"A little human custom called modesty," said Rita. They exchanged glances, then shrugged and did as she had told them. Rita waited, sprawled on the lumpy motel mattress, while they changed.

Cale emerged first, grinning a little self-consciously. "How do I look?"

Rita snorted. The clothes definitely were too big,

but anything was better than those attention-drawing jumpsuit things they'd been wearing. Seeing her expression, Cale's face fell.

"I cannot pass for an Earthling?"

"Oh, no, you'll pass. This is just a little large, that's all. Who knows, maybe in a few years baggy clothes will be all the rage."

In truth, he looked great despite the overlarge clothes. There wasn't anything they could do about his distinctive eyes, unfortunately, but the temples . . . Rita rose from the bed and went over to him. "Loosen your hair," she said.

He did so and the black locks tumbled down his shoulders. Rita took a sudden breath. Good God, but Cale was beautiful. Perfect, chiseled features, that long black hair, and those eyes . . . She forced herself to concentrate.

"You'll have to wear it down from now on, and maybe I can cut it a little around your face. Your temples . . ." She pointed to her own. "Ours aren't quite so deep."

"Ah. A disguise!"

They grinned at each other like conspiratorial children. A cough interrupted them. They turned and saw Rafe, looking uncomfortable in a button-down oxford-cloth shirt and khaki pants. He was scowling as he plucked at a sleeve.

Rita had done better at guessing his size, and the clothing actually fit. Despite his obvious impatience with the human clothes, he looked pretty good.

Rita looked him over critically. "That'll do for now. But I don't think preppy is really your style, Rafe."

"Now what happens?" asked Cale, coming to join them.

"Well, my apartment's pretty small, but you're welcome to stay with me. I live alone, so there won't be any problems."

"I think there will be nothing *but* problems," said Rafe. "Rita, I've said nothing because I feel we owe you far too much. And we needed your help yet again to get us to safety. You've provided clothing so that we may blend in unnoticed. That's fine, and we're grateful. But what do we do now? Cale, have you even thought about this?"

Cale sighed and ran a hand through his hair. "I— no. But now I think I do know what I have to do. Somehow, I have to get home—stop the Dragit before this invasion happens."

"What are you going to do? Hijack the space shuttle?" asked Rita, annoyed. "Cale, I understand what you're going through, but you and Rafe are stuck here. You have to make the best of it, stay alive, and count yourself lucky."

"If it were only myself, Rita, I would do that," replied Cale. "But I am the leader of my planet. Billions there depend on me for wise leadership, and billions here on your planet depend on me to save their lives—though they do now know it yet. The Dragit wants conquest, pure and simple. He wants this planet, and he'll do whatever is necessary to get it. I have a duty to more people than just myself, and I have to think of them."

"It's good to hear you speak like an Oosha again," approved Rafe.

Cale shot him a look. "I am Oosha," he replied in a mild voice, though his eyes flashed a warning. "Whatever I say, I say as Oosha. Don't forget that, Rafe."

"No, my liege." Rafe did not appear in the least bit chastised. Rather, he looked pleased.

Rita felt like an outsider. She turned, walked back to the bed, and plopped down on it. She would offer no more suggestions unless asked. Something was different now between her and Cale. He was the same man who had slain a Mangler in the cave, who had held and kissed her so gently. And yet—he wasn't. That man had no title; he was merely Cale, injured and alone. Now he was Cale-Oosha, "ruler of us all" in his native tongue, and Rafe seemed to be doing everything he could to drive a wedge between the two of them.

Maybe it was for the best. Maybe Rafe had had the right idea all along. Maybe, if Cale was going to just take off and head for the stars, she'd better concentrate on getting over him. Damn fast.

She felt ill. She recalled the unspoken promise she thought she had felt in the strong clasp of his hand: *I will not leave you. I shall not fail you.*

Yeah, right.

Rafe and Cale were talking in hushed tones. Rafe had seated himself in the rickety chair provided by the motel, and Cale was perched precariously on the edge of the ancient desk. Rita could have listened if she'd wanted to, but instead she lay down on the bed, rested her cheek against the pillows, and tuned them out.

Then an idea struck her. Petulantly, she at first refrained from mentioning it, but finally she rolled over onto her stomach and propped her chin up on her arms.

"Hey." They didn't hear her. "Hey!"

"Yes?" Cale turned and looked at her, the vaguest hint of annoyance on his features.

"You guys are overlooking one thing."

"And what might that be?" It was Rafe, staring at her with narrowed eyes, arms folded across his broad chest. Clearly he didn't think anything she had to suggest would be worth listening to.

Rita sat up. Her face felt flushed, and she realized she was angry at Cale. She forced the feeling back. "You may be able to contact someone and get out of here. But if you're going to be here for any length of time—and I'm afraid you are—you're going to need an identity."

"I do not understand," said Cale.

"This country is all tied up in red tape." Before Cale could question the phrase, she continued, adding, "Laws and regulations. I'll do what I can, but I can't feed all of us for too long. I'm only a student and my part-time job doesn't pay very much. Plus, thanks to you guys, I'm going to have to buy another car." It was a low blow, and it wasn't fair, but she didn't care. Cale flinched a little, but she went on.

"You'll need some kind of identity card to eat, get money, drive, get into places—you name it. Now, in the movies, people always seem to know someone who'll get them a fake ID, forge a birth certificate, all that stuff, but I don't know anyone. But believe me, that's the first thing you're going to need."

Rafe was listening to her now and taking her seriously. "You raise an excellent point."

Damn right I do.

"What do we do about it?"

Rita thought, cocking her head to one side and considering. "Let's see—we'll want a cover for you. Students, I think, since you're here. I'll teach you how to drive, you'll need to know that. And a social security card—"

"All these licenses and cards," interrupted Cale. "How are they issued?"

"By computer. But I'm no hacker. I don't even have access to—" She broke off. Rafe and Cale were grinning at one another.

"I do," said Cale.

"I cannot *believe* I'm doing this," moaned Rita. She sat slumped against the wheel, her head on her hands. She had turned off the car lights. Beside her, alert and tense as a hound on the scent, sat Cale. Rafe was in the backseat, leaning up between them. "I can't help feeling that I'm doing something illegal."

Cale had donned the strange glove he called the Exotar. On the way over to the County Building, he had explained some of its functions and history to her. The Exotar had been the symbol of sovereignty worn by the ruler of Tyrus for eight hundred generations. It was crammed with all kinds of sensors, and Cale had warned her never to attempt to try it on—"it will determine that your genetic code is not of the Tyrusian royal line and crush your hand." The remarkable glove fit either hand. It gave the wearer strength— Rita remembered how Cale had fought off a Mangler in the cave—and allowed him to hone and direct his powerful mental capacities.

Altogether, a most intriguing tool. Now Cale's dark head was bent over the silvery metallic glove, the fingers of his other hand lightly caressing what appeared to be a gem set in the middle of the palm. At her words, he spared her a quick glance. "Does someone own the air on your world?" he asked.

"No," replied Rita, embarrassed.

"Then how can it be stealing?" asked Rafe. "You yourself said we needed identities. We're getting them."

"How?"

Cale turned in the seat and directed the glove toward the darkened building. "Every Earth machine emits electromagnetic signals, including your computers. The Exotar can scan these fields and learn about the machine that emits them. In other words—I am teaching the Exotar how to talk to your computers."

He tilted his hand slightly. "There are many cables coming from here."

"They're probably phone lines." At Rafe's raised eyebrow, she floundered. "We use them to communicate. You talk in one end, the phone line breaks down the sounds and reassembles them on another end."

"Primitive, but effective," said Cale. "Do these—phone lines have any link with the computers?"

"Yeah, I think so," said Rita. "I took a computer class last semester. We're hooked up to something called the ARPANET—it stands for Advance Research Projects Agency Network. It's kind of electronic mail. The profs at various universities can communicate with it."

"Ah, that is perfect!" He cocked his head, examined the Exotar, and nodded, satisfied. "It has learned all it can from this place. Where is this ARPANET of which you speak?"

Her brow furrowed. "It's in the Computer Center, back on the campus. But I don't have access to that room."

"That is not a problem," said Rafe. "Please take us there."

Rita didn't move. "I'm not going to be a party to breaking and entering."

"We don't understand the structure of your bureaucracies," said Rafe. "We need you to navigate us through them."

"Rita," said Cale, gently, "we will harm no one and nothing. You have my word. Please."

She stared at him for a moment. "Damn it, you better be right." She shoved the car into gear.

This time they parked and walked. It was spring, and it was still a little chilly at night. No one was out and about at this hour, though Rita kept looking over her shoulder. She'd get expelled if they were caught—or worse.

They ducked into the shadows of the Computer Center, waited for a moment, then Rafe said, "Clear." Quickly they went to the door. Rafe kept watch while Cale raised Exotar-clad fingers to the door. He closed his eyes and concentrated. Rita gasped, softly, as the locked door unlocked itself and opened to them.

"How . . . ?"

"Telekinesis of the most basic sort," replied Cale. "Your planet's attempts to keep intruders out are extremely—"

"Primitive, yeah, I know. Come on."

They went inside and Cale took the lead, tapping in information on the Exotar and listening intently to what it "said." It took them to a large room, where again Cale unlocked the door using the powers of his mind. It was a little scary, when Rita thought about it.

Cool air blew out, stirring Rita's dark hair, and she heard the hum of the air-conditioning. She shivered in earnest and rubbed her cold arms. The computers had to be kept cool; she seemed to remember hearing that from someone. She followed Cale as he stepped up onto a raised platform inside the room itself. Rafe followed closely, shutting the door after them once they were all safely inside. Rita's heart pounded furiously. It was pitch-dark inside. She began to grope for a light switch.

Suddenly, Rita realized that she could see—at least a little. The Exotar was emitting a soft, pale blue glow. Cale bent his face over his arm, and the light bathed his features in the cool radiance. He looked utterly unearthly in the illumination—strange, alien, beautiful, aloof. The light cast shadows on his high, deep temples, offset by the widow's peak of dark hair, and made his slanted eyes look even more exotic.

She found the light and switched it on. The mainframe stood in the far corner of the room. From various points in the ceiling and the walls, cables stretched down the mainframe like black snakes. Beside it was a table with a stupid terminal—no, "dumb terminal," that was the correct phrase Rita had learned in her class. It had a keyboard, a modem, and a phone. A large dot matrix printer sat silently to the left of the table, and a cardboard box beneath it held a large sheaf of computer punch paper.

The walls were filled with tape drives, each about

the size of a soda machine. A soft clicking noise issued from them as the tapes advanced. The rest of the room was crowded with shelves, trash cans, and file cabinets.

Cale moved with a cat's grace, heading directly for the dumb terminal. "This looks like it might be an interface, yes?" Rita nodded. He extended his hand and passed the invaluable Exotar over everything— the computer, the tape drives, and all the tapes on the shelves. Absorbing their programs, no doubt.

At last he was done. He seated himself in front of the dumb terminal, his eyes quickly taking in the setup. Hesitantly, he picked up the phone. This seemed to be the first thing that had confounded him. He tapped at it, put his hand over the mouthpiece, placed it on the terminal. Smothering a grin, Rita stepped forward. With great gentleness, she said, "Here. Let me." She placed it into the modem cradle.

Cale raised his hand, spread the fingers, and placed it tentatively on the keyboard. At first, nothing happened. The little green cursor blinked on and off. Cale narrowed his eyes, concentrating. Abruptly, the screen lit up. Characters raced across the screen at a speed Rita had never seen. She hoped he wouldn't destroy the computer.

Cale seemed quite pleased. He turned to Rafe and Rita and stated confidently, "This will not be a problem." As they watched, the screen cleared. The unmistakable sound of the modem connecting issued forth, then again the screen lit up with flashing characters. The modem dialed several numbers and then the Salt Lake County's main computer menu appeared on the screen.

"There it is," said Rita excitedly, pointing. "There's the Department of Motor Vehicles. You did it!"

Cale glanced up at Rita and grinned, suddenly looking very human and very boyish. "Now do you see?"

Rita understood completely. Somehow, the Exotar

was acting like a hookup—and Cale was able to get into the county records. Quickly she walked him through it until they came to the driver's license form. Rita paused. "Who are you?"

"I am Cale-Oosha," he replied innocently.

"No, no, you're . . ." She paused, thought. "Here. Put this in. Caleb Gray. Might as well give you a name that sounds like yours so you'll answer to it without thinking. Age"—she glanced at him, guessed—"twenty one. That'll get you into the bars if you want."

"Bars?"

"Never mind." She cited her own address, guessed at his weight, and finally it was completed. "Now you, Rafe. Raphael—Raphael Smith," she said, rather lamely, "age—thirty five." Soon Rafe's, too, was complete. "Perfect. Now all you need to do tomorrow is go in to the DMV, tell them you lost your card, and ask them for a replacement."

"What next?" asked Cale, positioning the Exotar.

"Social security card next." She dug through her pocket, coming up with crumpled pieces of chewing-gum wrappers, dimes, keys, and a scrap of hotel statio-nery. She'd called Information to get a public, easily available number for the Social Security Administra-tion in D.C. and handed it to Cale. He positioned his fingers over the gem on the Exotar. The next thing Rita knew, the computer was dialing numbers. They sat back, relaxing a little. This could be a long wait.

The minutes ticked by as the three sat in silence. Rafe rose and cracked the door, peering out cautiously into the dark corridor. The Exotar-directed computer meticulously went through every extension in the so-cial security listing, attempting to contact another computer. Twice, it did so, but a cursory examination proved that they were not the correct ones.

Finally, it connected—then there was a sudden si-lence. Cale's high brow furrowed.

"What's wrong?"

"Nothing I cannot handle. Merely some security protocols. The Exotar will bypass them." A pause. "Complete."

They were in. Rita walked Cale through the process of forging new social security documents for himself and Rafe. He was about to enter Rita's address again when Rafe's hand came down on his shoulder.

"Wait." Rafe glanced at Rita. "I trust the proficiency of the Exotar, but just in case—do you have a secondary address where we can have the cards sent?"

"I don't understand," said Rita.

"I do," said Cale. "Rafe—do you think there might be trouble?"

"I'm an old soldier," said Rafe, "and you don't get to be an old soldier without preparing for every possibility. I think it would be wise to have them sent to a friend of yours, Rita. Just in case Cale has triggered something. I do not wish to have your government coming in search of us."

"Hey, better the social security folks than your uncle's goons," said Rita. "I guess Carrie wouldn't mind." She gave Cale her friend's address, and he completed the form.

They went back to the school's computer. It seemed that "Caleb Gray" was a senior in the field of astrophysics. With a 4.0 average. And Rafael Smith had served in the Air Force for a time and now was studying in the field of law enforcement.

"Find mine," said Rita. Cale called it up. For a moment, Rita was tempted to boost that 3.0 average up to at least a 3.5, but she resisted the urge. "I'll stay where I am." She sighed.

"These grades—they are important?"

"Yeah, you could say that. I don't keep them up, I could lose my scholarship."

Cale turned to her, his eyes searching hers. "Yet you do not wish to change them. Why?"

"It's not honest. I should earn my good grades."

He smiled, softly. "You have integrity, as well as courage. I am honored to be in your company. So— what now?" asked Cale.

"Now," said Rafe, "we see if we are truly alone on this forsaken planet after all."

CHAPTER FOUR

• • •

April 12, 1981
Broken Rock, Arizona
The Navajo Reservation

Edward Robert Rainsinger, MD, M.Ph., born to the Turquoise Mesa Clan, born for the Deep Water People, stepped off the bus onto the hot Arizona soil and stared, squinting, into the bright blue sky.

Dinetah. Navajoland. The Rez. He couldn't believe he had really returned. As his eyes watered from the powerful sunlight, so strange after years spent on a damp, gray East Coast, he felt almost giddy with happiness. He had made the right decision.

The trip to Broken Rock from first Flagstaff and then Tuba City had been hot, bumpy, dusty, and arduous. Sweat had darkened and almost immediately dried on his fine Egyptian cotton shirt, and he had removed the Pierre Cardin tie and jacket very early on into the journey. Eddie's short black hair was damp, and he fluffed it with long brown fingers. He was grateful for the Ray-Bans.

Was it really twelve—no, thirteen—years since he'd left, a wide-eyed, naive Indian youth who thought he could change the world? The only thing that had changed had been himself, from a teenager to a man of thirty-one, with the softening body and tired spirit that often went into such a transformation.

No, that wasn't quite true. Broken Rock was different from the way he remembered it, that much was certain. In 1967 it had still been a small Navajo town. Because it wasn't Monument Valley or Canyon de Chelly, tourists had avoided it. Now, because of the improved roads and all the other things that made the world seem so much smaller, it seemed like there was a McDonald's on every corner and sunburned tourists at every bend in the road.

But the land—

It had changed not at all. Eddie felt a sudden rush of kinship with all the generations that had gone before. Surely, had they stood here, they would have seen exactly the same site as he now did—the looming, comfortable, familiar curves of Turquoise Mesa, so named for the shadows that fell across it in the early morning and evenings. How many of his people had grazed their sheep in its shadows, built hogans and sweat lodges, and turned to gaze at its towering shape for reassurance that all was as it should be, that they were walking in beauty?

"*Yaa'eh t'eeh*, stranger!" called a voice. Eddie was started out of his reverie and glanced about, the hot blood of embarrassment warming his face. His eyes widened with pleasure as he saw his high-school friend, William Tsosie, leaning up against an ancient car and waving.

"Bill!" he called back. A smile stretched across his face, and he hurried to embrace his old buddy. The two men hugged one another tightly, unashamed of their affection, and when at last they pulled back it was only to grin into each other's faces. They both began talking at once.

"You've put on weight—"

"Look at the lines on your face!"

"Never thought I'd see you here again—"

"Never thought I'd be here." The words were true, and as Eddie said them, he sobered a little.

Bill Tsosie had been one of the reasons he had returned to the Rez, after leaving it with something almost resembling hate in his heart. Bill, with his long letters, somehow managing to capture the sun and the dust in an envelope and send it to green, soft Virginia. Bill, with his dry accounts of his own med school experiences, the horrors of his residency, and, finally, the poignant accounts of life at first the Indian Health Service and then the Drake Free Clinic.

Bill's grin, too, faded a little. He put a hand on his friend's shoulder. "I'm glad you're here. We need you. Do you want to get some lunch before I drop you off at the hospital?"

They got into Bill's car and headed for the nearest fast-food place. Eddie was full of questions, and Bill, who had returned to the Rez to help open the Drake Clinic two years ago, had plenty of answers.

As he chewed his burger, Eddie vowed that he would not, absolutely, positively *not* ask about Alana. That had ended years ago.

"How's Alana?" he asked.

An unreadable smile spread across Bill's broad face. He didn't answer at once, just helped himself to more fries.

Stupid. Stupid stupid stupid—

"She's fine, Eddie. She's still here, of course."

Okay, you asked about her, Eddie, but you can stop right there and—

"She, uh, married or anything?"

"Nope." Bill brought the crispy fries to his mouth and crunched with great concentration.

"Bill . . ."

"She's the same as ever. Still stirrin' up trouble, is our Alana. Too late, though. It's the eighties. The Indian is trying to get in on all this technology, not fight old wars. Alana, though, she doesn't give up easily."

"No," said Eddie, softly, "she never did." His mind's eye was filled with an image of Alana as he had last seen her, her beautiful raven hair, adorned only with a single eagle feather, her dark eyes snapping with betrayal and hurt, her tall, slim body taut with righteous anger, even though she was wrong. *You sold out to the* bilagáani, *Eddie Rainsinger. You're turning your back on your own people.*

Alana.

"How's her dad?"

"Ah, Hosteen Yazzie is too prickly to die," replied Bill with a twinkle in his eye. "Mother Earth won't take him. Too bitter a taste." He puckered his lips as if he'd just bitten into a lemon.

They laughed together, though both of them loved the old medicine man and knew it. Hosteen—Elder—Delbert Yazzie had intimidated the hell out of Eddie once upon a time. Tall, imposing, whip-thin, and seemingly born as old as the piñon, Yazzie's gruff exterior hid the warmest of hearts. He was something of a local legend. Yazzie had been one of the famed "Code Talkers" of the Second World War. It had been the only code the Japanese had been unable to decipher, a mixture of Navajo slang and Army code. The Navajo had many veterans among them from WWII, Korea, and the Vietnam war. They served proudly and well, and the hostile reception many Vietnam vets had faced upon returning home was nonexistent on the Rez.

Eddie sipped his Coke. He was starting to relax. He hadn't been sure of his reception here, and Bill's warmth and acceptance was doing much to reassure him.

"Eddie"—Bill traced patterns in his ketchup with his fries—"why are you back here? When you left for U. Va. I thought that that was the last this place would ever see of Eddie Rainsinger, especially with the falling-out between you and Alana. I got all your letters while you were in med school. I followed you through your residency by mail. What about the CDC? You were on the fast track—the Epidemic Intelligence Service.

Special Pathogens Branch, wasn't it? Thought you were going to go be a virus hunter in Zaire or something."

"So did I." Eddie shrugged, searching for words. "When I left here, all I knew was that I wanted to get out. I thought there was a better life for me out there. I mean, look at this!" He plucked at his fine shirt, gestured to his suit jacket. "Top quality. I was leasing a Jag. But you know something? I started to lose sympathy for my patients. I'd tell them to quit smoking, they wouldn't. Start exercising, quit drinking, all logical things to improve their health—and nobody listened. They had all the money they needed to eat right, to join exercise clubs, to play *polo* if they wanted, and they squandered it. It was a very cushy practice, and yet I was starting to hate it. That's when I remembered my attending physician talking about working in the field of public health—doing research." Eddie smiled, remembering. "It was like the man was in love with viruses. He kept marveling at what incredible life-forms they were, how masterfully they adapted. And he got me interested, too."

Bill nodded. "I remember you writing about it. Last time I heard you on fire like that it was when you had first started dating Alana."

"Well, I was about halfway through the CDC fellowship program when—when I decided it wasn't really what I wanted to do."

Bill narrowed his eyes. "Something happened."

Eddie shrugged. "I just wanted to come home, that's all."

Bill continued to scrutinize his friend. Finally, he nodded. "Okay, Eddie."

Eddie was grateful. He didn't want to talk about what had happened, but he didn't want to be rude to Bill, either. Obviously, though, his childhood friend was sensitive enough not to push.

"So," said Bill, changing the subject, "you coming to the powwow tomorrow?"

"Me? Nah, I just got back. I want to settle in first."

"Alana'll be there."

"Okay."

It was hot at midday and Eddie's throat was parched. He'd finished the soda and was now chewing on the ice. Years of steamy Virginia summers had made Eddie forget just how dry it was out here. He had missed that deep heat that baked into the bone.

Eddie crunched his ice, feeling awkward. Bill wasn't here yet, and there were many people, especially the younger ones, whom he didn't know. He directed his attention to the dancers, took a deep breath, and tried to relax. To listen to the drums.

After a few moments, his heart seemed to want to beat in time with the steady rhythm of the drumming circle. Out on the grass, a few dozen dancers stepped, one foot, then the other, their bodies bowed slightly, their bright regalia a riot of colors. Once, he'd been able to distinguish the costumes and the dances: Fancy Dance, Grass Dance, Traditional, but now they all looked the same to his eyes. Singing was going on, too, but the words were lost to him. Forgotten.

"Wait till you see the kids up next," said Bill beside him. "They're amazing little dancers. Come on, there's someone I'd like you to meet."

Though this was a Navajo powwow, it was not a religious ceremony and was open to the public. Eddie had seen a few white people on the fringes of the crowd, though for the most part they didn't look like tourists. They mingled freely with the People, and looked and acted as if they belonged here—belonged here almost more than Eddie himself.

It was toward a cluster of such whites that Bill steered him now. A tall gray-haired man, dressed in jeans and a sport shirt, conversed with a small, neat woman. Both carried paper plates of fry bread, though they were too busy talking to have eaten the delicious treat.

"Doctor, Kelly, may I present my old friend Dr. Edward Rainsinger. Eddie, this is Agent Kelly O'Connell and Dr. Elliott Drake."

"Of the Drake Free Clinic," said Eddie, hoping his discomfort wasn't visible. He stretched out a hand and Drake shook it. "We spoke on the phone. Please call me Eddie. Miss O'Connell, a pleasure." Turning, he shook hands with the FBI agent. She smiled warmly. Petite, only a little over five feet, with startling blue eyes and dark hair, she was quite a looker.

"Please—just Kelly. Welcome home, Eddie."

"Thank you."

"I must say," said Drake stiffly, drawing himself up to his full height of well over six feet, "I'm surprised to see you here, Dr. Rainsinger."

Eddie kept his smile steady. Before accepting a job at the IHS hospital, he'd wanted to join Bill at the Drake Clinic. Despite his stellar career and glowing recommendations, Drake had turned him down. Even now, he wasn't sure why.

"Well, when that pull to come home kicks in, you find a way," he replied pleasantly. "I'm sorry we didn't connect, but I'm looking forward to my volunteer hours at the clinic."

Something flickered in the depths of Drake's eyes, then was extinguished. Eddie felt petty, but pleased. Drake, for whatever reason, might not want to hire him, but he couldn't stop a licensed physician from volunteering at the clinic.

He glanced back down at the shapely FBI agent. "That fry bread looks great. I'm going to go get some. Enjoy the powwow, Kelly."

With a nod to Drake, he turned and headed for the table where the bread was being served. Bill started to follow, but was halted by Drake's cool voice: "Dr. Tsosie? A moment, please."

Eddie bought a piece of bread and walked with it to the sidelines to continue to watch the dancing. He took a big bite of sugar-dusted, honey-drizzled fry bread and smiled as the powerful sweetness hit his tongue. He loved this stuff, even though part of him stood by and detachedly calculated every calorie and gram of fat in the dietary bomb. Honey dripped down his chin onto his T-shirt. And, of course, that was the precise moment when Alana showed up.

She, like he, was in her early thirties, but one would never guess it. Almost as tall as he was, she looked exactly as he remembered her. Her hair was long and loose, save where she had bound the single eagle feather into the thick black mass. Her aquiline features bore no wrinkles except around the eyes, and even those served her beauty rather than detracted from it. Her body was more muscular than Eddie had recalled; she'd been paying a lot of attention to keeping it toned. She wore a T-shirt whose no doubt inflammatory statement was partially obscured by a jean jacket. A turquoise bracelet, jeans, and boots completed the ensemble. No regalia for her. Alana Yazzie was not a dancer, a potter, or a weaver, though she honored those traditions of her people.

Alana Yazzie had always been, and clearly remained, a warrior.

Eddie's mouth, already filled with fry bread, went dry. "Hello, Alana," he said. He sprayed her with crumbs and was immediately mortified.

She looked him up and down, as though he were a horse she was considering buying. *"Yaa'eh t'eeh,* Eddie. *Nil nantl'ah."*

Embarrassment flooded him. "It's been a long time," he said, swallowing most of the lump of fry bread. "I'm—I'm not exactly fluent in Navajo anymore."

Her brilliant brown eyes narrowed and she nodded. "As I thought," she said in English. "They've made you soft, Eddie."

A spark of anger began to burn inside him. "Hey, I've got an idea. Let's try this again. I say, 'Hello, Alana,' and you say, 'Hello, Eddie. Boy it's good to see you again.' And then I say—"

"It *is* good to see you again," she replied, utterly startling him. She put her hands on her hips, and he could see what was written on her T-shirt: *The only FBI on the Rez should be Full-Blooded Indian.* "I thought we'd seen the last of you when you and I—"

"Well, you didn't. I'm like a bad penny. Keep showing up."

"Father wants to know if you would like him to perform an Enemy Way." She nodded her head to the left.

Following her gaze, Eddie saw Hosteen Yazzie sitting on a corner of one of the refreshment tables. Long white hair fell in two braids down his back. The "Rez hat," a black hat worn by nearly all of the Navajo men, perched atop his head. He did not wear sunglasses, never had, and his face was a mass of wrinkles attesting to the fact. Yazzie was fond of jewelry, and wore more of it than his daughter did—a concho belt of turquoise and silver, a bolo tie also made of a big chunk of turquoise, rings on almost every finger. Yazzie held a big cup of black coffee in his wrinkled, beringed hands. The steam rose and curled like a snake about his face.

Eddie felt a sudden tug of affection. His own parents had died when he was a child, and when he had begun courting Alana when he was just sixteen, Hosteen Yazzie had become a father figure to him. Everyone had thought that Eddie and Alana would marry, but their differences had just been too great. Eddie had left without saying good-bye to Hosteen Yazzie, and had always regretted it.

As if feeling the younger man's gaze on him, Yazzie turned slowly. His wrinkled face wrinkled further into a smile. Then, just as slowly, he turned his attention back to the dancing.

"Eddie?"

"I heard you." Eddie had forgotten much about his people, but not the sings. An Enemy Way sing was performed by a medicine man for an individual who, for any reason, had been away from the People for any length of time. It no longer really meant "enemy" in the sense of hostility, but it did apply to anyone who was not *Dineh*—not Navajo.

Like the whites.

The rite was meant to purge the patient of any ill effects incurred by being away from the sacred land. But suddenly something in Eddie got angry at the implication—that there was something wrong with leaving the reservation to pursue an education from a race of people who had knowledge and were willing to impart it. What the hell was there to purge of that?

"No, thanks. I'm fine."

"You aren't walking in beauty, Eddie, I can see it in you," Alana persisted. She stepped closer to him. Other women might have worn alluring perfume. Alana smelled only of the dust of the land. "I remember how adamant you were about leaving. Something must have happened to bring you back to us, and that something has left its mark on you."

"And you *are* walking in beauty?" Eddie retorted, stepping back and lifting his hands. "How long is your rap sheet now? How much harmony are you in when you're sitting in prison? How balanced are you when you're hating an entire race of people?"

Her face went very still. "There is no shame in being a warrior."

"Alana, there is no war!" Eddie, frustrated, ran his fingers through his hands. Heads were turning, and he lowered his voice to speak again. "You want to change things? Fine. I respect that. So get on the Navajo tribal council where you've actually got some power to do something. If you're right, then a lot of people see the same things you see, and they'll vote for you."

"Spoken like a *bilagáana*," said Alana, her voice dripping contempt. "You never wanted to be an Indian, Eddie. You always wanted to be a white man. Move off the Rez, go to a white man's school, practice a white man's trade—"

"What I have learned *off* the Rez I can bring back *to* the Rez. Don't you see that? I can help our people!"

At that, she snorted derisively. "Help them? Eddie, you can't even *talk* to them!"

He froze at her words, staring at her mutely. Then, without another word, he turned on his heel and stalked off. He threw the partially eaten piece of bread into the trash and headed for the still-shiny pickup truck he'd just bought. Breathing shallowly he climbed into the cab and took off.

This had been a mistake. A horrible mistake. Eddie Rainsinger no more belonged on the reservation than a horny toad belonged in the rain forest. But he was here now, for good or ill; had turned his back on a promising career filled with everything he'd always wanted to do to come back to the Rez and take care of back pain, sinus infections, and the occasional broken bone.

What have I done? thought Eddie as he floored it, stirring up clouds of dust. *What have I done?*

CHAPTER
FIVE

• • •

April 13, 1981
Charles Air Force Base
The Utah Desert

"I believe your instructions were to permit me to have unlimited use of the facilities of this base," said Saris in a silky voice. "That includes access to all of your men, all of your supplies, all of—"

"I know what it means, damn it," snapped Konrad. He glared with real hatred at the spidery man who lounged before him. Every move Saris Krai made, every word he uttered bothered the colonel. This was his base. His mission. The Dragit had no right to elevate this *mik-tah* over him, especially not for a handful of deserters.

But that was precisely what the Dragit had done, and Konrad had to live with it. That didn't mean that he was going to lift a finger to help make Saris's task one whit easier. He was a bounty hunter as far as Konrad was concerned. Let him earn it.

"How many humans do you have here on a regular basis?" asked Saris.

"We've managed to keep it down to a very few, and they are only on the base during the day. The total is less than three percent. The majority of the area is classified as top secret and requires clearance to enter. We've made sure that only Tyrusians get that level of clearance for Charles."

"How secure is this base from the prying eyes of any *Erdlufi* intelligence?" asked Saris.

The very question was an insult. Konrad took a deep breath and tried to calm himself. He wasn't about to let Saris know just how upset he was. Normally, he could keep his composure around the man, but this morning Konrad was exhausted. He'd been up all night, typing out the damned report for the Dragit, and had had to stand at attention while his master thoroughly chewed him out before departing. To put it mildly, Konrad wasn't at his best.

"Completely. For the outer perimeter, we have in place barbed wire and electrical fences with sentries posted at critical junctures. We also have video cameras active twenty-four hours a day. If anyone gets past that, we have the Tyrusian force fields erected at every entrance. Of course, there are always the Manglers. We also have alarms and—"

"None of which," interrupted Saris, "served to keep out one lone female in an automobile. How do you explain that?"

"She didn't get past the force field," retorted Konrad. "It was Cale who reached *her,* not the other way around. And even he wouldn't have been able to manage it without the Exotar. Several routine duty shifts had to be adjusted for the Oosha's arrival and—"

"It seems to me," said Saris, leaning back in the Earth-style chair and placing the tips of his long fingers together, "that with a planned assassination and coup about to occur at the base, you might wish to have more security, not less."

"We did!" protested Konrad. Damn, Saris was getting to him. "We had security where we deemed we needed it—on the inside. Who would have thought an *Erdulfa* would pick last night to trespass?"

"Who indeed?" echoed Saris. "But she did."

"Anyway, the point is moot," replied Konrad. "She and Cale-Oosha are dead."

"Has this been confirmed?"

Konrad laughed harshly. "The Jeep crashed into a helicopter, Krai. Both vehicles—or should I say, what was left of both vehicles—then plunged two hundred feet into a chasm. A Mangler wouldn't survive that, let alone human or Tyrusian flesh and blood. Cale is dead, the meddling Earth female right along with him. Our security works. I thought," he added archly, "that you were here to track down deserters, not criticize the Dragit's own programs."

"Ah, quite right," smiled Saris. His lips were thin, and the smile stretched almost literally from ear to ear. Konrad, who had become used to Tyrusians who resembled humans, was unsettled by Saris's—well—alienness. "Then permit me some of your men and a vehicle. I wish to explore the area. Afterward, I wish to interrogate some of your men who knew the deserters. They might have some important information for me that hasn't yet been—forthcoming."

"We've combed the area thoroughly. You won't find anyone hiding within the perimeters of the base. I suggest—"

"*I* suggest you silence yourself before you say something you might regret." Saris rose and walked to Konrad's desk, placing his hands down and leaning in toward the colonel. "If I report that you are obstructing this investigation, the Dragit will be most displeased."

Konrad stared into the elongated purple eyes, not bothering to disguise his loathing of the man. But Saris was right. This was the Dragit's pet project, at least for today, and it would be unwise for Konrad to block its execution.

But he didn't have to go out of his way to help Saris, either.

"Very well. Take two men and one Jeep."

The thin, high eyebrows drew together, and Saris began to protest. "Rafe and the rest of his cronies did a great deal of damage to the base before they died," said Konrad, not letting Saris speak. "We have shifts working around the clock to effect repairs. Two men and a Jeep are all I can spare." He smiled and shrugged. "Truly."

He could tell that Saris suspected otherwise, but there was nothing he could do about it. Without another word, Saris stalked out. Konrad watched him go, his eyes narrowing speculatively. He thumbed a switch.

"Lieutenants Harrison and McCoy, report in."

"Harrison here."

"McCoy here, sir."

"Report to the surface. You're to be Saris Krai's escorts wherever he needs you to go. And gentlemen—"

"Sir?" Two voices speaking in chorus.

"I want a full report on all his activities and discoveries. *All.* He scratches his nose, I want to know about it. Understood?"

"Aye, sir."

"Aye, sir."

"Konrad out." He leaned back in his chair. McCoy and Harrison were good men. He really couldn't spare them now, but if there were any men whom he could trust to report Saris's activities down to the letter, it would be these two. And right now, that was more important than repairs to the base. If Saris's sniffing about turned up anything at all, Konrad was going to be the one to report it to the Dragit.

"Colonel?" The voice belonged to Lieutenant Dawson, the man Konrad had put in charge of his own investigation—unknown to Saris.

"Go ahead, Dawson."

"Security reports that one truck and several other items such as com orbs and holographic camouflage units were taken. Instructions on how to proceed, sir?"

Konrad was hit with a mixture of emotions—elation and frustration. Here was a solid lead on at least one section of the deserters. But he had to conduct the search covertly. If Saris got wind of this, he'd step in and snatch the victory right out of Konrad's hands.

"Sir?"

"Dawson, I want you to begin tracking this. Find these men as soon as possible and bring them back to me alive. But remember—you must not do anything that will alert Krai to these activities."

"That will cut down on the effectiveness of our search, sir."

"I realize that, but it's more important that we keep this operation secret than that we find any one group of deserters."

"Understood, sir."

Saris knew when he had been insulted. He also knew his enemies. Konrad was guilty on both counts.

He squinted in the hot sun as he sat in the primitive Earth vehicle called a "Jeep." The driver and his companion were tight-lipped, human-looking Tyrusians who clearly distrusted him as much as their colonel did. It mattered not to Saris. Unlike Konrad and, truth be told, the Dragit, Saris felt no need to surround himself with aides, valets, or sycophants of any sort. What he needed to do, he did alone. Always.

So he tolerated the dust and heat, the extreme jouncing of the primitive vehicle, and the silence of his mistrustful companions, and remained silent himself save to issue orders in a disdainful tone of voice. The letter of his commands was obeyed, if not the spirit, and that was all he required.

They wound up the road that the late Oosha had taken with his little *Erdlufa,* and when they reached the spot where the Jeep and helicopter had met in their fateful collision, Saris ordered, "Stop!"

The Jeep slid to a halt with much grinding of rock beneath its wheels. The dust clouds it had stirred up now began to settle. Saris fought back the urge to cough as he climbed out of the vehicle. Meticulously, under the sharp-eyed gaze of Konrad's men, he scrutinized the path the ill-fated Jeep had taken. It was an easy path to follow, with the shards of broken glass and the gaping hole in the guardrail, but Saris dropped to hands and knees and brought his face nearly to the earth in an effort to analyze it all completely. He strode to the edge of the cliff and peered downward. In the bright sunlight, the shadows seemed even darker, and the wreckage hiding in the depths below was all but swallowed.

Without a word to the airmen, Saris began to climb down. His long fingers found holds where ordinary Tyrusian digits would not, and his skeletal body was made mostly of muscle, bone, and sinew. It was unlikely that he would fall, and the confidence he felt in his skill gave added surety.

It took a long time for him to reach the bottom of the crevice, even though he climbed swiftly. Finally, he let himself drop the last several feet, landing perfectly. He flicked on a small handheld light and cast the illumination about. Twisted, blackened, sharp metal wreckage met his gaze. Carefully, Saris stepped over the chunks of debris, occasionally reaching to move aside a piece that obscured his examination.

Konrad was right. No one could have survived this. His light found what was left of the Tyrusian pilot—little more than a charred bone or two. There wasn't even a smell of decomposition down here. The wreckage was strewn everywhere. Had this been an open space instead of a confined crevice, debris would be scattered for yards. Some of it undoubtedly was. Saris felt certain that years from now some soldier would stumble across bits and pieces of this historical event. Unperturbed by the violent scene, Saris continued to pick his way through. He found no immediate remains of Cale or the girl, but considering the immensity of the destruction that was no surprise.

Finally, his light fell on a small piece of metal. It was crumpled and mostly singed black, but upon peering more closely at it Saris saw that there were letters still partially visible. He committed them to memory: R K HN. The rest were unreadable.

He would say nothing of this find to Konrad, but once he had finished with his tasks here, he would see what he could learn from those four letters.

Saris took a few more moments, to make certain he had missed nothing else of import, then nodded to himself. This place had told him all it could.

R K HN.

He would not forget it.

Saris Krai turned and calmly began to ascend.

Lieutenant Sean Anthony was a handsome enough fellow, and had the look of intelligence about him. He also had the smell of fear.

He sat upright and stiff, his eyes focused straight ahead. The bandage around his head had been removed, and the small area where the doctors had been forced to shave his head to treat the wound looked comical compared to the spit-and-polish image the youth clearly wished to present.

Anthony was only the third person Saris had interrogated this afternoon, and the Dragit's valet was still fresh.

For several minutes, the two of them had been alone in the small, claustrophobic room Saris had selected as the interrogation area. Anthony sat on a chair; Saris circled him repeatedly, never taking his purple gaze off the youth. So far, that was all. And so far, that had been sufficient to produce a slight sheen of sweat on the young man's high, deep-templed forehead.

Saris noted this and nodded to himself. This one would be productive. He sensed it.

Finally, he paused directly in front of Anthony. "Your head," he said. "Does it hurt?"

"No, sir."

"Don't lie to me." Saris's mental powers were beginning to unfold, to become alert to the subtleties of the mind in front of him. He read the boy's lie like a whiff of carrion in a garden; something disturbing, out of harmony. "Does it hurt?" he repeated.

"A bit, sir!"

The mental "scent" was gone. Saris nodded. Now Sean Anthony was telling the truth. Saris had established what the lieutenant's mind was like both in truth and in lie.

"Tell me again what happened. I've read the report, but I'd like to hear it from you."

Anthony licked his lips. The gesture didn't go unnoticed by the interrogator.

"Early this morning, Kaslik, Stephens, and Doc—we called him Doc, but he's—"

"I know, continue."

"We were watching the arrival of the Oosha."

"As you should. What happened?"

Anthony swallowed. "We watched the coup occur, sir."

"And where were your sympathies?"

"I—I will follow the Dragit."

"But your friends—they had other plans?"

"Yes."

"Did they ask you to go with them?"

A hesitation, then, "It was over too quickly, sir. One minute I was watching the screen, the next one of them had struck me on the back of the head with what I think must have been an arbus."

The "scent" of a lie was powerful. And this one

was an out-and-out lie, not a mere twisting of truth. Slowly, drawing out the moment and the young man's escalating fear, Saris put on his temple piece. His mental capabilities doubled, tripled.

"I think you're lying to me, lieutenant. Is there anything you'd like to retract?"

"No, sir!" Too loud, the voice; too strong, the denial. With the grace of a panther, Saris was on him. His long fingers closed about the youth's head and he jerked Anthony's face up to meet him, stared into the widening, frightened eyes.

And began to probe.

An image, of four friends watching the screen . . .

"No! Stop, please, I beg you!" Anthony started to lift his powerful soldier's hands in an attempt to claw at Saris, but a quick, almost scornful command from the Dragit's assassin made those hands fall.

Watching with horror, all of them, as the Oosha came under attack . . .

Anthony's face went slack and his eyes rolled into the back of his head.

"We've got to make the same choice, gentlemen . . . What's it going to be?" The one called Doc, slamming down his weapon, stating "Shoot me if you want, but I sure as hell didn't sign on for this Earth duty to be an Oosha-killer."

"Ah, Doc," purred Saris. "The first to desert."

Ashley following suit, then Kaslik, with reluctance and fear . . . "Only if they catch us, Kaslik. Only if they catch us."

"Ah, but my dear, I *will* catch you," said Saris. Beneath his long fingers, Sean Anthony began to convulse. Blood trickled from his nose.

"I'm scared, Doc. Ashley says they'll have to find us—but damn it, you know they will! We know how thorough we Tyrusians can be . . . hit me on the back of the head with that thing real hard, will you?"

"Fear, not loyalty, eh, Lieutenant?" Saris gripped

the man's skull harder. Blood was now coming from Anthony's eyes, nose and ears. It dribbled onto Saris's fingers. "More. Tell me more. Tell me their plans, where they were going . . . !"

"Knock me out and that way I've got a reason for not stopping the three of you. Good luck. And don't worry—I won't betray you." The image of Ashley's beautiful face, as the arbus came crashing down on his skull.

The poor fool. The poor, stupid fool. He already had.

Satisfied that he had gotten everything he could from Lieutenant Sean Anthony, Saris let go. The body, no longer supported by Saris's hands, toppled limply from the chair. Saris reached into a breast pocket, withdrew a handkerchief, and meticulously began wiping the blood from his hands. He went to the door and knocked on it. When it was opened, he said to the waiting airman, "Get rid of this and clean up the area. Then bring me whoever is next."

CHAPTER SIX

• • •

April 12, 1981
Salida, Colorado

Sarah Sayers stood in the corner, hugging her thin elbows and grinning like a madwoman. Sarah was tall and willowy, as the cliché went, with pale skin, pale blue eyes, and long pale blond hair. In contrast, she was dressed in a clinging silk dress that was patterned with bold primary colors. She looked like a dryad gone neon, but the effect was striking—exactly what she wanted.

All about her were the happy sounds of milling crowds—the murmurs, the tinkling of glasses, the soft Wyndham Hill music in the background. Milling crowds represented, tonight, the realization of Sarah's ultimate dream.

They were here for her. Or at least, for her art. Three years ago, she'd arrived with a single suitcase and a truckload of determination, and now she was here in the Salida Arts Group building as this month's featured artist. And there was actually a *crowd*. Sarah's smile almost hurt her face, but she found herself incapable of not smiling. This was not a New York or L.A. crowd, to be sure—no tuxes here, or strapless gowns. Just a host of the townspeople, in their sensible shoes and Sunday best. But they were stopping in front of her bold, almost abstract pieces, pausing in front of her graceful watercolors, and—best of all—reaching for wallets.

Paul Marsh, the owner of the gallery, sidled up to her and handed her a glass of champagne. Paul was also a bit of the walking cliché, of the tall dark, and handsome variety. "Why are you lurking here in the corner?" he chided. "Come out and meet your adoring public!"

She shook her head, but accepted the champagne. "I like watching them. I want to see what they're drawn to, what they're willing to shell out money for. What makes them pause, or laugh." Sarah shrugged her thin shoulders. At Paul's slight frown, she added, "I'll come mix and mingle in a little bit, I promise."

"Okay. But don't be too long," he said, then turned with a bright white smile to shake the hand of Ted Jonas, the president of the local Lions Club.

Sarah turned, sipping the champagne, and walked to the long, two-story window. It faced in a southwesterly direction, and the slope of Methodist Mountain humped upward, blocking Sarah's view of the starfield. She'd painted the mountain many times, drawn by its rounded top that was in such stark contrast to the hard, sharp juts of its neighbors, the Collegiate Peaks. She took another sip of the champagne and had started to turn around when something flashed in the corner of her vision.

She turned abruptly, staring back out the window. There it was again! A shooting star, heading toward Earth with tremendous speed. Sarah smiled to herself—a good omen. She'd just started to articulate a wish when the shooting star did the impossible.

It began to slow down.

Sarah's pale blue eyes widened and she tightened her grip on the champagne flute. Before her eyes, the meteor slowed to a stop and began to hover directly over Methodist Mountain.

A UFO. My God, I'm seeing a UFO. . . .

Now the light began to move again. Sarah stepped closer to the glass, lifting a thin hand to block out the glare of the room behind her. She saw now that it was no meteor. It was definitely a ship—a cylindrical ship, looking almost like a cigar. It was mostly white, but now that she looked closely she could see a variety of colors. It zipped around the mountain, disappearing from her view for a moment, then reappeared, hovered again, and then sank slowly in for a landing.

Though it was warm in the room with the press of people, Sarah started trembling uncontrollably. She couldn't tear her eyes from the place where the—the alien spaceship had landed. More than anything, she wanted to rush to Paul, to her fellow artists and townspeople, and cry out loud *They're real! Those people aren't crazy, the UFOs are real!* But she stood, still in awe over what she had seen.

This had been for her. For her eyes only, here on her night of nights.

"I'm going to paint you," she whispered, the image of the spaceship still burning in her brain.

And she did.

Jaran K'Lara sat at the command center of the badly damaged escape pod, his right hand closed so hard over the com orb that his fingers cramped. He ignored the pain, because he had to; just like he had to ignore the screams and sobs behind him, the hot smell of burned flesh, the knowledge that some of his friends were dead. Because he had to.

He had turned off the autopilot once they had penetrated Earth's atmosphere, because the last thing he wanted was for the ship to land where it had been programmed to—in the middle of Charles Air Force Base. He wasn't sure of the geographical layout of this planet, only that Charles was located in a place called Utah. He decided to avoid this Utah altogether and opted for its neighboring area, called a "state," that was known as Colorado.

He kept his thoughts as calm as he could, and the com orb responded, albeit jerkily. As they drew closer to Earth, he could see the bright light that indicated large population centers. These he wanted to avoid at all costs. Thus far, the *Erdlufi* had no knowledge that there were aliens among them, and Jaran didn't want his damaged, terrified, non–English-speaking "crew" of refugees to be the humans' first encounter with Tryusians.

He directed the ship as best he could, thinking directions, height, distance, speed, and finally set down in a mountainous area some distance away from the nearest large population area. There were some lights here, but not many. The pod descended, circled a large mountain, then Jaran spotted a clearing and brought the ship in for a landing.

He misjudged the distance and the vessel landed hard, crashing through trees and finally bouncing to a stop on the rocky earth. Jaran grunted as he was propelled forward a few inches, then caught by the protective restraint of the force field.

Silence. They'd made it.

Jaran closed his eyes and let out the breath he hadn't realized he'd been holding. He thought to himself, *now comes the hard part.* He felt a faint tingling as the force field surged slightly, then dissolved.

He turned in his seat and groaned softly at the disaster that met his gaze.

When they had been struck by the fire from the Royal Yacht, he had known that part of the ship had been blown away. What he hadn't realized in the dim, flickering emergency lighting was that the blast had also blown away several of the refugees. There was a huge, gaping hole in the side where once some half dozen people had been.

Many of those who were left had been injured in the scramble simply to get to the escape pods. They stared at him with pale, frightened faces. The sobs had subsided into silence, which Jaran found more unsettling.

Quickly, he counted: seven, including himself, Gevic, and Shalli. And Shalli looked bad. Seven. He desperately hoped the others aboard the Yacht had made it.

"Where are we?" asked a quivering voice.

"A place called Colorado. About five hundred miles as the humans measure from Charles Air Force base."

"Did any of the others make it?" asked Gevic.

"I don't know," replied Jaran, "and I don't think it would be wise to initiate contact. I'm certain that Konrad and the others back at the base know of our flight, and they might be listening for Tyrusian com orb signals." He rose and straightened, bracing himself for the dreadful tasks that awaited.

The first thing they had to do was tend to the injured. This encompassed nearly everyone to one degree or another. Shalli was the most gravely hurt. Carefully, Jaran cut off her uniform and applied a thick foam from a canister contained in the medikit. This immediately deadened the pain, and Shalli's face, creased with silent suffering, softened a little. A few seconds later the foam had thinned and hardened, forming a protective layer beneath which the injured flesh would heal rapidly. They treated others with burns in a similar fashion, placed broken limbs in computerized casts that straightened the bones, set them in place, and began at once to mend the damage. Scrapes, cuts, and other minor injuries were cleaned, treated, and left to heal on their own. Tyrusians healed quickly, even if a wound was untreated.

The next task was harder. They buried the dead under cover of the night. It was cool in this place, and

Jaran shivered with the unexpected sensation. Those who often traveled to other worlds, liked the diplomats he had attended, no doubt grew used to strange climates and being out in the open. Jaran had grown up in an artificial climate on Tyrus, after which he had spent nearly all of his adult life aboard the Royal Yacht. He knew nothing of winds, or the phenomenon called "snow," or cold, and knew that for most of his compatriots here tonight the sensations were equally alien.

They dug holes with the use of the arbuses, and in shivering silence placed their dead within. Then they covered them with the cold earth, tree branches, stones, whatever they could find. It was a sobering task, and more than one person wept. Once this was done, Jaran herded his people—strange, to think in such terms—back into the pod. They obeyed, the burials having taken the edge off the panic and replaced it with a somber sort of calm. They looked to him, fear and hope plain on their faces.

Jaran licked his lips, met the eyes of each of them, and began.

"It isn't the best of all possible situations," he began, "but as for me, I'd rather be here than aboard the Royal Yacht, standing in line to be executed. I hope all of you feel the same."

Soft murmurs. Heads nodded. Despite the injuries and the unsettling deaths of their friends, they were all still with him.

"We have made it safely to this planet Earth. The vessel has obviously taken damage, but with any luck, we'll be able to repair it. We are in an artificially designated plot of land called the United States of America, in a subdivision known as the state of Colorado. That's about all I know right now, but once I have some time, we'll search the computer records to see what we can learn."

"We won't have the knowledge," said Baris, a big,

dark-haired man known for casting the worst possible spin on any situation. "The way the master computer is set up aboard the Yacht, there's a warning that's sounded when there's a need to evacuate. That's when the computer begins unloading critical information into the escape-pod computers."

"We're all aware of that, Baris," said Jaran, with a slight edge to his voice. He really, really didn't need Baris's gloomy forecast right now. He needed optimism. They all did. "The upload also starts when the pod is opened manually, as we did. Some information was indeed uploaded into the pod's computers before the Dragit's men interfered."

"I imagine it won't be useful," said Baris, looking almost pleased at the thought.

"I'm hoping it will be," countered Jaran. "Does anyone here know English?"

They all shook their heads. "There is a translation program that's automatically installed into the computer database. Between that and doing a lot of listening, we should be able to pick it up. It'll be useful to know how to talk to the aliens if we have to." He was not overly worried. Tyrusians, even the less educated, had the ability to learn languages quickly. It came easily to them, and nearly everyone spoke over eight languages fluently. English should not be too much of a problem.

"What about food?" asked someone.

"That is not an issue." Jaran was relieved to have something utterly positive to report. "The pod is equipped with enough food and water to feed twenty for a full month. That should last us for several months, if to comes to that."

"Do you think it will, Jaran?" asked Gevic. "What are you planning to do, anyway? What's going to happen to us?"

That was the tough one. Jaran took a deep breath. He hoped most of them would agree with him, but didn't dare hope that his plans would be universally applauded.

"We have landed on a planet whose inhabitants don't know we exist. I think that we should avoid encountering the natives if at all possible. I don't think our holographic camouflage program is damaged, so we should be able to hide fairly well. Our focus should be on repairing the ship and seeing if we can get it flightworthy again. I hope that will be soon. In the meantime, we know we weren't the only ones to flee the ship. Somewhere on this planet, there are others of our kind. With any luck, we'll be able to find them." He took a deep breath, and said, "My goal is to find Cale-Oosha. I believe in my heart that he managed to escape."

That did it. Everyone began talking at once. Some, like brave, injured Shalli, expressed joyous relief that someone else shared her hope that the Oosha had survived. Others, primarily loudmouthed Baris, thought the whole concept ludicrous and potentially suicidal. Jaran let them express themselves for a few moments, then rose, holding out his hands for silence.

"Quiet," he said. Then more forcefully, "I said *quiet*!" They were silent. "We never saw the Oosha die. And I for one don't think Commander Rafe would let him die no matter what the odds." He smiled a little, and saw a few answering grins. Rafe was not a man any of them would want to tangle with. "I also firmly believe that Tyrusians are better than the events on this planet would lead us to believe. Not everyone on the Royal Yacht was ready to fall to the Dragit, and I simply can't believe that everyone on Charles would be a ready partner to regicide. Someone down there, maybe only a few, maybe several dozen, refused to participate. I have to believe it, or I lose all pride in my people."

He stood straight and tall, firm and rock-steady in his faith in his people. "Everyone here chose potential death over siding with the Dragit. Everyone. And until we have proof of the rightful ruler's death, everyone here should be willing to believe that he's alive. To that end, we will listen—monitor all frequencies. Our enemies will be looking for us—but our friends will be, too. Once we have our ship repaired we'll be in a lot less danger, and perhaps we can begin sending out our own messages."

He fixed each of them with a steady gaze. "I will tolerate no challenge to this plan. We must all work together toward a common goal, or be destined to fail. If anyone wants to leave—to try to blend with the humans as those at Charles have been doing—then you are free to go. I'll send you off with food, water, and whatever else we can spare, and wish you luck with all my heart. But I will not allow anyone to stay here and drain the morale of the rest of us. We need hope and faith now as much as we need food or technology. Am I understood?"

They nodded slowly. A few looked as if they might choose to take him up on his offer, and that was fine with Jaran. If they didn't want to stay, he most certainly didn't want them around.

"Good. Now—let's see just how badly we were hit."

While others went about the task of investigating the damage, he went to sit beside Shalli. She managed a feeble grin for him.

"I should be . . . one doing this," she said, waving a hand in the direction of the computer panels.

"Don't worry about that," said Jaran. "The ship's been damaged enough that I'm sure there'll be plenty left for you to do when you're better."

He grin widened, and her eyes sparkled with a hint of her old mischief. Then the smile faded. She reached a hand up to Jaran, touched his cheek.

"So brave," she said. "So smart. We're lucky . . . you're leading us."

A sudden rush of emotion swept though him, and

Jaran began to shake. She'd come so close to being killed . . . Impulsively, he pressed his own hand over hers and brought the mechanic's strong, callused fingers to his lips. She did not pull away.

Doc couldn't believe how lucky they had been, and wondered when that good luck would run out.

During the coup, things had been a little crazy back on the base. He, Ashley, and Kaslik had been able to commandeer a truck, load it up with as much food, water, tools, and weapons as they could carry, and speed off unchallenged into the Utah night. They drove until the first tendrils of the sun's light had begun to fill the sky, then had pulled over, activated the holographic camouflage device that would completely disguise them, even to Tyrusian eyes, and tried to sleep.

To Doc's surprise, he did manage to sleep a little. They rose, stiff from sleeping on the floor of the truck, around dusk. Breaking into the rations, they perched on pieces of equipment and assessed their options.

"They'll start looking for us. They probably already are," said Kaslik.

Ashley elbowed him. "Thanks for the optimism, Kaslik."

"I'm serious," Kaslik protested. "We should get as far away from here as possible."

Doc shook his head. "I'm thinking we stay right here. They'll be expecting us to put distance between us and them. They'd never think to look right in their own backyard."

"Doc's right," said Ashley. "I say we sit tight for a few days. Listen in—we know all the channels. We can find out if—" she paused, then continued, "if the Oosha made it out all right. And I'm willing to bet we weren't the only ones who had a conscience. There are others of us out here, I'm sure of it. We should try to find them and—"

"And what?" asked Doc. "Try to overthrow the Dragit?"

She gazed at him evenly. Her beauty always made Doc's stomach do funny things. "Yes," she said, calmly.

Kaslik and Doc met each other's eyes. "Ashley," began Kaslik, in that exaggeratedly calm, almost professorial voice of his, "I don't think you fully understand the implications of—"

"I understand perfectly!" snapped Ashley. "I understand that for thirty years our people have been fed a lie. This has *never* been for the betterment of Tyrus; it's always been for the betterment of the Dragit! Do you think for one minute that Cale-Oosha would have been allowed to live even if he had agreed to this invasion scheme? I don't."

"So you think he's dead, then?" asked Doc.

"Maybe," said Ashley reluctantly. "But I bet when word gets out about the assassination—"

Doc snorted, and Ashley glared at him. "Dear, innocent Ashley, word won't get out. Such a terrible accident the young Oosha suffered. Isn't it tragic? How fortunate that on his deathbed Cale-Oosha called his uncle to his side and gave him his blessing and, incidentally, the crown of Tyrus. Remember the Hundred Days of Mourning? Tyrusians will mourn their young ruler—and then follow the rightful heir. The Dragit."

Ashley paled. "My God," she said. "Doc, damn you, I think you're right. But I still can't help thinking that if we got out of there, others did, too. We have a lot of technology in this trunk. Maybe enough to contact those others—maybe enough to get a message out, to let our people know what really happened."

"Maybe," echoed Doc. "And maybe we'd just better concentrate on how we're going to survive long enough to—"

His comment was abruptly cut off by a loud

whooshing noise from outside. At the same moment, the truck lurched badly to one side. Doc swore. A flat. Somehow, even though they weren't moving, they'd managed to get a flat.

"What the—" managed Kaslik.

"Flat tire," said Doc. "Come on. We better go assess the damage."

Ashley was the first out, opening the door and jumping lightly to the earth. It was the right front tire. Doc was behind her, still holding the bricklike ration in one hand, followed by Kaslik. Ashley planted her hands on her hips and glared at the offending tire.

"Looks pretty bad," said Kaslik.

"Wait a minute," said Ashley. She knelt to examine the tire more closely. "Doc, come look at this. Are you thinking what I'm thinking?"

Doc knelt beside her and the blood drained from his face. This was no accident. The tire hadn't been pierced by a rock or piece of glass. Along its tread was a wide, deep cut.

Just as Doc was about to warn Kaslik, they all heard a throaty, menacing growl.

Slowly, Doc and Ashley turned.

The Mangler had backed a terrified Kaslik against the truck. It couched at his feet, a macabre parody of the faithful hound adoring its master. Except this hound was about to rip out the "master's" throat.

In an effort to better understand humans, Doc had taken to reading some of their popular literature. Sometimes, in tense moments, the human authors described time as suddenly moving very slowly, almost stopping. He had dismissed this as utter nonsense— except that now, when he ought to be moving at the speed of light, doing something to save his friend, he felt as if time were standing still. Stupidly, he thought, *Well, those humans were right about situations like this after all.*

None of them had an arbus. They had come barreling out here to inspect a "flat" and had been prime targets for the ambush—for so it had to be. Sharp Mangler talons had ripped the hole in the tire, and the clever creature had simply waited for his dinner to come to him.

Suddenly the brick-ration was grabbed out of his hand and before he fully understood what was happening, Ashley had moved forward. "Hey! Mangler!" she cried. "Hungry? How about this?"

Snarling, the beast whipped its deformed head in her direction. It craned its neck—what it had of a neck—and caught the ration Ashley had tossed at it. With a slobbery gulp, the food bar was gone. A thick tongue crept out to lick its lips. In a detached, thoughtful part of his mind, Doc noted that one of its fangs had been broken off. Probably while chewing on one of Doc's friends.

But, miraculously and improbably, the creature had turned its attention from Kaslik and sat staring fixedly at Ashley. Its dewlaps lifted in a soft snarl. Ashley kept her gaze locked with that of the Mangler. "Doc," she said in a shockingly steady voice, "get me whatever food we have."

Doc ducked back into the van. He did as Ashley had requested, gathering up every foodstuff he could lay trembling hands on. He also grabbed an arbus. Stumbling back out, he almost fell, but caught himself just in time.

Doc's near fall had made the creature nervous. It backed away from Kaslik, who had stayed completely motionless except for his darting eyes, and moved toward Ashley. Its limbs reminded Doc of a spider's— long, thin, awkward, yet full of unspoken threat. "Toss him another one, Ashley," Doc hissed to his friend. "I got the arbus trained on him—"

"No."

"What? Are you crazy?"

Ashley shook her head, still gazing at the Mangler,

not even sparing Doc a glance. "No, I'm not. He shouldn't have responded, he should have just gone straight for Kaslik—but he didn't. He went for the food."

"And Kaslik is damn lucky, but—"

"Here, boy. Here, Blue," called Ashley. Doc now saw what Ashley had already observed—that the Mangler's skin was not the usual shade of gray, but rather a sort of slate blue hue.

The creature snarled.

Ashley tossed him another ration bar. As before, Blue snapped it up with astonishing grace and accuracy. "Good boy," crooned Ashley. "Kaslik, start moving toward me. Slowly."

Kaslik nodded, swallowed, and started inching toward his two friends. Blue finished the bar and swiveled his huge head toward Kaslik, his dark eyes boring into the Tyrusian. Kaslik froze.

"Come here, Blue. That's the boy. Keep coming, Kaslik, he won't hurt you. At least I don't think so."

"How reassuring," breathed Kaslik, but he kept coming nonetheless. He, like Doc, had a lot of faith in Ashley. Blue ate a third bar.

Damn Mangler likes those bars better'n I do, thought Doc crazily.

Ashley fished out a fourth bar. But instead of tossing it to Blue, she held it out to him.

"Ashley! For mercy's sake—" Doc's voice broke, pleading. He couldn't move fast enough to get to her in time, and even if he did, a sudden movement would startle the Mangler and he might turn on his benefactor. Sweating, Doc felt a rush of fear crash over him. *Ashley . . .*

The Mangler moved forward. Doc expected it to lunge forward and snatch the bar, but it surprised him by reaching out a clawed forepaw—the same forepaw, no doubt, that had ruined the tire—and delicately, gently, plucking the proffered food from Ashley's hand and bringing it to its tooth-filled mouth.

Ashley grinned. "I think we've just found another refugee," she said. "Welcome to the Resistance, Blue."

CHAPTER SEVEN

● ● ●

May 15, 1981
Salt Lake City

"Aw, come *on,* you guys!"

Rita slammed the door behind her and Cale started, both at the sound and at the strain in Rita's voice. He and Rafe were seated at the kitchen table. Every inch of exposed Formica was covered with wires, cables, tools, maps, and the Exotar. Guiltily, Cale realized that not only had he and Rafe commandeered the table, they had also taken possession of the counters, the coffee table, and the sofa. And large areas of the floor as well.

"People are supposed to live here, you know." She slipped her backpack off her shoulders with a quick, practiced move of her thumbs and swung it to the floor.

"Rita," said Rafe, "we discussed this, and I explained to you that we would need room if we were to attempt communication with others of our race. Our communication module is imperfect, but we have made some progress nonetheless."

Rita didn't answer him. She opened the refrigerator, peered in, and selected a Coke. She popped the top and took a sip.

"Rita," began Cale, rising.

The look she shot him pierced him to the heart. "Save it." She stalked off into her bedroom, again slamming the door.

Cale gazed after her. Rafe put a hand on the youth's arm. "Let her be," he said in Tyrusian.

"But she's right to be angry with us," said Cale, replying in the same language. "We're—we're parasites. We destroy her vehicle, we put her at risk, we eat her food and spread our tools all over her house. I would be angry, too." He paused, and a frown furrowed his high forehead. "I hope that is all. She has seemed upset since we first came to this Salt Lake City."

"Cale," said Rafe, putting down the tangle of wires on which he was working, "may I speak honestly with you?"

Cale smiled warmly. "Rafe, you were my father's friend and now mine. Speak as freely as you would like."

"First I need to know—what passed between you and Rita in the cave? Before I found you?"

A blush warmed Cale's cheeks, and he looked down, busying himself with the Exotar. "That is private," he said.

"I wouldn't ask if I didn't think it was important."

Cale sighed. "I woke up there, after Rita and I made our escape. I don't remember even walking there, once we had jumped out of the Jeep. She cooked for us, and we ate, and we talked. Then the Mangler came." Now he glanced up, his eyes alight. "She fought at my side, Rafe! She helped me kill the Mangler. Then, when it was over, she looked so vulnerable and frightened—I went to her, to comfort her, and she looked up at me and said, 'I was afraid for you.'" He shook his head, still marveling at the words. "For me, Rafe. Here she is, not even aware that other beings exist on other worlds until that night. She rescues me, faces danger, fights off what to her must seem a monster, and she is fearful for *me*!"

Rafe said nothing, only watched his ruler with sharp eyes. Cale continued.

"I was amazed. I was so proud of her. And—I felt something else. I—I kissed her, Rafe."

"You *what*?"

Cale's cheeks felt like they were on fire, but he met his friend's disapproval head-on. "I kissed her. And I do not regret my actions."

Rafe groaned and rubbed his eyes. "Cale, you had no right to do that. She is not of any Tyrusian noble house. She has no standing, no—"

"She is brave, and intelligent, and I have never seen her like before! The women I have courted, the so-called 'Of-Proper-Rank' females—what insipid, soulless things they are compared to my Rita!"

The telephone rang. Both of them jumped, startled. Inside the bedroom, Rita picked it up.

"Cale—Rita knows nothing about Tyrusian bonding customs. To her, this kiss may have meant nothing. We have seen their television. We know how little a kiss, or even a sexual encounter, means to the *Erdlufi.* Did it ever occur to you that she might not share your affections? That she might have returned your embrace simply because she found it physically pleasurable? That it really meant very little to her?"

All the color drained out of Cale's face. His gut tightened, and he felt ill all of a sudden. He shook his head. "No," he whispered. "I—I had not thought of that."

"Maybe you had better think of it."

"But—why would she be willing to help us so?"

"You said yourself, she has a good heart. She helped you because you were in trouble—not because you are who you are. She would have done the same for anyone."

Cale was stunned. Rafe had to be mistaken. He had

held Rita in his arms, saw her fear for him plain on her beautiful face, felt her tremble as he kissed her. Surely, she cared for him! And yet . . . she had held herself aloof recently. She seemed to become angrier quicker, with less provocation, and sometimes with no provocation at all. He couldn't read the glances she gave him when she thought he wasn't looking; didn't know what emotions to ascribe to them.

"You need to remember who you are." Rafe's voice was gentle and held a trace of sorrow. "We're trying to find some support for your cause here on this planet—maybe even a way for you to get home, rally those loyal to you, and plan a war to win back your rightful crown. You owe your people your loyalty, Cale. You owe them an Ooshala who is also a Tyrusian. You owe them an heir who—"

Cale's head came up, and his purple eyes snapped fire. "I owe Rita my life. Do any of my other duties exceed my duty to her?"

"And what if she does not love you in return?"

Cale was silent. It was an awful thought. To have finally found someone he truly loved, and not to have that love returned—he almost wished he had died at the hands of his uncle, never tasting that dreadful, wonderful emotion at all.

In the silence came a soft sound. Cale listened. It came from Rita's bedroom.

"She is crying," he said, hurting as though the pain were his own. He rose and began to walk to the door, hand already outstretched to knock.

"Cale!" Rafe's voice cracked sharply, like a whip. "She may not want you."

For a long moment, while Rita's soft sobs continued on the other side of the door, Cale gazed at his friend. He loved Rafe like a big brother, and knew the older man had wisdom he himself had yet to earn. Rafe's level head and good judgement had saved Cale's life many times already on this planet.

And yet—the sound of his *Kia* in pain, whatever the cause, drew Cale inexorably. Maybe Rafe was right. Maybe Rita didn't care for him, except as she might care for a lost, injured animal. But if she was hurting, he had to be there, had to offer what comfort he could and let her be the one to turn him away.

"I know you think you know what is best for me, Rafe," he said quietly, affection warming the words. "And you may be right. She may not want me. But"— and he smiled sadly—"I must go to her, nonetheless."

Rafe uttered on oath, rose, and headed for the front door. Cale watched him leave, regretful over the argument, but unable to heed Rafe's advice. He turned back to Rita's bedroom and knocked at the door.

The knock was soft, gentle—like so much about Cale. The very tentativeness of the sound was like a fresh wound in Rita's already slashed soul. She wanted to snarl, "Go away," but found she couldn't summon any words at all. They simply couldn't get past the lump of agony in her throat. She rolled over and buried her face in the pillows, still crying.

"Rita?" The sound of the door opening. "Rita, I am sorry—I could not help but hear—please, what is wrong?"

The door closed, and the mattress sagged beneath his weight. Still, she didn't turn to face him. She couldn't bear *that* on top of the news she'd just received. Hot tears trickled down her nose onto the wet pillow.

"Rita, please. I cannot bear to see you hurting so."

She took a deep, shuddering breath and sat up, fumbling with the pillow, clinging to it as she wished she could cling to Cale but didn't dare. The room was dark, save for what light filtered through the blinds. It was enough to see him, though. She met his eyes, knowing that hers were puffy and reddened, and marveled anew at the aquiline, regal beauty of him.

"I got a phone call," she said, her voice thick.

"Bad news?"

She nodded. "My mom—she was killed in a car accident a few days ago. It took them this long to track me down."

"Rita—*Kia*, I am so sorry! You have never spoken of parents—I did not know—"

The words came easier now. She realized she wanted to talk to him, wanted him to know about this part of her life. "My parents got divorced when I was six. I went to live with my dad in California. That's where I grew up. He died of cancer a few months ago, just after I'd turned eighteen. My mom didn't even show up for the funeral."

Cale was silent, letting her speak. His wordless comfort calmed her. "I'd seen her only a couple of times since I was six. She lived in a little town called Glenport, in Massachusetts. I know she loved me, but she always seemed confused, like she didn't how much to say or do or show. And yet—I just learned that she left everything to me. Several thousand dollars, her house—everything. To a daughter she hardly knew."

"She was afraid," said Cale gently. "Clearly, she loved you very much, but because she was not able to watch you grow, she did not know who it was you had become. I am so sorry, *Kia*. You have lost your mother twice."

Fresh tears welled in her eyes. She wiped at them, pressed the cold soda can to her hot cheeks. It felt good. "Your parents—is an Oosha allowed to be close to them?"

Cale smiled sadly. "Yes, indeed. My mother died when I was young, but my father and I were quite close. I loved him very much." A shadow passed over his features. "In the light of what has happened here on Earth, I begin to wonder about his death. Perhaps my uncle hastened it along."

"Cale—that's an awful thing if it's true. I'm sorry."

"You said your father died of cancer?" She nodded. "What is that?"

"It's a disease. We don't know much about it. Cells—turn bad, and start turning other cells bad. Sometimes you can treat it, but . . ." Her voice trailed off. Tears were threatening again, and she didn't want to cry in front of Cale any more.

Cale's face had a stricken expression on it. "Cale? What's wrong?"

Suddenly he slipped off the bed and to her utter shock he was on his knees before her. "Rita, you must forgive me!" he cried. "Curse my uncle . . . and curse me and my father, for not seeing his true face sooner!"

"Cale, what is it?"

"This cancer of which you speak . . . it is known to us. Or rather, was known. We—" He glanced down, then back up to her, his throat working. "We have known how to treat it for almost a hundred of your years. The environment was so damaged before we moved into the domes that various cancers were almost common. Our physicians developed a cure for it. Had my father made contact thirty years ago, when your planet was first discovered, I do not know how many millions of lives we might have saved. Including your father's. I am so sorry." He turned his face away, guilt and shame writ plain on his face.

Rita couldn't speak. Her father had been fairly young when he died. The thought that he might still be here, alive, laughing, along with so many others—and the Dragit had taken that away from her—

Cale thought the Dragit had killed his father. Rita knew that the bastard had all but murdered her own.

She took a deep breath and deliberately forced the anger down. Perhaps Cale and his father should have recognized the evil in the Dragit, but they hadn't, and there was no point in blaming Cale for her father's untimely death.

"Oh, Cale," breathed Rita. "It's okay. It's not your

fault." Awkwardly, she reached to touch his black hair. It was as fine against her fingers as cool silk. He had cut it, and only when his hair was brushed back, as Rita did now, could one see his deep temples.

At her touch, he lifted his head, and her heart leaped as their eyes met. For a long moment there was silence between them. Rita thought about all she knew of this man, if man he could rightly be called. For over a month, he and Rafe had lived with her. She had watched him devour thick books at a single sitting, watch television with a keen interest, exclaim in horror at the world's brutalities, and laugh like a child at its delights. He was so different from her, from anyone she had ever known, and yet there was a familiarity about him that made him feel at times like she'd known him all her life.

Cale-Oosha. A ruler of a planet, with the weight of the world—two worlds, now that Earth was threatened—upon his shoulders, to whom responsibility was second nature, yet who was so ready to laugh and care.

Except about me.

The thought shattered the moment, and a broken sob escaped Rita's lips. Cale moved faster than she could have imagined, and suddenly she was in his arms and they were on the bed. His long fingers tangled in her brown hair and he kissed her deeply, searchingly, and she wondered if the wetness on her face was entirely due just to her own tears. He broke the kiss just as unexpectedly and his warm weight was gone.

"I am sorry," he gasped, "my behavior is unacceptable. Please forgive me."

"Damn it, Cale, what do you *want* from me?" Rita could cheerfully have strangled him. He blew hot, then cold, then hot again—

"Of course. I am an idiot. You know nothing of our customs. You don't know what it means when—"

"Cale!"

He grinned, suddenly, and then the smile faded. "I am afraid, Rita," he said simply. "I've lived through a coup, betrayal, fighting off Manglers, living on an alien world, and you frighten me so much more than any of these things."

"Me? Why?"

"Because," he said simply, "I love you."

"Oh," said Rita in a small voice.

"I should not have kissed you, now or in the cave. I did not lie when I said it was a Tyrusian custom. It is the second step in the six-step courtship we call *Kia-thamaa*. I had not even performed the first step, asking formal permission to kiss you, I did not know if you were even willing to enter the *Kia-thamaa*—"

"I was willing," said Rita.

"Oh," said Cale. And he started to grin again.

"So," said Rita, a little breathless now, "what's the next step?"

He hesitated. "Rita, the *Kia-thamaa* is an extremely serious rite. It is not like your television shows *Dallas* or *General Hospital*. The aim is a lifetime pair-bonding. Speak now if you do not wish to pursue this. Bonding with an Oosha is quite different from bonding with anyone else. Especially this Oosha. I come with trouble at my back at the worst, the responsibility of minding a world at the best." He smiled sadly. "It will, how do you humans say, break my heart, but I will accept it."

It was ridiculous. She should decline, at least for the time being. She should take time, get to know Cale better, know what they would have to face together, before—

But no. That was wrong. She had known she belonged with him back in April, when she impulsively said, "Take me with you!" She loved him. She would stand by his side here, or on Tyrus, or wherever his duty took him.

"So, what's the third step?"

His eyes were bright in the dimness of the room. "You make me so happy, *Kia.*"

"What does *Kia* mean?" He had called her that earlier, when she told him about her mother.

"Beloved," he said. "*Kia-thamaa* literally means 'beloved always.' The third step, we have also already performed. We have shared our histories. At least, a little. Tell me more."

So she did. She recalled favorite memories of her father, some that made Cale smile sadly and others that made him chuckle. She spoke also of what little she recalled of her mother, and felt comforted by his wordless sympathy. He in turn spoke of life as a prince and then, at too young an age, a king. Through his words, Rita saw a world full of both beauty and sorrow, great accomplishments and great misfortunes.

The sun went down as they spoke. At one point, Rita leaned over to switch on the bedside lamp. Cale's hand stayed her.

"No. All segments of the *Kia-thamaa* must be conducted under natural light if possible, firelight if necessary."

"I've got a candle or two around here," said Rita. She went to the closet and fished about for a bayberry-scented candle that usually came out only at Christmas, carried it back to the nightstand, and lit it. The warm glow cast shadows on Cale's sharp features.

For how long they talked, she didn't know. At last, she thought she had shared with him everything about her—except one thing. Eric. Slowly, not meeting his gaze, she told him of the only other man she'd ever been serious about. She spoke in halting sentences about her pain at the breakup, how empty and alone she felt.

"Never again," he said softly. Her mind flashed back to when she and he had emerged from the cave, before Rafe's unkind words had begun to cast a pall over their newly found happiness. She remembered his long fingers curling about hers, the words he had not spoken, but she had sensed: *I will not leave you. I shall not fail you.*

Rita suddenly, stupidly wished that a meteor would land on the apartment complex, for certainly she would never be this happy again in her life.

"Now, the fourth step," said Cale. "We pledge ourselves to one another." Their hands had met and clasped while they were talking. Sitting cross-legged on the mattress across from Rita, Cale gently turned her hands up and rested them on her knees. Carefully, he placed his own hands, palm down, on hers. He met her gaze and smiled, seeming almost incandescent to her somehow.

"Rita Carter, you appeared as if sent by a benevolent god in the darkest moments of my life. You are my light. What I can do to make you happy, I will; what I can give you, is yours. Now I am a king without a throne, all I have is my poor self. But that I give most joyously. Will you have me?"

Tears stung Rita's eyes. "Cale-Oosha," she whispered, "I will." She licked dry lips. "I was alone in the world, with few friends, and I didn't realize how lonely I was until I met you. I think I was yours from the moment I first saw you. Will you have me?"

"Beloved, always," he said softly. His eyes, dark in the dimness, caught and held her gaze. Suddenly he chuckled.

"What's so funny?"

"The fifth step is repeating those vows formally—a wedding, I believe is the human term. We have no one to marry us."

"Oh." Rita tasted disappointment, but Cale was still smiling.

"That means I, as the rightful highest temporal authority over every Tyrusian, have to marry us." He laughed. "So, I say that we are married. The fifth step is completed."

"Not much of a wedding," teased Rita. Her mirth turned to chagrin at the disappointment on Cale's face.

"I am sorry—I did not think—weddings are important to humans. If you like, I can dissolve—"

"Oh, no! We'll just have to have a really fancy wedding when we return to Tyrus," she said, emphasizing the "we."

"Yes, my Ooshala—my queen," he breathed. Rita's heart sped up as Cale's strong hands tightened on hers. He moved forward, taking the lead gently but purposefully. She sensed that if at any time she protested, he would stop—but she didn't want him to.

He laid her down on the bed, gazing at her and stroking her face softly. "Beloved always," he whispered.

"Kia-thamaa," she echoed in his language. "The sixth step?"

He chuckled, his breath warm on her face. "The best part, so I have been told."

"You've never . . . ?"

"I have never been pair-bonded," he replied simply.

Rita had a sudden, awful thought. They were two different species. Clothed, he looked human, but . . .

"Cale? What if—what if the pieces don't fit?"

He laughed aloud at that, then brushed his lips over her forehead. "Let's find out."

CHAPTER EIGHT

• • •

June 25, 1981
Charles Air Force Base
Utah Desert

Saris Krai stretched in the uncomfortable chair. The hour was early, but it was the only hour when his time was his own. Over the last two months he had been moderately successful in carrying out the Dragit's orders. Fourteen "jumpers" had been found, and six of the fifty deserters. All, of course, had been executed after Saris had drained them of any useful information.

He had developed a routine that almost always brought results. He had his team monitoring every know Tyrusian frequency twenty-four hours an Earth day. Inevitably, the various scattered factions of those loyal to Cale-Oosha—"Ooshati," they called themselves—would wish to link up with others. Some had expressed a naive hope that somehow Cale had managed to survive. They would break the silence that was their safety, and Saris and his men would be listening.

Sometimes they spoke in English, more often in their native tongue. Some of the more clever ones came up with codes that took a while to decipher. But always, in the end, the loneliness would be their undoing. It was then ease itself to prepare an ambush—although, twice, someone or something had warned the prey of the predator's approach. With the history of enmity that lay between them, Saris suspected that Konrad might be deliberately sabotaging his attempts to recover the traitors. If this was so, then the man was good at covering his tracks. Saris had nothing to take to the Dragit about Konrad's suspected interference, and until he did, he must remain silent.

Now, in the precious time alone to himself he had in the early hours of the morning, he sat at one of the special computers designed to interface with the humans'. The things were childishly simple to break into. Saris placed a long-fingered hand over the com orb and concentrated. Finally, he had a chance to pursue that lead he had discovered on his first day on the base. He had learned that the crumpled piece of metal with the letters on it was called a "license plate," and that every car in the United States was registered with such a plate.

Numbers and letters flashed before him at a pace that a human brain would find impossible to acknowledge: every registered license plate in this United States of America with the letters R K HN. Saris leaned back in the chair and waited. There were hundreds of combinations. He formed a thought and the search narrowed to the states in the vicinity: Utah, of course, Colorado, Nevada, Arizona, Wyoming, New Mexico, Idaho. He would begin with Utah and expand his search from there.

Now it was down to a few dozen. It would take time to sort through them all, and it might lead to a dead end. On the other hand, it might not, and Saris Krai was nothing if not patient.

Saris started with Salt Lake County. It was the nearest major population center and the likeliest. The minutes slipped by in the darkened room. R85K HN2,

R22K HN4, R62K HN3 . . . they went on and on. At each one, he checked the name on the registration. Many were men. That did not discount a wife and child, but from what he knew of human culture a woman driving alone, at night, in the desert struck Saris as an independent sort. He then checked the age and "race" of the women. The term amused him— humans were all of one race, weren't they? Silly, to put such arbitrary divisions according to skin color or shape of an eye.

The girl who had helped the Cale was of the "Caucasian" or "white" race, according to the human classification. That eliminated more possible suspects. He had been told that the car registered was a "Jeep," which narrowed his search further. Diligently Saris began checking the few remaining white, young females who owned Jeeps in Salt Lake City. He paused at one—a personalized plate that said ROCK HND. Rock Hound, he guessed—someone who was interested in geology. Who might be out in a desert with interesting rock formations in the middle of the night. . . .

He pulled the address and cross-referenced it with all others in the database. If this mystery girl had someone living with her, they could perhaps be contacted and—

Saris's purple, slanted eyes went wide in shock. Surely, fate was smiling upon him. Rita Carter, age eighteen, white female, owned a Jeep. Living at that same address were one Caleb Gray and one Rafael Smith. His heart pounding with excitement, he quickly checked for an obituary for said Rita Carter in the local paper. There was none.

She was alive and well, living in Salt Lake City with a Caleb and a Rafael.

Cale. Rafe. Alive.

Saris couldn't believe his luck.

June 26, 1981
Salt Lake City, Utah

The sky was bright blue, and the yellow sun smiled down on everyone in the world except Rita Carter. As far as she was concerned, it could have been pouring rain.

She had hoped she'd been wrong when, after several weeks of picking up the phone and then putting it down again, she had finally made an appointment with her doctor. However, Dr. Simpson had confirmed her worst fear.

Her lips curved in a grim smile. This would give Rafe even more fodder, she thought as her mind went back to the morning when . . .

. . . *she and Cale, knowing that Rafe's wrath awaited them outside, had finally emerged from the bedroom. He was at the kitchen table, methodically working on getting their crude communication device up and running, and did not turn around at first.*

Cale cleared his throat. "Rafe—"

Now Rafe did turn around, and Rita cringed inwardly at the anger on his face. "You don't have to tell me. Believe it or not, I noticed when you didn't come out to sleep on the sofa last night, Cale."

Cale sighed. "It is not what you think. We have completed the rite of Kia-thamaa. Rita has done me the honor—" and here he paused, looked over at her and squeezed her hand reassuringly—"the very great honor of becoming my wife." Then, softly, with an edge of warning, "You should greet your Ooshala."

To Rita's increasing dismay, Rafe blanched at Cale's words. "You—performed Kia-thamaa? Cale, you are bound for life! There is no dissolving this once all six steps have been completed! You hot-blooded little fool, what have you done?"

For the first time since she had met him, Rita watched

as Cale grew truly angry. He stood straighter and his eyes flashed a warning to his friend. Gone was the tender lover of the night before, the gentle man terrified of her rejection. This was a king indeed, a king capable of giving orders that would have life-and-death consequences. He suddenly frightened her, and she shrank back from the power he radiated.

"Commander Rafe, you dishonor yourself, your Oosha and your Ooshala! Had we been on Tyrus I would strip you of your rank and place you under Laai-rass!"

Rita didn't have the foggiest notion of what Laai-rass might be, but judging from Rafe's reaction, it was very bad and very dishonorable.

"But I know your heart is good, and, to be brutally frank, I need every loyal Tyrusian I can find now. You are lucky we are on Rita's homeworld, not ours. I have chosen Rita with my head and my heart. I am no foolish hot-blooded youth, but an Oosha, born and bred. I knew our laws before I knew how to write them, Rafe, and my father was the best teacher I could have had!" Now his visage softened somewhat, and he added, *"Except for you. Rafe, you know what you taught me. Can you think I would not listen at a time when such knowledge would best serve me?"*

Rafe's jaw worked. He was trying hard to compose himself. "No, my Oosha."

The simple admission seemed to dissolve the last bits of Cale's fury. He was not a man to hold on to a grudge; forgiveness came naturally to him. "Then, old friend, trust me to know what I am doing. Trust me to know that Rita, although she is not of noble birth, is noble of heart and spirit. She is brave and kind and wise, and we Tyrusians are lucky to have her." He smiled, a little sadly. *"How many jik'taasi can you think of who would have a deposed Oosha, anyway?"*

At that, Rafe chuckled a little. "You may be right at that," he admitted. "But, my liege—what about an heir?

Should anything happen to you, there is no heir save the Dragit. Whatever your qualities, my Ooshala, you are not Tyrusian. You may not be able to conceive Cale's child."

Rita blinked at that. It had never occurred to her that one of her duties might be to serve as Royal Broodmare, popping out heirs for the kingdom. But now that she thought about it, that was the single duty of every queen that had ever been, wasn't it? Rita had never thought about children, never particularly wanted them, and the thought that it might now be her job to produce them unsettled her. She turned to look at Cale, to see his reaction. He smiled at her, and as always, the world went away when he did that.

"It may not be a problem at all, Rafe. All I knew about humans was that we might be able to negotiate trade treaties with them. I had no idea I would fall in love with one. The scientists back home will no doubt have the answer. If Rita cannot conceive naturally—we are after all the people who genetically engineered Manglers. Certainly, we can learn how to blend human and Tyrusian DNA."

Rafe began to protest, but Cale held up a hand. "Your concern is legitimate and appreciated, my old friend. But for now, instead of arguing about something you cannot change, I would rather you greet your new Ooshala."

Rafe nodded his understanding and rose. He was a big man, and Rita suddenly felt very small, very young, standing next to him. She felt even more uncomfortable when the warrior dropped to his knees and took her hand. His fingers were strong, his palm, callused. He uttered something profound and solemn-sounding in Tyrusian, then repeated it in English.

"Hail unto the bride of my king. Rita Carter, of Earth, lady of the stones, I, Rafe, Commander of the Oosha's Royal Guards, give you heartfelt greetings." He paused, and to Rita's shock his pupil suddenly di-

lated. She saw, dancing against the blackness of the pupil, a dappled field. The Rafe's eye returned to normal and she realized he was again speaking. "If I serve you with my skills, it is well; if I serve you with my life, it is better. I am yours to command, even unto death."

"Rafe, I—Cale?"

"Accept his—I think the ancient term for it in your tongue is 'fealty.' "

Rita turned back, feeling awkward. With as much dignity as she could muster, she said, "Commander Rafe, I accept your, um, offer of loyalty. I thank you." She only wished it had come from Rafe's heart, not as a gesture to appease his ruler. She liked Rafe, even though he frightened her a little—okay, a lot. She wanted him to like her. But even as Rafe nodded his understanding of her acceptance, she saw a spark of something in his eyes that told her that they were a long, long way from ever being friends. . . .

"Hey!" The shout and the blaring horn startled Rita out of her reverie. She'd crossed the street so deeply engrossed in her reverie that she hadn't even checked for cars.

"Sorry!" she yelled, and scurried across. The driver, angry and probably scared himself by the close call, gave her an obscene gesture. Even though she knew there was no personal malice behind it, Rita's heart sank even further. No one in the world was being kind to her today.

Rita and Cale wouldn't even be home yet. A week ago, to everyone's shocked delight, their simplistic, jury-rigged communications system had finally borne fruit. They had intercepted a signal from what appeared to be a small group of deserters from Charles Air Force Base. Hours of intense listening had followed. Rita had tried to get into the spirit of things, and she *was* excited for Cale, but as she couldn't understand a word of the conversations on which they were eavesdropping, she had finally slipped away to

make coffee. Tyrusians, she found, adored the brew—
at least these two did. When the time came for negotiations with Tyrus, the small country of Colombia
might have the edge over everyone else.

"Coffee," she said to herself. "Damn it. I even had
coffee this morning. And a glass of wine with dinner
three nights ago. . . ." If only she could take it back,
knowing what she did now.

Her thoughts went back to that long night, listening
to a steady stream of Tyrusian babble floating up from
the Exotar. Later, his whole body radiating excitement, Cale had told her what they had learned.

There was a group of four deserters living in the
Utah desert. They had managed to link up with several "jumpers," people who had served aboard the
Royal Yacht that had brought Cale to Earth and who
had been ignorant about the coup. Upon learning of
it, many had fled the Yacht in escape pods. This particular group was located somewhere in Colorado.
They had effected repairs on the damaged pod and
the plan was for both groups to rendezvous at a certain point in the desert not far from Salt Lake City.

Rafe had been more suspicious, as was his nature.
"It could be a trap," he had warned. Nonetheless, he
agreed with Cale—they needed to check it out. They
had only listened and had not attempted to contact
anyone. The plan was to show up at the rendezvous
point and observe from hiding. If these groups were
really freedom fighters—Ooshati—then Cale would
announce his presence and they would pool their resources. If not—

"Be careful, Cale," said Rita under her breath, as
she had said yesterday morning when she held him
and kissed him good-bye. They would not be back
until this evening, if all went well. She wouldn't let
herself think about what might go wrong.

She hadn't told him about the doctor's appointment,
passing off her recurring queasiness as nothing impor-

tant. Would he have gone to this meeting if he knew? How would he react when she told him? And Rafe—

Sighing, Rita fished for her keys and ran up the steps to the apartment building. She unlocked the doors and opened her mailbox. As she climbed the stairs, she sorted through today's letters: a flyer urging her to subscribe to *National Geographic,* an offer to join a book club, bills, bills, and more bills, and—Rita leaned against the stairwell wall and opened the letter from someone named Phillip A. Preston, Esq.

The note was brief and to the point.

Dear Ms. Carter: This is to inform you that there has been no contention as to the division of the estate of Helen J. Carter. The title to the house in Glenport and the acreage on Maple Island should be arriving soon and will be forwarded on to you. As per your request, the stocks held by Helen Carter have been liquidated and the resulting sum is $122,489.87 (One hundred twenty-two thousand four hundred eighty-nine dollars and eighty-seven cents). Ten percent (10%) of this sum has been wired to your account. The rest will be released from probate in approximately thirty (30) business days.

If you have questions, please do not hesitate to call. Sincerely, Phillip A. Preston, Esquire.

Rita glanced at the date and chuckled, even though her eyes sparkled with tears. The date was May 20. Trust the Post Awful to be late with news like this. Over a hundred thousand dollars! Rita supposed she was rich. Her heart lifted slightly. Money wasn't everything, but it was something, and it would mean that they wouldn't have to skimp on little things like, oh, food and shelter anymore. Rita's paycheck had been stretched about as far as it could go.

She continued up the stairs, the smile on her lips softened by sorrow. *Thank you, Mom. But I wish you had lived to see your grandchild.* She turned the corner and froze.

Her door was ajar. Rita was a practical woman at the most relaxed of times, and since she began harboring two fugitives from Tyrus she'd been extra careful. She'd locked that door and checked it, she knew she had. Fear spurted through her.

Unless Cale and Rafe had returned early? No, Cale might not think about things like closing and locking doors, but Rafe, the warrior and guardsman, certainly would have.

She tried to calm herself. University towns always had their share of break-ins. Sons of bitches might have taken the TV and what little bits of jewelry she had, and that was all right. She had the money to replace everything in that apartment and then some.

Dear God, please let it be burglars.

She'd taken care to cover their tracks. Hell, everyone at Charles thought Cale and Rafe dead—she'd heard as much from Cale after a night of monitoring signals from the base. And no one had the slightest idea who Rita was and where she lived—did they?

Shaking, Rita reached out and gently pushed open the door. It swung slowly open with an ominous creaking sound to reveal something that made her gasp.

The place had been ransacked. She felt bile rise in her throat at the sight of the violation. The sofa cushions and pillows had been slit open and their stuffing strewn about. The little table and chairs in the breakfast nook had been overturned, the contents of the hall closet dragged out and examined. The cupboard doors were all open and their contents emptied. Flour and sugar coated the countertops like snow. Even the refrigerator had been emptied.

Her legs wobbling, Rita went into the bedroom. The same destruction met her eyes. The mattress and pillows had been cut open like the sofa out in the living room. The dresser drawers had been pulled out, and all her silky, lacy underthings lay exposed. The thought of someone rummaging with careless, angry fingers through her clothing made her feel like vomiting.

Dizzy, she stumbled and caught at the door frame. Her foot crunched down on something, and automatically she jumped away and glanced down, thinking it might be a piece of jewelry or a button.

It was a temple piece.

There was only one temple piece in the apartment, and Rita would have bet her entire inheritance that Commander Rafe would not have walked out of this apartment without his. Slowly, she bent and picked it up.

"Oh my God," she breathed. "They've found us."

Behind her, she heard heavy footsteps coming up the stairs.

CHAPTER NINE

● ● ●

June 25, 1981
Black Rock Desert, Utah

Cale took another sip of water from the very useful canteen and wiped his brow. The sun was merciless in this place's deserts, and he was grateful Rita had reminded him and Rafe to use a lotion that screened out the sun's harmful rays. After spending their first full day on Earth exposed to its beautiful sunlight, both of the Tyrusians had experienced bad burns. Rita was surprised, as it was a cloudy day and they had not been outside much at all. Cale realized what had happened—after generations of living in climate-controlled domes, Tyrusian skin was very sensitive to so-called natural elements. He found the heat almost unbearable, but he took a deep breath, calmed himself, and endured.

He and Rafe had borrowed the patient Carrie Dalton's vehicle for the trip. They had arrived yesterday morning at this, the meeting site, and had carefully scouted the area. It was a natural basin, flanked on all sides by the dramatic rock formations that Cale was beginning to realize were common to the area. It was thoroughly exposed, which was no doubt why the Tyrusians who seemed to be the meeting's organizing force had selected it. Rafe had come up with a strategy. Cale, utilizing the Exotar's ability to create a holographic camouflage, would move in to a close vantage point and observe what transpired. If, after listening for a time, Cale was certain that this was indeed a large meeting of Ooshati, he would reveal his identity.

Rafe, meanwhile, was ensconced in a rock formation some quarter of a mile away. He was armed with his arbus and a high-powered rifle with a scope, which he had purchased at a pawnshop along with many other weapons. One of those weapons, a handgun, was with Rita at the present moment, under her bed should anything untoward occur.

Cale took another sip of lukewarm water and frowned. Something was not right with his Ooshala. One of the traits he most loved about her was her willingness to fight by his side, to be his equal in the dangers as well as the hoped-for benefits of his position. When the three of them had discussed the plan, Rafe had, naturally, begun by saying that it was too risky for Rita to come with them. Cale waited for his *Kia-thamaa* to protest, as was her wont. Instead, Rita shocked all of them by agreeing with Rafe. She would stay behind, she said. She was armed with the handgun, she would be safe enough. Cale and Rafe needed to concentrate on the task at hand; she would only be a distraction.

That was not the Rita Cale knew, and he worried about it. When this was over, he would have a long talk with her and try to determine what was wrong.

A distant sound made him tense. Yes, it was definitely the sound of a vehicle approaching. He glanced down at the wristwatch Rita had bought him. Three o'clock—nearly a full hour before the designated meeting time. Someone, like he and Rafe, had decided to come early. Instinctively Cale leaned back into the shadow of the overhanging rock, although with the holographic camouflage unit activated, no one would see him unless he moved. He lifted a pair of binoculars to his eyes.

It was an Army truck. He tensed, then forced himself to relax. If this were an ambush, they would hardly send in one truck so early. Many of those attending the meeting were deserters from the Army—people who had followed their consciences and refused to kill their Oosha. He should be pleased that they had been able to steal a truck.

The truck slowed, stopped. Waited.

"I hate this," said Ashley, fidgeting. "Why can't we just go out *there* and wait?"

"Too dangerous," said Kaslik absently. He was seated at the control panel, his hand resting on a control orb as he mentally put the machine through its paces.

"We're sitting ducks no matter what," she shot back. Blue, who had been resting his deformed head on her lap, growled a little in support of his adored mistress. Absently, she stroked the short, fine, blue-gray fur. He closed his eyes, the growl mutating to a croon.

"Despite your penchant for colorful *Erdlufi* phrases," said Kaslik, "you know I'm right."

Ashley sighed. "I suppose so."

"Let's go over it one more time," said Doc. "Kaslik and Blue stay in here. Ashley and I go out to the meeting area once everyone's arrived. How's that setup coming?"

"Very well," replied Kaslik, his hand almost caressing the control orb. "I've expanded the area I can monitor to two miles. If any Tyrusian vessels enter that perimeter, we'll know about it. I've entered the energy signatures of the escape pods whose crews have contacted us, so those particular vessels won't trigger the alarm. It wouldn't do to fire on people who are on our side."

"Good," approved Doc. "Now we just wait. I hate waiting."

Time passed. Cale began to realize he had to start rationing the water. More and more vehicles drove up—pickups, vans, sedans, and even motorcycles. One by one, they came, parked—and waited.

And then the pods came—long, cylindrical shapes that dropped out of the sky to land at shocking speed. Almost immediately, once they had touched ground, they "disappeared." Those aboard had activated their own HCUs and blended into the landscape. Cale's heart sped up. So many—so many who had escaped the "inescapable," who were, he hoped, still loyal to him.

"So many!" breathed Jaran as he guided the pod in for a landing outside the natural circle of stones.

"I hope we're not walking into an ambush," grumbled Baris. Jaran and Shalli, who were seated to his right, exchanged glances. Shalli rolled her eyes, and Jaran winked. So far, none of Baris's dire predictions had come true. She reached to touch his face, gently, so as not to break his concentration. He gave her a fleeting smile and gently brought the pod down. Dust billowed up around it.

"Don't worry, Baris," said Gevic. "This is what we've been working toward ever since we jumped."

Jaran moved his fingers on the control orb and began to view the area. "There's Kiri and Feydan!" he exclaimed.

"Feydan?" Now that they had landed, the force fields had been deactivated and Gevic and the others crowded in to see. He began to laugh. "You're right. Son of a Mangler, but I'm glad to see he made it!"

The tension in the ship eased as the seven of them began spotting their friends—friends they had feared dead or turned traitor. Only Baris now grumbled dark thoughts, and he was largely ignored.

"Everyone's starting to get out of their vehicles," said Jaran. "Let's go."

He stroked the control orb and the door opened. Nervously, everyone checked their weapons before stepping into the bright sunshine. As Jaran rose, Shalli surprised him by grabbing his elbow and pulling him back into a tight embrace. She kissed him fiercely. "Yes," she said.

"Yes?" Jaran was shocked. He knew exactly what she was referring to. Three weeks ago, he had summoned his courage and performed the first step in *Kiathamaa*. She had denied the request and, now, utterly shocked him by kissing him—quite enthusiastically—of her own accord. She was willing to pair-bond with him!

"Yes," she repeated. "I love you, Jaran. I didn't want to start something we couldn't complete, but it's likely that there will be someone here who can marry us. So come on—let's go!"

And suddenly, to Jaran, this hostile world seemed bright and full of hope. He could even permit to hope that, maybe, today, his adored Cale would appear. Maybe.

The hour had come. Tyrusians began to get out of their cars, their trucks, their ships, and slowly walked into the basin. Some of them wore weapons, but none was drawn. Cale saw fear, apprehension, determination, and veiled hope on the sharp Tyrusian features. When they had all assembled, he did a quick count. Thirty-seven. Far more than he had realistically expected, but fewer than he had hoped.

A man and a woman in military garb, the ones from the first Army truck that had arrived, seemed to be the organizers. The man began to speak and Cale immediately recognized the voice from the conversations on which he and Rafe had eavesdropped.

"Well," said the man who had identified himself as "Doc," "I'm right pleased that so many of you could attend our get-together."

Despite the tension, there were a few smiles and even a chuckle or two. "I'm hoping that we're all on the same side here, or this will be a mighty brief reunion. Just so everyone knows, my friend over there"—he turned and pointed toward the Army truck—"has got a warning system set up. If any unrecognized Tyrusian vessels enter a two-mile radius, this"—he held up his com orb—"will start beeping like crazy. We'll have about four seconds if they come in at full speed. Just enough time to draw our weapons. And believe me—I'm prepared to use mine."

Another stepped forward—a tall woman in human clothes. "Any news of the Oosha? Did he escape?"

"I'm afraid not," said another, clad in filthy military garb. "An *Erdlufa* helped him get out of the compound, but they were both killed later. Their vehicle collided with a helicopter. No one could have survived that."

A moan rippled through the crowd. Some began weeping openly. Doc's throat worked and he turned away. "Dammit," he swore.

A young man stepped forward. He looked very familiar to Cale, but he couldn't quite place him. "I refuse to believe that," he stated firmly in a clear voice that carried through the muttering.

Beside him, a woman placed a hand on the youth's arm. "Jaran—" she began, in a sad voice.

He shook her hand off. "No! Has anyone seen the body? Do we know for certain? Perhaps Cale-Oosha was not in the vehicle—it might have been a trick!"

Jaran! Now Cale realized where he knew him. Jaran K'Lara had been one of the many stewards aboard the Royal Yacht. His father had been personal attendant upon Cale's father. The memories came back—Jaran's bright face and enthusiastic demeanor made Cale smile as he reminisced. But something had changed about Jaran. He stood straighter, and there were lines on his face that had not been there before. Here was a leader of men, not a mere steward, and suddenly Cale was overcome by a wave of pride. He needed someone like that on his side.

"I know what I saw," retorted the man who had brought up the subject of Cale's "death." "No one could have survived that. Are you calling me a liar?"

Jaran held up his hands in a placating gesture, but his expression did not change. "No. I believe you. I believe you are reporting what you saw. But if you did not see a body, then there is a chance—a slim one, admittedly, that he is still alive." He scanned the crowd, his eyes searching out those of his people. "I follow the Oosha until his death is a proven fact. And if that tragic day comes, then I follow what he and his father stood for. The Dragit is not and never will be *my* Oosha."

At that, the murmurs swelled into a chorus of approval. Everyone here, it seemed, hated the Dragit.

Cale was deeply moved. He took a deep breath and was about to rise from his position and confirm loyal Jaran's hopes when suddenly Doc's com orb began emitting a shrieking wail. Doc swore.

"Friends, now's your chance to show where your loyalties lie. That's the Dragit's ships coming in!"

As Doc had bleakly predicted, there was indeed just enough time for those assembled to draw what weapons they could. The ship came out of nowhere, dropping from the stratosphere like a stone and swooping down upon the Ooshati with a dive that would have done a raptor credit. The ship came to a dead stop and hovered. A door slid open in its belly and a dozen figures dropped out.

Cale stared, horrified. Even as he watched, the fig-

ures seemed to sprout wings and float toward the
earth, firing arbuses as they came.

He knew who they were. Here, on this planet, they
were clad in trench coats and fedora hats, their temple
pieces disguised as sunglasses. On other planets they
would wear other things, but their intent was always
the same: to kill. These were the *ga'lim,* the Tall Men.
They operated in secret, in the dark places of the government where Cale and his father did not often like
to look. That they were here meant only one thing: the
Dragit did not intend for anyone assembled to escape.

A few of the Ooshati broke and ran back for the
safety of their vessels, but the majority stayed and
rallied. Their faces were grim as they lifted rifles, shot-
guns, pistols, and arbuses toward their enemy and
began firing. The Tall Men were good with their
"wings," which were actually complex, compact glid-
ing devices. Only one was struck, and the blow was
glancing. But several below screamed and fell as the
Tall Men fired their own weapons.

One of the Tall Men spasmed, lost control, and
slammed into a rock formation. Cale heard a distant,
powerful *crack* from a rifle report. By now most of
them were folding their ManWings and touching down
to the earth. They hit the ground running, and more
and more Ooshati either died or were injured.

Suddenly there was a bright flash. Cale was tempo-
rarily blinded and when vision returned, he realized
that he could see every vessel that had approached—
even those that had been protected by their holographic disguises.

And now, people were turning to stare at *him.* One
of the Tall Men smiled, a terrible sight, and headed
straight for him. The Dragit's ship had issued a dampening field that had deactivated every HCU in the
area—including the one from the Exotar. He was now
as visible as if he had stepped forward crying, "Hey,
look at me!"

His eyes narrowed as righteous anger rose in him. He stepped forward and began to lift his Exotar-clad arm, prepared to fight.

He didn't get the chance. The Tall Man hadn't gone three steps before his head exploded in a crimson shower of blood, bone, and brain. Cale heard the echo of the rifle and said a silent prayer of gratitude for Rafe's marksmanship.

A second Tall Man died an instant later in the same manner. Cale concentrated on the various sharp pieces of rocks in the area. With a thought, they rose and rushed toward his enemies, slamming into their heads with, if not the force of one of Rafe's bullets, sufficient power to cave in a skull.

The silence of the desert had erupted into a cacophony of screams, weapon fire, and gunshots. Pandemonium reigned. The single thought on everyone's mind was not a complex question like loyalties of right of succession, but simple, immediate survival.

Cale's eyes sought out another stone. He had just focused his attention on it and pulled it free from the soil when his control of the object was suddenly . . . *severed.*

The sudden bright light that engulfed him burned his eyes. He felt as if he had suddenly been wrapped in a thick blanket, barely able to move. A confinement beam. The *ga'lim* were not to kill him, then, merely capture him. Capture him and give him like a present to the Dragit.

No!

Jaran had never before been involved in a battle. Even on the extremely rare occasions when the Royal Yacht had come under attack by hostile forces, what role did a steward have to play in such things? Now, though, he felt a peculiar calm steal over him. He had been trained to fight and had diligently performed target practice with his arbus, and now that training stood him in good stead. He and Shalli raced, firing as they went, for what little cover the rock formations provided. Panting, they crouched behind the rocks, popping up and firing when they could.

Gevic was the first of their group to die.

Jaran saw him go down, firing his arbus as he went. He had startled one of the Tall Men, who whipped around and fired. Gevic got it full in the chest and stumbled backward, dead before he hit the earth. The Tall Man hastened to his side and frowned. Clearly, death had not been the objective.

"Gevic!" cried Shalli. Her voice was thick, but she blinked hard and refused to let the tears fall. Her hand was steady as she continued firing.

"They want us alive!" Jaran yelled to be heard over the din. Shalli nodded that she had heard, but continued to fire.

Light flooded the area. Jaran turned his head away, and when he looked again, he saw what they had done. They had stripped the Ooshati of their HCUs. Everyone's vessels and vehicles were exposed now, and the ship began targeting them, blowing them up with ease. Jaran swore and looked around.

A lone figure standing against the rock formations caught his eye. He was dressed in human clothing. The youth had no weapon, but the sun glinted off his right hand and—

Cale! "Shalli!" cried Jaran. "Look! It's the Oosha! He *is* alive!" Elation flooded him. Just as quickly it soured to bile in his throat as he realized that the Tall Men were angling toward him. "He's unprotected," breathed Jaran, reorienting himself so that he could fire at the Tall Men closing in on his beloved ruler.

At that moment, there was a sharp *crack* and the Tall Man closest to the Oosha stumbled. He suddenly had no head. As he fell, Jaran whooped aloud. He was willing to bet anything that Commander Rafe had survived as well, and was protecting his Oosha here on Earth as he had done on Tyrus. Who else would be such a good shot?

Just as quickly he realized that the Oosha was far from defenseless himself. Cale calmly began using the Exotar to direct his energy and hurled deadly rocks at his enemies.

A white light again flooded the area, but this time it concentrated solely on the young ruler of Tyrus. A cone of light poured forth from the ship, encircling Cale-Oosha. The Oosha began to struggle.

"They've got him in a confinement beam," cried Shalli. Jaran stared, frozen, unable to react. What could he do? Futilely, he lifted his arbus and began firing at the ship. It accomplished little, but he could think of no other way to help his Oosha.

Cale's struggles ceased. Jaran glanced from the ship down to the young ruler. His eyes were closed, his face slack with the deepest of concentration. Cale stretched out his Exotar-clad hand and splayed the fingers hard. There came a deep rumbling sound and the color of the light flushed to bright blue. For a brief instant, the image of Cale seemed to ripple, then, suddenly, the ship above him rocked violently. The beam disappeared. Cale fell to his knees, and Jaran realized that the sand, up to a five-foot radius around the Oosha, was suddenly reflective. Cale's mental energy had broken the confinement beam—and turned the sand about him to glass.

He was on his hands and knees now, bright blood trickling from where the hot glass sliced and burned him. He shook his head, utterly disoriented. Of course—such an effort would be extremely draining. Until he had gathered his wits again, the Oosha would be completely defenseless.

A Tall Man realized this at the same moment as Jaran did.

Jaran didn't pause to think. He began to run, his

eyes trained on his ruler, his legs propelling him forward faster than he could have imagined.

"Jaran, no!" screamed Shalli behind him. Her voice was faint, drowned out by the pounding of his heart and the urgent scream of his single thought: *Protect the Oosha.* Loyalty to the royal family ran in his blood, was all but encoded in his genes. His hope that he would find Cale-Oosha alive and well had been realized, but now it was about to be shattered, and Jaran would not—could not—permit it.

The Tall Man, a particularly ugly and menacing specimen, had not gone for a weapon. Clearly, the Oosha was more valuable alive. He did, however, have a pair of *naakai*—manacles made out of light, like the ramps that descended from Tyrusian ships. They were unbreakable—even for a man of Cale's formidable mental abilities. Once they snapped shut about the Oosha's wrists, his struggles would be useless.

Now Cale had managed to get to his feet, though as Jaran watched he stumbled and nearly fell. The Tall Man was almost there.

With a wordless cry, Jaran launched himself at the Tall Man. Startled, the ugly head whipped around and the lips curled in a snarl of frustration. The man transferred the *naakai* to one hand and raised his arbus with the other. As Jaran's body descended on the Tall Man, bringing him to earth, the arbus fired.

It was, as the humans would term it, point-blank range. Funny, Jaran thought, that he would use *Erdlufi* words at the moment of his death. To his surprise, he did not die immediately. He went very, very cold and when the Tall Man struggled out from beneath his body, Jaran toppled limply over into the sand.

From his position, he could still see the Oosha. His heart spasmed as he watched the Tall Man raise his arbus and fire at the youth. But Jaran's leap had bought Cale precious seconds in which to recover. The arbus fire hit his Exotar-clad hand and ricocheted back to its source. The Tall Man fell backward, dead.

Jaran closed his eyes in relief. The he felt hands closing on his arms. "Jaran!"

He was so tired. With an effort, Jaran opened his eyes and managed a faint smiled for his Oosha.

". . . alive," he breathed. "I knew . . . they couldn't . . . kill you."

"And they won't kill you," replied Cale. His purple-blue eyes were filled with concern. "Don't let go, Jaran. Stay with me."

"Jaran—oh, no, please no." The voice was Shalli's, and cracked on the last word. Her face swam into Jaran's darkening vision.

"Shalli," he breathed, the intensity of his love for her startling him. "*Kia-thamaa.* I only wish . . ." He lifted his hand to touch her face, but could only raise it an inch or two. She caught it and kissed it fiercely, her eyes bright with tears.

His last words were for his Oosha. "I kept believing," he rasped. It was so cold. "I am glad . . . I saw you before I died . . . *Kia Cale,* it is an honor to have served you."

"Jaran, you saved my life. What can I do?" Cale's eyes, too, were shiny, and the sight moved Jaran. He fought to remain conscious.

"Protect Shalli . . . others. They followed me. I followed you."

"I will. I swear it."

Jaran summoned his evaporating strength and reached up with his other hand. He placed it on Cale's chest, over his heart, in the oldest sign of fealty in Tyrus's long history. There was blood all over his fingers. Swiftly Cale returned the gesture, placing his gloved hand over Jaran's heart. "If I serve you with my skills, it is well; if I serve you with my life, it is better."

And then Jaran K'Lara closed his eyes. The frightened sound of Shalli's voice and the warm touch of his king went away in a swirl of cold darkness.

It was utter chaos.

Doc and Ashley had headed for what cover they could the minute Kaslik's alarm had sounded. It became obvious, though, that the Tall Men would either kill or capture them unless they reached the safety of the truck. They exchanged a wordless glance, and Ashley nodded in the direction of their vehicle. Doc nodded, once.

"You go, I'll cover," she said. Ashley was a superior shot with an arbus, and Doc saw the logic in her words. Besides, she outranked him. He took a deep breath and went.

He ran as fast as his legs would carry him. The Army truck was a camouflage-colored dot in the distance, utterly visible now that the dampening field was in place. It seemed so far away. Behind him, he heard Ashley, hard on his heels, firing like mad.

And then, suddenly, he didn't hear her. He stumbled to a halt and whirled, screaming her name.

She lay facedown in the sand, the arbus an arm's length away. There was a smoking hole in her back. Her blue eyes were wide.

Doc charged forward and scooped her up in his arms. She was heavier than he would have thought—not an ounce of superfluous flesh on her, only bone and muscle and sinew and heart—

On shaky legs he ran for the truck. Kaslik saw him coming and had it running, reaching to pull him up. His face paled when he saw Ashley. "Oh, no," he breathed.

"Go, go!" yelled Doc. Kaslik slammed the truck into gear and they tore off. Doc, still cradling Ashley, was slammed up against the side of the truck. Blue had come out and reached out a clawed hand to touch

Ashley. With an almost human gesture, the Mangler shook the woman's shoulder.

Her head rolled limply against Doc's chest. He was a medic. He knew she was dead, had been dead even before he had reached her. He had put both his and Kaslik's lives in jeopardy by going back for the body, but somehow, against all logic, he had hoped that he was wrong, that he could save her. . . .

She was cooling against him. Blue growled, softly, in the back of his throat, then lifted his head. A long, keening howl, softer than the blood cry with which Doc was familiar, issued forth from the creature. Without realizing what he was doing, Doc reached and laid a hand on the Mangler's head.

"I'll take care of you, boy," he said in a thick voice.

The truck jounced along at top speed, but Doc was hardly even aware of the discomfort. The pain in his heart was too great. No doubt Kaslik would want to rally, to try to make contact again, but Doc knew he couldn't. Never again would he lose someone he loved. Life was too short for that kind of pain. He and Blue would take to the desert and let Kaslik go on his way.

Doc had had enough of killing—and dying.

"Cale—Oosha." Pause. *"Majesty!"*

Cale shook his head and lifted his gaze from Jaran's dead face. The young woman beside him—Shalli, he thought her name was—had tears running down her face, but her full lips were set in determination.

"Majesty, what now?"

What now, indeed. Cale looked about him. The *ga'lim* appeared to be distracted. They kept looking at him, but the Ooshati who remained were firing on them, and what man would turn his back on an attacking enemy?

Bodies littered the basin, though some Ooshati had managed to escape. Cale felt as though he were sur-

rounded by the screech of tires. One vehicle sounded
as if it were approaching him—

He rose and his heart lifted a little. Carrie Dalton's
car, with Rafe at the wheel, was coming toward them.
Cale picked up Jaran's body and turned to Shalli.
"How many of you?"

"We started with seven. Now—I don't know."

Rafe slammed on the brakes and the car swerved
to a stop. "Get—" His gaze fell upon the body and he
swore. "You can't bring him, Cale. I'm sorry, but—"

"Rafe, he died saving my life!"

"I will take him." Shalli stood straight, but her lips
quivered. "He was to be my *Kia-thamaa*. The duty—
the honor—is mine."

"Your people—I promised to protect them," said
Cale, anguished. An idea struck him. Shalli was wearing her temple piece. Cale raised the Exotar, concentrated, and touched it to her temple piece. There was
a crackling sound.

"What . . . ?"

Cale smiled, a tired, ancient smile. "For the mo-
ment, get your people to safety. I will find you. And
I will take you to a place where we will *all* be safe.
This, I swear."

"I will await your summons, Cale-Oosha." Shalli
stepped back as Cale got in the car. He barely had
time to close the door when Rafe peeled off. In the
rearview mirror, Cale watched, his heart aching, as
Shalli crumpled, weeping, beside the body of her
beloved.

"Are you injured?"

Cale shook his head, looking down at his shirt. "No.
It—it's Jaran's blood." Bleakly, he glanced up at Rafe.
"He saved my life. He died in my arms, Rafe."

Rafe didn't take his eyes off the road—if road it
could be called. "He is only the first. Many more will
die. Now, you understand what's really at stake."

Anger flared inside the youth. "Do not condescend to me!" he snapped. "I have always known!"

"You've known here," replied Rafe mildly, tapping his deep temple. "Now," he said, placing his hand on his heart, "you know *here*."

Cale saw the truth in Rafe's words, but could not find words of his own to answer him. Rafe filled the silence.

"They knew you were coming."

"Impossible," said Cale. He began to unbutton his bloodied shirt, pausing to regard Jaran's red handprint with a fresh wave of pain and guilt commingled. "We have never initiated any communication. They probably detected the Exotar's emissions."

"Nevertheless, a confinement beam is hardly standard issue aboard Tyrusian vessels. They were expecting you to show."

Cale was silent, pondering this. A fresh wave of horror broke inside him, and he turned wild eyes to Rafe. "If they know about us, then they know about—"

"Rita." Rafe's mouth set in a hard line, and he floored the accelerator.

CHAPTER
TEN

• • •

June 15, 1981
Salt Lake City

Saris Krai had watched with complete satisfaction as everything unfolded according to plan.

He had sent his best men to cover the meeting in the Black Rock desert, but had not gone himself. There was no need to alert Konrad as to the seriousness of this particular gathering. It was the largest one Saris had heard of—several parties were rendezvousing there—and he had every reason to believe that Cale would show as well. It was physically close to the Salt Lake City address that the young ruler had chosen, the size would interest him, and Saris did not make the classic mistake of underestimating his foe. Cale-Oosha was not a fool, nor was his commander of the Royal Guards. If Saris had figured out how to listen in on Tyrusian conversations, most certainly the Oosha had as well.

And if he was not there, then Saris Krai would be patiently waiting for him at his "home address." He had observed the woman, Rita Carter, leave earlier this morning. The apartment was searched thoroughly. There was no sign of Cale or Rafe, not even a scrap bit of Tyrusian technology. Now Rita was returning, her body language screaming dejection. Her hands were shoved deep into her jeans pockets, and she was so lost in thought that a car nearly ran into her.

And what might distract the little heroine? Fear for her Tyrusian friends, perhaps? Watching her confirmed Saris's suspicions. Rafe and Cale were at the meeting site—walking into Saris's carefully laid trap.

She muttered to herself as she fished for her keys. Saris strained to hear; something about "coffee" and "wine." Earth beverages. Rita unlocked the doors; Saris watched her retrieve her mail. He began to smile as she ascended the stairs. With a nod, he signaled that they should begin recording.

The Tall Man seated next to him in the black sedan obeyed the silent order. At once, the exterior of Rita's apartment appeared on a small, handheld screen.

"Now, Rita Carter," Saris said to the screen, "I will know your mettle by how you react." He leaned forward eagerly.

Rita came around the corner and stopped dead in her tracks. Fear flitted over her face. She stared at the door, left slightly ajar by Saris's order, then glanced down the corridors. Taking a deep breath, Rita reached out a hand that shook and opened the door.

"Camera two," said Saris.

At once their view shifted to the interior. Rita gasped, then entered slowly, her eyes roving everywhere. Saris's men had been under no instructions to be subtle—quite the reverse. Saris watched intently as Rita wandered through her ravaged apartment, finally coming to the bedroom.

He had debated with himself about the placement of the temple piece. It was important that she notice it, but he had to take care to make it look as though it had been accidentally left behind. At first, he had placed in on the dresser, then at the last minute he had changed his mind and simply tossed it at random on the floor.

Rita stumbled and caught at the doorframe for support. Her foot stepped precisely on the temple piece. Saris nodded. He'd made the right decision. Now—would Rita Carter disappoint him?

He watched as she picked it up, clearly aware of what it was, and pocketed it. "Oh my God," she breathed, "they've found us."

Excellent. Clever girl. Saris leaped out of the car, opened the locked door with a thought, and began to ascend the stairs. Normally silent when he moved, he made an effort to tread heavily. He wanted to see her reaction. Would she hide? Throw things at him? Go out the window? Whatever she did, it would tell him something invaluable about her.

He was almost at the door now. He reached out—

—and she took him completely by surprise by flinging the door open and leveling a gun in his face.

Saris blinked. Rita's face was pale with terror, and the hands that clutched the gun were trembling, but nonetheless, it was in his face, and he hadn't expected it.

For a long minute their gazes locked. Rita didn't look away. Then, slowly, Saris stepped backward and smiled. He raised his hands and let her pass.

Rita didn't seem to trust her good luck. She still pointed the handgun at him in deadly silence, then glanced quickly down the stairs. She began to back toward them, then, after throwing him one more glance of mixed terror and determination, she ran down the steps, taking them two or three at a time.

Saris followed, his feet light on the steps. She was running now, halfway down the block. Smiling to himself, Saris returned to the car.

"Do you want us to follow her?"

"No, let her go for the moment," said Saris. "I can find her anytime I want. We have more important prey to hunt."

"She's not answering." Cale's voice was artificially calm, and Rafe knew his liege well enough to know what that meant. Cale was on the verge of breaking. And Rafe didn't know that he could blame him.

Once they felt they were a safe distance away from the disastrous meeting and the Tall Men, Cale had stripped off his shirt, washed off Jaran's blood with water from the canteen, and insisted that Rafe pull over the minute they saw a phone. He had returned some minutes later looking ashen. Rita had not answered the phone.

Rafe tried to calm him. "She may simply be at class."

"She has no classes today."

"Then she could be out grocery shopping. Cale, we shouldn't assume the worst."

Cale gave his friend a ghost of a smile as he pulled the door shut. "You always do," he said.

"That's true," replied Rafe. "But I'm not always right."

The hours passed as they sped up I-15 toward Salt Lake City. Cale fell silent, clearly torn between wanting to arrive as soon as possible and wanting to stop, phone, and hear Rita's voice. Six times they had stopped now, and each time Cale returned, shaking his dark head.

Rafe tried to distract him. "We cannot stay in Salt Lake City anymore, regardless of whether they've tracked us down there or not."

Cale said nothing. He stared out the window and his eyes were unfocused. Thinking of Rita. Wondering why she wasn't answering the phone. "Perhaps they've caught her," he said suddenly.

Rafe shook his head. "Then they'd make her answer the phone, tell you everything was all right. They'd want to use her as bait." He regretted the blunt words as he saw Cale's jaw tighten and his eyes close. However, he did not apologize for them. Cale had just survived his second battle. He'd held a friend who lay dying, had taken responsibility for those who had followed that friend. Now was not the time to ease up on the boy. If anything, Rafe had to push harder. It was easy to be a king when you were safely ensconced in your royal quarters on a planet inhabited by people loyal to you. It was harder to be a king when a usurper sat on that throne and every minute your life—and that of others—might be in danger.

It was for this reason that Rafe desperately wished Rita had sent them on their way after that first night. She was intelligent, caring, and practical, certainly, and once things had settled down Rafe would not have disapproved of Cale's courting her. It was unusual, but so were the circumstances.

But now Rita was an impediment as far as Rafe was concerned. Cale should be planning the next step, determining how to gather his allies now that they had been most brutally scattered, concentrating on regaining his throne. Instead, all his fears were concentrated on Rita. Rafe was about to open his mouth when Cale's soft voice broke the silence for him.

"We must find a place where we can train. It has been helpful to use the university's gymnasium, but we need a private area. I know how to use the Exotar, but there may come a time when I do not have it. I need to practice with the *zi-nor* and *har-nor,* with hand-to-hand fighting, with these human weapons as well. And so must Rita. She does not like these weapons, but she must know how to use them. She must be able to defend herself if I am not there."

Rafe was pleased. The boy had surprised him. Then the import of Cale's words registered.

"Rita—damn it, I told her to do target practice twice a week! Does she even know how to use the handgun?"

"I believe she knows the basics. But she never did train with it. As I said, she does not like these things." He smiled sadly. "We have had long talks, she and I, about saving whales and the environment. She is right,

Rafe, to be concerned about such things. Look at what happened to Tyrus because we failed to heed the warnings."

Rafe felt himself growing angry at Rita again. "She may be right, but she can't save the whales if she's lying dead from an arbus blast!" At Cale's stricken look, he softened his voice. "There is a time for that, Cale. But that time isn't now. You know that."

"Yes," sighed Cale. "I do. My poor *Kia-thamaa*. She did not know what kind of can of worms she was getting into."

Rafe smothered a smile. Cale spoke English very well indeed, but the subtleties of American slang sometimes seemed to elude him.

Cale sat up in his seat and pointed at a gas station. "There. Let me telephone her again."

It was past dark when they finally arrived. Rafe turned off the lights and moved with agonizing slowness down the last street before Rita's. Cale fidgeted, but stayed silent. He trusted Rafe to do his job, and for that Rafe was grateful.

Finally, Rafe parked about two blocks away. He reached in the backseat, found the binoculars, and began to survey the area.

"Do you see anything suspicious?" Cale asked, dropping his voice to a whisper even though there was no need.

Rafe nodded. "Up ahead. A black sedan with four very large men in trench coats in it."

Cale moaned softly. "I should never have left her. I should have insisted—"

"Rita is your Ooshala, not your servant. She doesn't obey you. Unfortunately." Now Rafe turned the binoculars to the apartment. "It's dark. I can't see anything inside. Here." He handed the binoculars and the keys to Cale. "I'm going to do reconnaissance. You know how to drive this thing?"

Cale nodded—a little uncertainly, Rafe noted. "If I'm not back in fifteen minutes, take it and get out."

"Be careful," said Cale.

"I always am."

Rafe was silent as a shadow as he made his cautious way toward the apartment building. The lights were on in other apartments, and Rafe could hear music and laughter issuing forth. Students, who comprised most of the tenants, went in and out by twos and threes. They seemed to sense nothing wrong.

Rafe didn't dare enter by the main door. The Tall Men in the car were clearly stationed to keep track of who went in or out, and Rafe was a known quantity. Instead, he veered around toward the back of the building, put on his temple piece, glanced about to make sure he was not being observed, and began to climb.

Rita's apartment was on the third floor. Quickly Rafe ascended the brick wall. He opened the locked window by concentrating, and slipped inside the bedroom.

He flattened himself against the wall and let his eyes adjust, though even in this dim lighting he could see that the room had been ransacked. Rafe moved carefully, in utter silence, taking care to disturb nothing. He knelt by the bed and reached under the mattress. The gun was gone. He hoped that was a good sign. Rising, Rafe edged out into the hallway and strained to listen.

Silence. If there was anyone here, he was being as quiet as Rafe was. With each second that passed, Rafe grew more certain that Rita was no longer in the apartment.

Rafe glanced quickly into the bathroom, pulling aside the curtain to make certain there was no terrified Rita, bound and gagged, placed inside. Only a no-slip shower mat and shampoo greeted him. Rafe turned his attention to the kitchen and living-room area, edging slowly down the hallway and placing his feet carefully. Holding his breath, he peered, with infinite slowness, around the corner.

The Tall Man had made himself at home in the kitchen. He had pulled up a chair and placed himself with a perfect view of the front door. His back was to Rafe. An arbus lay across his lap, and he sipped a cup of steaming hot coffee. The big mug had a picture of Earth on it with the phrase, "Love Your Mother" written in flowing script. It looked tiny and obscene in the Tall Man's huge hands. Rafe was suddenly very angry.

Rafe debated his options. He could leave, quietly, and the Tall Man would be none the wiser. Or he could kill him now. But if he did so, he'd have to be silent.

A sudden thought struck him. Whoever was behind this was thorough. There was a good chance that the place was "bugged," as the humans would term it. He might have been spotted already. If he killed the Tall Man, even quietly, it could be picked up on video.

The Tall Man took another sip of the brew and grunted in satisfaction. Rafe had seen enough. If Rita were here, the Tall Man would be guarding her. Time to get out of here.

As quietly as he had come, Rafe edged back toward the window. The Tall Man was luckier than he knew.

"What did you find?" asked Cale as Rafe opened the door.

"They've been there all right. The place was torn apart. I saw a Tall Man, eyes glued to the door, but no sign of Rita."

Cale closed his eyes in relief. "There's only one person she trusts—one friend she has. Let's see if Carrie has heard anything."

Rafe still did not turn on the lights as he pulled away from the curb.

*   *   *

Rita jumped when the knock came on Carrie's door. They were up in the bedroom, talking in agitated whispers. The two friends exchanged glances, then Carrie smiled reassuringly. She patted Rita's hand and said, "Stay here. I'll go check it out."

"Remember what I told you," said Rita, "if they're big ugly guys in trench coats, we go out the back way. Okay?"

She had told Carrie some of what had happened— enough to warn her friend, should the goons and their leader who had ransacked her apartment show up here. The tiny, scholarly woman had become Rita's only friend. She had to go to a place where Cale could find her, but she hated the thought of doing anything to put Carrie in jeopardy. So she told about the "thugs" who were following her and Cale, but did not mention their extraterrestrial origins.

Carrie rose, smiled uncertainly at Rita, and closed the door. The seconds ticked by. Rita clutched a pillow and gnawed at her lower lip. She could hear the muffled sounds of voices from the dining room, but they were so low she couldn't tell if it was Cale or not.

Then the door was flung open. Rita shrieked, then recovered herself almost immediately.

Cale!

Sobbing, she launched herself from the bed into his outstretched arms, flinging her arms around his shoulders and even wrapping her legs about his waist. He crushed her to him, kissing her neck fiercely.

"Are you all right?" they both said at the same time.

"What the hell is going on here?" said an utterly confused Carrie. She and Rafe had followed Cale into the bedroom. Rita gulped and slid down Cale's body to stand shakily on her own.

"Carrie," said Rafe briskly, taking charge of the situation, "Can you leave us alone for a few minutes?"

Carrie eyed him. "Okay. I'll go brew some coffee—I've got the feeling it's going to be a long night for you guys. But when you're done, you've got to tell me what's happening." With a last look at Rita, she stepped out and closed the door.

Cale and Rita began talking at the same time. "There was this guy—Rafe said the place had been ransacked—who was he and how did he—"

"Silence!" bellowed Rafe. They started and looked at him. "Time is growing very, very short. Rita, tell us what happened."

She took a deep breath and steadied herself, then told them about coming home to the wreck that had been her apartment. She described the man who had shown up at the door, and the ugly thugs waiting in the black sedan outside. Her voice caught when she told them about leveling the gun in the stranger's face. Cale squeezed her hand comfortingly, but sat in silence until she was done.

"You're sure he was Tyrusian?" asked Rafe.

Rita nodded vigorously. "He couldn't have passed for human. He had really slanted eyes, and his temples were very deep and very high. Oh, I almost forgot. . . ." She dug into her pocket and came out with the temple piece. "They dropped this. I thought you might be able to use it."

Rafe raised an eyebrow as he accepted the temple piece. "That's levelheaded thinking, Rita. We certainly can use every piece of Tyrusian technology—especially now."

"Rita," said Cale, "we're going to have to leave."

"I know. I've emptied my bank account and bought a pickup. I tried to think of everything I needed to bring and put it in the backpack, but I'm sure I forgot something. Whatever it was we can buy it."

"Wait a minute—you bought a truck?" Rafe's brows drew together. "We need a vehicle, but if you've applied for a loan they can trace you!"

"I bought it with cash from an ad in the paper," explained Rita. She reached over and grabbed her backpack. It was full of green bills. Cale and Rafe stared, their eyes wide. "My mom's inheritance cleared, and we've got about a hundred grand in cash now. So we can go wherever you think best."

A slow smile spread across Cale's face. He leaned forward and kissed Rita on the forehead. "My brilliant Ooshala!"

"How do you think they found us?" asked Rita of Rafe.

"Could be anything. We could have been spotted on the campus, they could have discovered our tampering with the social security computer—anything at all. But they knew where to find us—both times."

Rita felt suddenly cold. "What—what do you mean?"

"The meeting," said Cale gently. "It was a trap. Dozens of loyalists were killed, and they almost captured me. Rafe believes they knew I was going to be at the site. If it hadn't been—" He looked away. "A friend of mine gave his life to save me. I held him as he died."

"Oh, Cale," breathed Rita, sympathy welling inside her.

The face he turned to her startled her. It was hard, determined, even though his eyes were bright with tears. "They cannot be permitted to win. I don't want anyone else dying for being loyal to me. We've got to stop it. We've got to go somewhere and get ready for the fight."

"Where might be a good place to go?" asked Rafe.

Rita thought. "We could go to Canada or Mexico, but that's more red tape. We might be spotted." An idea suddenly occurred to her. She turned and fished through the backpack, spilling fifty-dollar bills. She brought forth an atlas and flipped through it. "I bought this today when I got the car. Thought we might need it. Yes, here we go—"

She pointed to a map of Arizona. "It's the state directly south of us. Right here"—she indicated a large area—"is the Navajo Indian reservation. Twenty-five thousand square miles of land and only about two hundred thousand people on it, most congregated in certain areas. Sparsely populated. A lot of it is very rural." She glanced up, her eyes flickering from Rafe to Cale and back again. "A good place for people to get lost in."

"*Kia*, you are amazing!" said Cale.

"Indeed," echoed Rafe, his eyes narrowing speculatively. "Quite amazing. What's happened?"

"What do you mean? asked Rita, thinking she knew full well what Rafe was getting at.

"You've never given me any reason to think you stupid. But this type of planning is remarkable."

Rita swallowed hard, her eyes downcast. "I'd like to speak to Cale alone, please."

Rafe shook his head, implacable. "No. There must be no secrets between us. Not anymore. Too much is riding on our survival."

Rita nodded. "Okay." She turned to Cale, took his hands in hers, and tried to ignore the belligerent visage of Rafe watching her intently. "Cale, I wasn't telling you everything. The reason I didn't come with you?"

"Yes?"

"I had a doctor's appointment."

His eyes widened. "You're not ill?" He gripped her hands hard, almost painfully, but she didn't pull away.

"No. The doctor says I'm doing fine. Cale—" Oh, the words were hard. She took a breath and simply blurted it out. "We're going to have a baby."

Stunned silence filled the room. Cale and Rafe stared in shock. "Well?" asked Rita, uncomfortable. "Doesn't anyone have anything to say?"

Cale uttered a string of lovely, liquid-sounding words that were totally incomprehensible to Rita. Judging by the softness of his voice, they were endearments. He pulled her close and rested his chin on her hair. Her ear pressed against his chest, and she could hear the rapid beating of his heart. She shut her eyes in relief.

Rafe also uttered a string of words in Tyrusian, but judging by the anger in his voice they were most assuredly *not* endearments. "Why now? Rita, how could you let this happen?"

Cale raised his head. "Rafe!" he snapped. "I played a part in this, too. Would you chastise me as well?"

"I would! You know what we're up against. We don't have time to worry about changing diapers when—"

Rita had had enough. Squirming free of Cale's protective embrace, she stood and planted her hands on her hips. "What is it you want from me, Rafe? First you're mad at Cale for choosing an Ooshala who might not be able to conceive. Now I'm pregnant, and you're mad at me for that! You asked what was different. I'll tell you. *I* am. I'm a queen and a wife and a soon-to-be mother, and I will not let *anything* harm my baby or my husband!"

Rita was crying now, hot, angry tears. She gestured frantically at her attire. She was wearing jeans, sneakers, and a black T-shirt bearing the word "Nukes" with a red universal "No" sign through it. "I've marched in peace rallies. I'm scared to death of guns. I hate violence. And I'm telling you, let's go somewhere, and you teach me how to fight. I'm ready to learn. And if that's not different enough for you, then to hell with you!"

She wiped at her red, flushed face. She trembled with rage. Behind her, Cale rose and put one hand gently on her shoulder, the other, clad in the Exotar, he placed on her belly.

"Do you carry the child here? As we do?" he asked.

"Y-yes," stammered Rita, startled out of her anger by his tenderness. Cale spread the fingers and closed his eyes. "What are you doing?"

"I am saying hello to our baby," said Cale. And suddenly the tears in Rita's eyes weren't those of anger, but of joy.

There was a knock on the door. "Come in," called Rita.

Carrie entered. She had four cups of coffee on a tray. "Coffee's ready. Are my explanations?"

Carrie's coffee cooled, untouched, as she listened in amazement to what Rafe had to say. Apparently, he and Cale were government agents in deep cover. Rita had found out about it, and now, Carrie knew, too. Such knowledge could be dangerous.

The men who were after them were enemy agents from another country They were large, and often wore sunglasses, even at night, trench coats, and fedoras. Carrie was to deny everything that had happened, though she could say she was friends with the "students" Rafael and Caleb. After a day or two, Carrie was to "discover" the break-in and report it to the police. Did she understand everything?

She nodded, shocked. Unable to resist, she pressed Rafe for more information—stuff like this was the mother lode to a poli-sci major. But Rafe merely smiled and said the less she knew, the safer she'd be.

They piled into Rita's new/old pickup. Rita embraced her friend tightly and whispered, "Be careful." Then they were gone.

Carrie was still up around ten o'clock when the knocking came on the door. Her heart leaped, and she froze like a deer in the headlights. Was it the ugly Tall Men Rafe had warned her about? Carefully, Carrie moved to the window and peered out. Relief flooded her. Standing on her step were two very clean-cut young men, probably from the neighboring Fort Douglas. Carrie often saw military men on campus as U of U and Fort Douglas were right next to one another. She scurried down the stairs, thankful that they wore MP uniforms, not trench coats.

She flung open the door. "Yes?"

One of them smiled, charmingly. "Sorry to disturb you, ma'am, but we heard a disturbance in this neighborhood as we were driving by and wanted to know if folks were all right. May we come in?"

A horrible thought struck her. "Let me see some ID," she said. Obligingly, they fished out their military ID. It was genuine, all right. The last of her fear gone, she stepped back. "Come on in."

She closed the door, saying, "I haven't heard any noise in the last couple of hours, but—"

Carrie turned around to come face-to-face with a pistol. The charming young men weren't smiling anymore.

"Tell us about Caleb and Rafael."

CHAPTER ELEVEN

• • •

September 9, 1981
Broken Rock, Arizona
The Navajo Reservation

The first light of dawn was just beginning to creep over the yellow sand when Eddie pulled into what passed for a parking lot at the Drake Free Clinic. This was his favorite time of day—before the heat and the responsibilities descended. It was fresh, full of possibility, and Eddie loved it.

He got out of his dust-covered pickup and slammed the door shut, not bothering to lock it. That was one wonderful thing that the Rez had over any city on the East Coast. The Navajos didn't have the same concepts of "stealing" as the *bilagáani* did. If one day Eddie's truck did turn up missing, he'd know more or less where it had gone—someone simply needed to get home and borrowed it. It was a totally different mind-set, and Eddie was beginning to relax back into it after so long away.

The door to the clinic, however, was not unlocked. Eddie wasn't sure if that was because sensitive and potentially dangerous equipment and materials were inside, or if because the Drake Clinic was run by an Anglo. He unlocked the door and stepped inside.

"Morning, Eddie," Bill Tsosie greeted him, favoring him with a quick glance and a smile. He was already in his white lab coat and the door to the supply room was open. "We can sure use you today. Care for some coffee? I'm brewing a pot now."

The heavenly smell, nectar to those in the medical profession, was indeed wafting toward Eddie's nose. "You bet. What are you doing here so early, Bill? Thought I opened this place up today."

"We're starting the first round of Dr. Drake's Famous Flu Shots," grinned Bill. "Cures what ails you. Come eight o'clock we're going to have a line the likes of which you won't believe."

"I'm not believing it now," said Eddie. He shrugged into his lab coat and washed his hands. Indians generally had to be dragged kicking and screaming into places like this. The Indian Health Service clinic at which he worked succeeded in treating people on a regular basis only because two-thirds of the staff were *Dineh*. Perhaps the allure was the word "free" in the Drake Free Clinic. Perhaps it was Bill. He didn't see how any of the Navajo he knew would trust a cold fish like Drake, no matter how brilliant he might be.

"Drake's been doing this for two years now. The success rate is phenomenal. Much better than the national average. You get Drake's Wonder Shot, you don't get sick. Period."

"What the hell's in it?"

"Drake says it's just the standard stuff, but he tinkers with it a little. Adds some vitamins, things like that. Whatever it is, it's working."

Eddie, who'd been reaching for a chipped mug, paused. "He's conducting *experiments* on these people? Damn it, Bill, doesn't he know that—"

"Hold on, Mr. CDC," said Bill, a slight edge to his voice. Eddie bristled. "I saw the list of ingredients when he first came up with it, and Drake hasn't done anything except play with the ratios much since then. There's nothing in here that could harm anyone. You think I'd let my people be used as guinea pigs?"

"They're my people, too, Bill," said Eddie in a low voice. Had it been Alana, the comment would have launched a tirade with the central, recurring motif of *You're more Anglo than Navajo*. From Bill, it merely produced silence.

Then—"You're right. I'm sorry. I know you've had problems with Drake, and frankly I can't for the life of me figure out why he didn't jump at the chance to hire you for the clinic. But he's a good man, if a little prickly, and he cares a lot about helping people. If he's a bit radical, what's the harm when the result is completely positive? I take the shots myself, Eddie, and it's nothing short of a miracle. So ease up on him, all right?"

"All right." A thought hit him. "Will he be in today?"

"Oh, you bet. He wouldn't miss a day of flu-shot week. Ego-stroking, you know."

Eddie swore silently to himself. He'd been careful about which days he chose to volunteer at the clinic, and had meticulously structured his schedule around Drake's nonappearances. He thought about bailing out, but if things were going to get as busy as Bill clearly expected, they'd need every pair of hands. Besides, if this shot was the miracle drug Bill described, it would be a positive way to come into a lot of contact with his fellow *Dineh*.

He helped Bill prepare the instruments and the clinic for the predicted onslaught. At seven, a full hour earlier than usual, Susie Benally, their plump but very pretty and extremely organized secretary, appeared.

"Ready for the crowds?" she chuckled. Susie wore a perpetual smile, and her voice, husky from years of cigarettes, also seemed to smile when she spoke. She was a joy to have in the office, Eddie had found, and one of their favorite friendly games was sparring over the issue of cigarettes.

"Sounds like you're going to be so busy you won't

have time to sneak a smoke," he teased, pouring her a cup of coffee loaded with creamer and sugar.

Susie threw back her head and laughed heartily. Eddie found himself smiling. "I'll find the time," she assured him. "Better be ready, Dr. Rainsinger. They're lining up already."

Disbelieving her, Eddie went to the window and peered out. Through the grimy glass, he saw about a dozen people standing patiently in line. He gaped. Navajos weren't early for many things. There was a joke among them about "Navajo time" being different from "Anglo time." And yet here they were. Even as he watched, stupefied, four more pickups pulled up, and people spilled out.

"Jeez," he breathed. "You two were right."

At eight o'clock the doors opened on what was to be one of the longest days of Eddie Rainsinger's life. He was glad he'd eaten breakfast at home, because that was the only meal of the day until he returned home, exhausted, at 7 P.M. But it was a good exhaustion. The tentative smiles on the faces of strangers, the welcome he felt even though he couldn't yet speak the language fluently—that was food for the soul, something he had badly needed.

Even Drake wasn't too bad. He'd stiffened and frowned when he saw Eddie, but after a few moments largely ignored him. It was far too hectic at the clinic to indulge in vendettas and active snubbing. By the time they closed the doors, they'd given 153 men, women, and children shots that would ensure that they had a healthy winter. Eddie feasted at McDonald's, watched some TV on his little, battered television set, and fell into the trailer's bed at ten. He slept deeply, and had no dreams.

Alana killed the ignition and hopped lightly out of her red pickup. The sand rose in small, dry puffs beneath her well-worn boots as she ascended the steps to the Broken Rock Trading Post.

Her feet fit into the grooves worn smooth by decades of Indian and Anglo boots, and if the old wood of the porch groaned and strained with each step, it was just one more familiar thing about this place. Three chairs were placed on the porch, with an ancient rain barrel between them serving as a table. A glass ashtray was overflowing with cigarette butts. Come evening, a *hosteen* or two would sit, sip a Coke, and add to the collection of butts. Now, the chairs were vacant. A cow skull adorned the low door, glowering impotently as Alana opened the door and stepped inside. She let it bang shut behind her. Everyone did.

"Good morning, Walter," Alana called in Navajo. She let her eyes adjust to the dimness, almost dark after the powerful sunlight of late summer. She could barely make out the skeins of colored yarn that adorned one wall and the narrow aisles of staples that led deeper into the trading post's dark interior.

"Good morning," replied the post's owner, Walter Johnson, in the same language. Walter poked his snowy head up from behind a pile of chicken-feed sacks to give Alana a friendly grin. Walter Johnson was the only Anglo Alana implicitly trusted. His was the first white face she had seen as a small, shy little girl visiting the trading post. He spoke fluent Navajo and had given her a piece of hard candy. In later years, it would not be so easy to win Alana Yazzie's trust, but Walter had succeeded and had been a good friend to the Yazzie family for many years. Even with his twinkling blue eyes and red cheeks, Alana tended to think of him as more *Dineh* than *bilagáana*. Walter knew and respected Navajo tradition and, frankly, behaved more like the People than an Anglo.

"How is Hosteen Yazzie? Is he well?" Walter dusted his hands off and moved to start stocking sacks of Bluebird Flour.

Alana's father always accompanied her on her weekly trips to the Broken Rock Trading Post. "He's doing a Blessing Way for Nathan Begay over in Window Rock," she replied. She paused at the small, enclosed display of jewelry at the counter. "I see you've got some more of Carla Bedonie's work." She gazed longingly at the intricate working of silver and turquoise, and thought, as she always did, that it would be nice to sit in a hogan and make beautiful things.

But it was not her destiny. For others to sit in their hogans peacefully working crafts, some had to protect that peace—fight for it, maybe even die for it. Alana was one of those.

"Hi!" said a voice right by her ear. Alana jumped, startled. She didn't have to even look up to know it was an Anglo. None of the People would sneak up behind you and brightly exclaim "Hi!" She turned her dark eyes briefly upon the stranger: a man of medium height, well built, with blond hair and blue eyes and a white smile. He was wearing a suit and looked very hot already. She avoided his gaze and did not reply, moving sinuously through the aisles of the Broken Rock Trading Post and continuing to shop.

In typical *bilagáani* fashion, the man opted to ignore what was perfectly clear, if nonverbal, Navajo for "please do not bother me."

"My name's Tom Alexander," he said, falling into step beside her. He stuck his hand out. Reluctantly, Alana reached and squeezed it gently, bracing herself for—and getting—the familiar crush of a white man's "firm handshake."

"I'm with the Bureau. I just got assigned here and was told that the trading post was where to meet people."

"People do congregate here," Alana agreed stiffly. Mentally, she went over how much feed to buy to supplement the flock's grazing. It had been an unusually dry summer. According to traditional *Dineh* thought, bad weather and lack of rain meant that the People were out of balance with the universe—not walking in beauty. Alana thought, with a wave of resentment somewhat but not particularly directed to the fresh-faced young blond beside her, that her people hadn't been walking in beauty for a long, long time.

"Can I help you with anything?" Agent Alexander was saying. "I'd like to get to know—"

"Thank you, I'm fine. I've been taking care of my sheep and my family for a while now, and I do not require the assistance of the Federal Bureau of Investigation to continue to do so."

His white face flushed. "Sorry," he said. "I meant no offense." He stood beside her a moment longer, looking as if he wanted to think of something else to say, then wandered off.

Alana's gaze followed him, boring into his back. It was considered rude to maintain prolonged eye contact, and staring in general was frowned upon, but Alana often disregarded conventions.

She liked to know her enemy, and most white people—certainly anyone from the Bureau—were her enemy.

A sudden thought struck her, made fear suddenly spurt adrenaline into her blood. Did this insipid white man know? Had someone leaked information, or been careless? Alana knew and bitterly disliked the tiny, perfectly groomed Agent O'Connell, but this man was an unknown quantity.

There came the bang of the door. Jimmy White Horse entered, looked about, then made his way to where Alana stood among the canned goods. Jimmy, one of the most promising of the young rodeo riders in the Broken Rock area, was twenty-five, ludicrously handsome, and had the hottest, quickest temper of any hand. Quietly, in Navajo, he asked, "What did he want?"

"To be friendly," she murmured back, pausing to look at Agent Alexander. He had fished out some change and was trying to coax a soda from the ancient, recalcitrant machine. He waited, then put in more coins. Another wait, then, frowning, Agent Alexander started shaking the machine ever so slightly. That was Walter's cue to get out the keys. Regulars knew better than to try that machine.

"That's a bad sign. When white people want to be friendly, they usually want something more."

Tom Alexander got his Coke and thanked Walter. But he didn't leave at once. He used the bottlecap opener on the machine to open the soda, took a sip, and began talking to Walter in a low voice. Once, his blue gaze flickered over to Alana, then back to Walter.

"He's asking about me," said Alana. "Jimmy, has anyone—"

"No," said Jimmy firmly. His brown eyes snapped with the anger of the righteous. "No one would betray you or I.N.N. But I think we should change the meeting site, just in case."

Alana nodded slowly, still watching Walter and the new fed boy talking. Walter shook his head and said something. Alana imagined the words: *Not Alana. Her father's a healer. Alana wouldn't be involved in anything like that.*

The door creaked open, banged shut. Another Anglo had entered—a young woman, just a teenager by the looks of her, with a swollen belly. She had the fresh, innocent look typical of an Anglo youth, but there was a tempering about the eyes and mouth that made Alana wonder at what recent lessons the child had undergone. Her skin had been deeply tanned by the sun, and her clothing, while clean, was not new. She wore a sleeveless sundress, and her arms were knotted with muscles.

Alana Yazzie sized up everyone. She wondered

what the girl was doing here. She didn't look like your standard tourist.

"Alana," said Jimmy, "I can host the meeting."

"Are you sure?" Jimmy had a promising career shaping up in the rodeo. She knew he believed in what they were doing, but she didn't want to jeopardize his chances.

Jimmy nodded. His dark hair fell into his eyes, and he brushed it back with a thoughtless movement. Alana was amazed anew at just how handsome he was. She knew Jimmy was interested in her, but also knew the attraction for what it was—a young man being drawn to his charismatic leader, nothing more. Unbidden, Eddie Rainsinger's face swam into her thoughts. If only he had burned with the fire that consumed young Jimmy. But he didn't hear the drums or smell the smoke of the pipe; he heard other songs, dreamed other dreams.

"All right," she said. "Tonight."

"Again!" barked Rafe.

Rita leaned forward, a task that was considerably harder now than it used to be, and put her hands on her knees. Rafe had taught her that trick, and she gulped air furiously as she tried to slow the pounding of her heart. Tendrils of dark hair were plastered to her sweaty face, and the look she shot Rafe was not a pleasant one. He couldn't be serious.

"I said, again," repeated Rafe. He saw her expression and smiled a little. "Good girl. Now, channel that anger into your workout!"

Pausing only long enough to gulp some water from the bottle strapped to her side, Rita obeyed and launched into a fourth run on the obstacle course Rafe had designed to whip all of them into fighting form.

He had worked with the natural roughness of the landscape. The first segment of the course was an area they had cleared of brush for a quick sprint. It led directly to a set of boulders. Rita set her jaw and scrambled over them as fast as she could. It was both harder and easier now—harder because she was tiring, easier because after three months of running this course every day she knew precisely where the hand and foot grips were. She landed easily and headed for the eight tires. Her feet felt as though they had weights on them, and her belly . . . !

Grunting, she launched herself straight up and pulled herself into the knotted branches of an ancient, weatherworn tree. It looked far too fragile to hold even her, but Rafe, Cale, and the others ran this course daily as well, and the tree had supported all of them.

"Report!" Rafe was there, squinting up at her.

Rita's throat was dry and dusty, and her voice was a croak as she replied. "To the north: Cale, Shalli, and Baris are doing target practice." Even as she spoke, she saw them take aim and fire. The reports cracked an instant later. "To the south: Our encampment is undetectable. To the east: nothing. To the west: nothing."

"Excellent. Get down and do your meditation and flexibility exercises. After that—"

"After that," said Rita wearily as she carefully negotiated the twisted branches, "we work on developing my mental skills." She dropped down. "How much longer do we have to continue that farce, Rafe? I think it's clear by now that I'm not a latent telepath."

Rafe studied her, his eyes searching her face. "It's not for you," he said. "It's for the baby."

"What?"

"The physical workout is for you. You're in pretty good shape, but you could be better. As your pregnancy advances, the baby's weight will become more and more of a hindrance, so you need all the strength and stamina you can build now. The flexibility is also important. The meditation and mental-testing exercises are for the child. Tyrusian children begin their mental development in the womb, right along with everything else. Children who are exposed to the proper stimuli develop faster. Had things gone according to plan," he added with a hint of bitterness, "you would be on Tyrus and we could supplement this with technological and medical stimuli."

"Had things gone according to plan," said Rita, reaching for her bottle of water, "I wouldn't be married to Cale in the first place."

Rafe gave her an unreadable look. "That is true."

In the silence, the report from the guns echoed. Rita realized that Cale and the others had been firing all this time. She had simply grown so used to the noise— one or the other of them was always practicing—that she simply had started to tune it out.

I'm getting used to the sound of gunfire, she thought with a twist in her gut. *God help me, but I am.*

The time had flown. Ever since they arrived on the reservation nearly three months ago, Rafe had seen to it that they had all been kept very busy. Things had started off badly when Rafe had discovered a tracking beacon implanted in the temple piece Rita had found in her apartment. Whoever that hideous man was who was after them, he had known they were heading for the reservation. Rafe disabled it shortly after arrival, but the incident had made an already tense situation even more alarming.

Then they had to try to find a place to settle. It had been harder than Rita had first thought. There were many places where the map indicated that humans were scarce, but Rita hadn't reckoned on the Navajo culture. Unlike the Hopi, whose reservation was actually enclosed within the Navajo's, the *Dineh,* as she had discovered the Navajo preferred to be called, were nomads. Certainly there were towns, but the desolation was deceptive. A huge expanse that Rita could have sworn would have to be deserted often yielded a small grouping of the traditional six-sided houses called "hogans," where the families would tend their sheep and grow what they called "dry" crops. This was very much their land, and place after place was examined and then rejected.

Finally, they had settled on this place—Turquoise Mesa. Too rocky for easy sheep grazing, too dry for even "dry" crops, its barrenness suited the purposes of the little band of Ooshati. Using the arbus and good old-fashioned elbow grease, they had dug a cave which they were able to camouflage well. Rita hated the lack of privacy—she was, after all, still a newlywed, albeit a pregnant one—but she had said nothing. It couldn't be helped.

Then the others had started coming. First was Shalli and her small band of four. Then others, some in pods with valuable equipment, others in four-wheel drives. Their number was now seventeen, and it was becoming increasingly hard to disguise their activities. Even the HCUs had their limits.

Rafe had become the drill sergeant of the group. Cale was their leader, but Rafe put everyone through his and her paces. He'd designed the obstacle course, he had organized the division of labor, and though he never wavered in deferring to Cale whenever that youthful king had conflicting opinions, it was clear who had the daily run of this particular show.

They had taken turns driving in to get supplies at the Broken Rock Trading Post. Rita hadn't been back five minutes, the pickup loaded to the gills with staples, before Rafe had been at her to get on with her workout.

Now she returned to the blessed coolness of the cave on legs that trembled. She sprawled on her sleeping bag, burying her hot face in the pillow. One hand crept up to caress her swelling belly.

"What a situation I'm bringing you into, little one,"

she said softly to her unborn child. "I hope you can forgive me."

"It's me."

"You shouldn't call on this line."

"The alternative was to have you paged, would that have been better?"

"I see your point. What is it?"

"I wished to update you on the condition of Operation Hamstring. The first stage has been carried out successfully. The situation will be monitored carefully as it unfolds."

"Outstanding. Good work. Any problems?"

"Nothing I can't handle."

"Be sure about that. Be very sure. The Dragit has a lot riding on this."

"I foresee no problems. What about you? The agent you spoke of—are you still worried?"

"That agent is not one of us, I'm certain of that. Could be a security risk."

"Watch your back."

"I intend to."

CHAPTER TWELVE

• • •

June 16, 1981
Charles Air Force Base
The Utah Desert

Konrad leaned back in his chair, steepled his fingers, and surveyed the two young officers who stood ramrod straight in front of him.

"You failed, gentlemen," he said in a deceptively soft voice. "And quite the abysmal failure it was, too."

With a sudden, violent motion, he slammed a copy of the *Salt Lake Tribune* on the desk. The headline blared: "University Student Found Slain In Apartment."

"You were just supposed to question this Dalton woman, damn it—follow up on the tampering with the social security computer! What the hell happened?"

The two men were pale. "Sir, she became hysterical once we mentioned the names of Rafael and Caleb. Swore up and down that she'd never heard of them. It was obvious she was lying. We tried to press her further, but she started throwing things and eluded our grasp."

"She locked herself in a room with a telephone, sir," said the second youth. "We—well, we had to stop her, sir."

Konrad took a deep breath and exhaled slowly. "Did you get anything useful at all out of the girl before you shot her?"

The first officer shook his head. "No, sir. Except that she clearly knew who they were, and was terrified about answering questions regarding them."

"Hmm . . ." Konrad scratched his chin thoughtfully. "She might have known who they were—or they could have told her something else. Now, thanks to my trigger-happy men, we'll never know." He picked up the newspaper and waved it at them. "Another student's apartment was broken into last night. You two got lucky—the police will probably try to link the events, call it a burglary gone bad. I never want to see a slip-up like that again, do you understand?"

They nodded. Disgusted, Konrad waved a hand at them. "Dismissed." He watched them go, frowning.

This was the sort of thing that bastard Saris Krai loved—seeing Konrad's men pursue a line of investigation and botching it badly. The thought of the spidery little man sitting alone in his office, tracking down the jumpers and the deserters, made Konrad almost physically ill. Good thing Krai didn't know about the lead Konrad had been pursuing. It was a slim lead, admittedly—Caleb and Rafael were, after all, perfectly genuine *Erdlufi* names—but combined with the tampering his experts had been able to detect in the social security computer link, it had been worth investigating.

And now, the one girl who knew anything was dead. The trail had grown cold.

Saris Krai surveyed the blip on the screen with satisfaction. The trail had begun to heat up.

He was furious with the *ga'lim* for losing Cale when they, quite literally, had him within their grasp. The royal line of Tyrus inspired amazing loyalty, it would seem; a young man who had been aboard the Royal Yacht had distracted one of the Tall Men long enough for Cale to recover. The steward had paid for his act with his life, which, as far as Saris was concerned, was not enough.

Thank goodness the little *Erdlufa* had been smart enough—or foolish enough, depending on how one looked at it—to pocket the temple piece Saris had left. The blip on the screen assured him that all was going as planned.

He wasn't certain where they were headed. The route was circuitous, as he expected it would be. No straight shot down an Interstate for Cale-Oosha. The three had taken the back roads, twisting and turning through Utah but clearly, gradually, making their way south. What was their eventual destination? Right now they had just crossed the state line into Arizona, near the Four Corners area.

And then, suddenly, the blip stopped.

Saris cried aloud in shock. What had happened? Frantically he placed a hand on the control orb and tried to search mentally for any interference that could have caused it to short out. Nothing.

Angrily, Saris cursed. Someone had manually deactivated the signal. Almost at once, though, calm settled on him as the significance of this registered. Rita certainly wouldn't have known what to look for. Only a Tyrusian would. And not just any Tyrusian, either. By now, Saris was certain that Cale-Oosha was with Rita Carter. Now he was almost as certain that Commander Rafe was indeed the mysterious Rafael Smith. He'd know what to look for, and he'd think to look for it.

"Cale and Rafe," mused Saris. "The Dragit will be so pleased."

He made up his mind. He reached for a com orb, a different, slightly larger crystal than the one that operated the computer system, and concentrated. A few seconds later, the stern visage of the Dragit, slightly distorted by the curve of the crystal sphere, appeared.

"This had better be important, Krai," growled the Dragit.

"Oh, indeed it is," Saris confirmed. "I require your permission to take this investigation off the base."

"Hmm. Is that really necessary?"

"I'm afraid so. I have a vital lead that I must follow up."

"Really? What is it?"

"Ah, great Dragit, let me conduct this in my own way."

"I don't like this . . ."

"Have I ever failed you before in this capacity?"

It was a rhetorical question, and the Dragit's face curved in a smile. He chuckled. "That you have not, Krai. Continue as you see fit. You have my full authority to pursue this matter. But Krai . . ."

"Sir?"

"I am very curious."

Krai smiled, a thin stretching of his lips over his teeth. "I hope to satisfy that curiosity very soon, Dragit."

As the Dragit's image faded, so did the forced smile on Saris Krai's face. He turned again to look at the image on the screen, a map of Utah and Arizona. His purple eyes narrowed. It was not the obvious place for them to go, but Krai hadn't gotten where he was by simply chasing the obvious. He was a firm believer in being prepared.

He placed his fingers on the control orb and the computer screen shifted. A few directed thoughts and Saris had what he was looking for—the database of all known languages spoken on Earth. He selected four and began the tutorials. He hoped he would avoid encounters—he hardly looked like a healthy, typical human—but it was just as well to speak the languages just in case.

Over the next hour, Saris Krai mastered Spanish, Hopi, Apache, and Navajo.

October 3, 1981
Turquoise Mesa
The Navajo Reservation

The wind was cold, laced with tiny white specks that promised a hard winter to come. The chill breeze stung Alana's cheeks, even as the tears stung her eyes.

She hated arguing with her father. And last night's confrontation had been dreadful.

She had returned late from a meeting of I.N.N. to find him waiting up for her. The smoke drifted upward and out through the small opening in the center of the hogan.

"Our way is the way of peace, daughter," he had said, his dark eyes boring into her. "Look how hard this old man strives to bring about harmony with his people. We are fortunate. We still have our ancestral lands, we are the largest and the wealthiest of any of the Nations. Your flock increases. Your beauty increases, but not your wisdom. These young boys you lead are troublemakers. You are out of balance. This is bad medicine, child, and you know it."

She didn't ask how he knew. He probably wouldn't tell her. Even to her, who knew him best and loved him best, he was an imposing sight, seated cross-legged at the fire, his white braids dangling down the middle of his back. The flames seemed to throw the lines on his face into sharp relief, and she sensed the anger and grief simmering just beneath her father's carefully controlled visage.

"I know how it must seem to you, Father," she said, stepping inside and stretching her hands out to the warmth of the fire. "But we are striving for the same thing. I would like nothing more than to be at peace. But it has been a long time since any of us walked in beauty. How can we be in harmony when we are second-class citizens in the eyes of the government?

And what about the murders in Farmington back in '77? Three people killed just because they were Indians. What about the smallpox in the blankets, the Long Walk, the—"

"Do not lecture me on the history of wrongs done our people," replied Hosteen Yazzie in a soft, warning tone of voice. "But your Independent Navajo Nation is only bringing about more disharmony. Balance cannot be achieved by fighting."

"It's the only way!"

"Are you certain? Has Changing Woman come down from the mountains and told you this? More like Coyote is playing with you! The more you flail, the farther away from your true goal you grow. There are other ways to bring about change. Better ways."

Her throat had closed up at that, and she had stalked off into the bitter night. She'd slept with the dog Bisoodi in the crude shelter they had erected years ago for the sheep in particularly hard winters. Covered with hay, inhaling the scents of dog and sheep, Alana had cried herself to sleep.

She'd known that one day Hosteen Yazzie would find out. She'd imagined that time—dreamed of her father standing with her, using his spiritual powers as a *haatalii* for the good of the cause. Instead, he had berated her as if she were nothing but a foolish child.

She'd slept little and rose early, taking the sheep, which had been given to her by her mother and her mother before her, and driving them out in a new direction. Alana didn't care where she went. She just wanted quiet, a place to think.

She opened a thermos of hot coffee and poured a cup. Sipping the steaming beverage, she perched atop a boulder that retained the warmth of the strong sun and thought.

Alana was confused. She had marched in rallies, spent time in jail, even authorized illegal activities such as burning buildings. But no one had been hurt—

not yet. She knew that, sooner or later, someone—
from I.N.N. or an Anglo—would get hurt, maybe
even die.

But this was a war, wasn't it? People had to die
sometimes, die for what they believed in—kill for what
they believed in?

Her father's blatant disapproval had shaken her
confidence. She was at a crossroads. She could follow
Hosteen Yazzie's advice and turn back from this violent path, or she needed to keep fighting and give
I.N.N. teeth. All, or nothing.

Alana took another sip of the hot, black coffee. She
stared at the landscape of brown and yellow and
white, rock and sand and sheep, and her heart cried
out, to whom she did not know: *Show me the way!
Show me my path!*

Scarcely had she formed the thought when, as if in
answer to her soul's prayer, she heard the report of a
rifle. Startled, she dropped the plastic thermos cup.
Coffee splashed on her jeans, hot and wet, and then
almost immediately cold and wet. *Who'd be shooting
out here?*

She patted the inside of her coat. The knife was
always there. Trembling, Alana forced herself to be
methodical. She screwed the lid onto the thermos and
put it away in her backpack. She pulled out her binocular kit and swung the binoculars around her neck by
the strap.

She lifted them to her eyes and slowly began pan-
ning, searching. Nothing. But the shots had come from
Turquoise Mesa, she was certain. Another rifle shot
cracked in the cold air. Her heart leaped.

There was nothing for it. Alana whistled for her
black-and-white mongrel. "Stay, Bisoodi," she told
him. He barked and settled himself down, ears pricked
and alert. He'd take care of the sheep while she was
gone.

She made her way carefully toward the direction of

the gunshots, taking cover where she could and sprinting across the open spaces. The sounds grew louder as Alana reached the curve of the mesa proper. Slinging the binoculars in back of her, she began to climb. It was chilly, but by the time she had found a place from which to observe, she was quite warm.

There they were. From here, they were too tiny to make out distinguishing features, but they were clearly humans, clearly shooting. She settled back into the stones and trained her binoculars on the interlopers.

And sucked in her breath at what she saw.

Some of them were using regular rifles. Others had what could only be semiautomatic or perhaps even fully automatic weapons. And the girl on the far end, the dark-haired, tiny one in some kind of ratty uniform—she was firing a weapon the likes of which Alana had never seen. It looked as though lightning exploded from the tip of the tiny, snub-nosed weapon, and where it hit, the target was vaporized. Gone.

Then a second one stepped forward, tall and handsome for a white man, and took aim at another makeshift target. He wore something shiny on his right hand and as Alana watched, hardly breathing, literally dozens of small rocks rose up of their own accord and launched themselves at the target. They hit a perfect bull's-eye.

How in the world—

Movement caught her eye, and she moved her binoculars to follow it. The pregnant girl she'd seen at the Broken Rock Trading Post was here. She was armed with a knife in each hand, and a large, dangerous-looking man seemed to be trying to teach her the finer points of hand-to-hand combat. The girl wasn't bad, especially given her condition, but she was nowhere near as good as her instructor.

Her first thought had been that the shooters were Anglo kids on a spree. Her second, after seeing so many gathered here, had been that this was perhaps some sort of secret government training camp. But that was also incorrect. The weapons were too advanced, and yet the clothes and uniforms were in tatters. And what secret government base would have a pregnant girl—a girl who was obviously no trained soldier—with them?

She would watch here for a while, and see if she could learn anything more about them. An idea was starting to form, but Alana reined it in. Alana Yazzie was nothing if not careful, especially when it came to I.N.N.

"Do you even have a home, Agent Alexander?"

Kelly O'Connell's voice was teasing. Tom Alexander glanced quickly at his wristwatch—well past seven—and then smiled up at his partner.

"No, actually. My cat's litterbox is right under your desk. Took you all this time to notice?"

"Seriously—you've worked late every night for a week. How about heading out for a bite to eat with me?"

"I thought you and Dr. Drake were . . ."

She shook her dark head vigorously. "Elliott? No, he's just a friend. My first friend here on the reservation. Even so, it's not against the regulations for partners to have dinner together. You're still so new here, I imagine you've got a lot of questions. The Rez is a different place."

"Kelly, thanks, but I really want to get this wrapped up tonight. I have a recurring nightmare of all the files on my desk falling down on me."

She shrugged. "Suit yourself. If you change your mind, I'll be at the café. Don't work too hard."

He watched her as she left, the smile fading from his face. A beautiful woman, yes; intelligent and congenial as well. But many people were attractive, intelligent, and congenial—and dangerous.

He heard the door close behind her, and, once he

was certain she was gone, he pulled out the real file he'd been working on, which he had kept hidden beneath the one marked YAZZIE, ALANA.

EYES ONLY: O'CONNELL, KELLY MARIE.
He opened it and began to read.

CHAPTER THIRTEEN

• • •

November 8, 1981
Turquoise Mesa
The Navajo Reservation

Rita felt like she weighed a ton. The daily runs on the obstacle courses grew harder as the baby grew bigger. She felt clumsy climbing over the boulders, lumbering as she stepped in and out of the tires. Hauling her swollen body up into the tree was almost impossible, but somehow she managed.

"Report!" called Shalli, who was Rita's training partner today.

"To the north: Rafe, Baris, Lyss are doing target practice," Rita called over the reports of the rifles. "To the south—hey, somebody left out all the cooking stuff at the camp."

Shalli sighed. "That would be Lyss. He gets an extra set of push-ups tonight. We can't afford to leave anything out longer than necessary."

"To the east," continued Rita, shifting awkwardly in the branches, "nothing. To the west, nothing." She began to descend.

"You're doing very well, Rita—considering," smiled Shalli. Rita glanced down at her belly, made a wry face, and dropped the last few feet to the earth. "I'll go find Lyss."

"Don't bother," said Rita. "I'll clean it up."

Shalli eyed her. "It's not your mess."

Rita shrugged. "I'm not good for much else right now." She held up a hand as Shalli began to protest. "I'm not running myself down, just stating a simple fact. All of you guys are better fighters than I am, and if Lyss is off training, I don't want to disturb him." She smiled wickedly. "I'll think of another way for him to pay me back."

"If you're sure—"

"I am. You go on—it's time for your target practice, isn't it?"

"Yes, it is. Very well, then—but it's your choice." She smiled and headed off northward, to the target range. Rita watched her go, the smile fading. She had spoken the truth to Shalli—she really *wasn't* good for much else other than simple campsite chores—but that didn't mean she had to like it.

Her feet were swelling. When she got back to the campsite, before she tidied up Lyss's mess, she would soak her feet and elevate them for a bit.

"You," she said to the baby growing within her, "are a lot of trouble." She rubbed her stomach and added softly, "And a lot of joy. I can't wait to see you."

This pregnancy thing was complicated. Rita didn't know what to expect. She had aches and pains, morning sickness, and mood swings that Cale assured her were hormonally induced. She'd never thought about a baby much, but she'd always assumed she'd have regular checkups, eat decent meals, and have the baby in a nice, clean hospital if she did ever decide to become a mother.

The reality was drastically different. Rita did have quite a bit of money, but no one knew how long this hideout would have to last. So they ate only what they needed, bought clothing and tools only when necessary. Rafe had even been reluctant to let Rita take the truck and drive into Flagstaff to stock up on maternity clothing. Her body changing daily, loaded with the hormones Cale had mentioned, Rita had exploded into hysterics and demanded the keys.

She'd gotten them, and for one glorious afternoon Rita wandered through a mall, sipping sodas and munching on pretzels and cookies. At one point, Rita found herself perilously close to sobbing when she gazed into a jewelry store. There were matching sets of wedding rings on display. Her own left hand, brown and powerful now from months of exercise, was bare. No cake, no rings, no "I now pronounce you husband and wife" for her. She'd forced herself to walk away, keeping the tears unshed.

Rita had also stocked up on books. The evenings, more often than not, were spent with the sixteen Tyrusians huddled around the radio and the com orb, listening intently for any signs that they might be discovered. Despite hours spent trying to learn Tyrusian, Rita still couldn't understand the language, and always felt particularly distant from her husband at these times. Better to curl up and read.

She found some maternity clothes she felt she could live with and splurged on baby clothes and items as well. Who knew when Prison Guard Rafe would relent enough for her to come back again?

But that was a month ago. Rita shivered—it got cold here in the desert, contrary to what she'd always thought—and blew on her hands as she strode briskly toward the encampment. She saw the glint of the sun on the pots and pans and grimaced. Rafe's paranoia was contagious, and all she could think was *that could be seen from miles around.* Lyss hadn't even washed them out. Sighing in frustration, Rita quickly lit a fire, dug out a clean pot, and began to boil water.

She leaned forward, impatient as always, and blew at the feeble flames. At that moment, a hand clamped down hard over her mouth and pulled her backward.

Another hand brought a knife up to her throat and pricked the soft flesh ever so gently.

"I'm going to take my hand away from your mouth so you can answer my questions," a female voice hissed in her ear. "But the knife stays where it is. You scream, I stop the scream before you can get it out. Understand?"

Terrified, Rita nodded, ever so slightly.

"Good." The hand came away, but the knife remained as was promised. "No, don't turn around. Answer me. Who are you?"

"I've got to see who you are," whispered Rita.

A snort of laughter. "You stay right there and you talk or—"

"I've got to see who you are or else you'll just have to kill me now!" Tears filled Rita's eyes and tricked down her cheeks. If whoever held her was Tyrusian, she would gladly die—gladly even take the baby with her—to save Cale and the cause. If it were a human, it might be different—they might be able to talk.

Her captor swore softly and then Rita was bent backward. A fall of long black hair tickled her face. She stared, huge-eyed, into the high-cheekboned, dark-skinned, brown-eyed face of a Navajo woman. She closed her eyes and relaxed a little with relief.

"You going to talk or do I have to persuade you?" The Navajo meant business. The knife pressed deeper and Rita hissed with pain as the bright blade broke the skin. She felt the blood trickling slowly down her throat into her shirt.

"My—my name is Rita Carter."

"Better than that, *bilagáana*. You look normal. What about your friends? Who are they? What are those strange weapons?" The knife pressed deeper. "They're all out practicing. No one is going to come rescue you. Talk or I will use this, I swear."

Rita opened her eyes, stared into the angry brown ones of the Indian woman.

Rafe was going to be so ticked off at her. Especially if she got herself and the heir killed. She thought about lying, but lying had never come easily to her. Best to just tell the truth.

"My friends look different from us because—because they don't come from this planet." She braced herself, expecting an oath and a quick, cold/hot slash of the knife. Neither came.

"Why are they here? Do they work for the government?"

"No." A sudden thrill of fear. "Do you?"

"Like hell," replied the woman. "What's their agenda? How do you fit in?"

"They're—" How to condense it all quickly? "They're freedom fighters. A tyrant is on the throne, and they're trying to depose him. It's a really long story." It sounded stupid put that way, but it was the truth. Rita had to hope the woman sensed it.

"They look ragtag enough for that," the woman said thoughtfully. "And you? Camp follower?"

Rita bristled. "One of them is my *husband*."

"Well"—the woman maneuvered Rita back toward the towering walls that surrounded the encampment—"get your *husband* and whoever's in charge in here. Go ahead," she prompted, prodding Rita with the knife. "Call him."

Rita debated trying to take the woman. She was getting pretty good at hand-to-hand combat despite Rafe's comments, but she knew she couldn't take the Navajo. Not yet. If the woman had a gun, she wouldn't have had to use a knife. So the others were safe—sort of.

Rita took a deep breath and cried, "Rafe!" She deliberately didn't call Cale. No need to tell the woman exactly who was in charge. Her cry echoed, died.

"Again."

"*Rafe!*"

"Let her go," came an answering cry. Rita couldn't see anyone. Damn, they were good.

The woman's back was pressed to the stone, one hand twisting Rita's arm behind her back, the other still holding the knife to her throat. "No way," she yelled. "Let me speak with whoever's in charge or Rita and her baby die! I have no love for Anglos, so don't push me!"

A silence. Then, Rafe showed himself. He stepped forward. "I'm in charge here, and—"

"No." Rita's heart sank as Cale emerged to step in front of Rafe. "We don't begin by lying, Rafe." He turned to face Rita and her captor. "*Kia*, you are bleeding. Has she hurt you?" His face was taut and anger and fear blazed in his eyes. Rita's heart hurt at his expression.

"No, I'm all right. It's just a scratch."

"That is well," said Cale. His words were for the Navajo. "Had you injured her, you would not leave here alive." His voice was calm, but icy. Rita felt the woman at her back stiffen.

"Your girlfriend told me what you're doing here. Care to verify it?"

"I am certain my *wife* and queen told you the truth. I am Cale-Oosha. I am the rightful ruler of the planet Tyrus. My uncle has usurped my throne. We are training to fight, so that one day I will win it back—for myself"—he gestured to Rita—"and my child."

"I've been watching you, Cale-Oosha, for a long time. I've seen what your weapons can do. I've watched people disappear into thin air and reappear minutes later. I've seen your ships, your skills. You look different from humans, and I hardly think a tale of alien freedom fighters is the sort of thing someone who thinks she's going to die would make up. But prove it. Show me something that can't be explained away as top secret U.S. government technology."

"May I approach?"

"Slowly." The woman's grip on Rita's arm tightened. "But remember, I have your—your *queen*."

"I am not likely to forget," said Cale. He stepped closer, moving slowly, until he was about six feet away.

"That's enough. So—show me."

Cale's pupils dilated. Even from this distance, Rita could see the swirling field deep within. It unsettled her when Cale or any of the other Tyrusians did that—and yet it was beautiful, too, like a glimpse into an inner universe complete with a whirlpool of stars.

The woman gasped.

"I do not think your government can do that," said Cale in a deceptively mild tone of voice. When the woman, still in shock, didn't reply, he said, "You have been observing us, you say. Why did you not reveal us to the authorities?"

"Because—because I want your help."

Cale raised an eyebrow. "Holding my wife hostage does not endear you to me or my people," he said. "What do you wish?"

"You're freedom fighters, right? Then you'll understand. I'm a freedom fighter, too. I'm trying to attack *my* goverment—overthrow it. I and those that follow me need to hone our fighting skills—we need weapons."

Cale shook his dark head in pity. "What is your name?"

"Alana. Alana Yazzie."

"Alana Yazzie, listen to me well." His eyes were intent, and they seemed to bore into her. He spoke slowly and distinctly, emphasizing the words. "The true government of this country is all that stands between you and obliteration. We are on the same side—against my uncle, the Dragit. He tried to kill me because I would not agree to invade your world and massacre your people."

"Oh, please!" Alana's voice was angry. "A sob story about strange visitors from another world who come to a place, take what they want, and kill those whose rightful home it is? Seems to me I've heard *that* one somewhere before!"

Cale looked puzzled. "Where? Has your planet been invaded by aliens before? Rita told me nothing of this."

"Oh," said Alana. "Oh. You really *don't* know about—you really *are* aliens, aren't you?"

"So I have told you. Must I repeat myself?"

"Teach me. Teach me and those who follow me how to fight."

Cale was growing angry. His expression changed only a little, but Rita knew every emotion that flitted across that beloved countenance.

"Your battle against your government is misdirected," he insisted.

"I don't think so. Teach me, or she dies!"

Cale's eyes searched her face. "I will teach you and those you bring. You have not betrayed us; I do not think you will. But I will not cease speaking with you about the wrongness of your cause. You are intelligent and brave. I think in time you will listen. Those are my terms."

"Give us weapons."

Cale shook his head. "No weapons. Knowledge only."

Silence. Then, "Fair enough," and Alana removed the knife from Rita's throat.

Rita sprang like an arrow from a bow into Cale's outstretched arms. He held her tightly, and she heard the rapid beating of his heart against his chest. He had been terrified for her and the baby. She'd been pretty scared, too, truth be told.

Nestled against the warm strength of him, she saw movement out of the corner of her eye. Rafe had lifted his arbus.

Cale saw it too and shouted, "Rafe! No! Alana is safe here. I have given her my word."

Rafe sighed unhappily and lowered his weapon. Cale stepped a little bit away from Rita and turned his attention to Alana. The Navajo woman still carried the knife. Cale stretched his hand, clad in the Exotar, and moved his fingers.

The knife leaped from Alana's hand and flew toward Cale's. He caught it easily. He gazed at the shocked Alana, and smiled slightly at the dawning realization that spread over her face.

December 19, 1981
Broken Rock Indian Health Service Hospital

Six-year-old Harry Chee looked awful. He turned sad, patient eyes up to Eddie as he entered and tried to smile. Without even touching him, Eddie could see that the boy was running a fewer.

"Hello, Harry," said Eddie to the child, and turned to address his mother. "Good morning, Mrs. Chee. Looks like Harry's feeling a bit under the weather."

Rachel Chee nodded. "He hasn't been well for the last few days."

"My throat hurts," rasped Harry. "And I'm thirsty."

"Open your mouth, sport, and let me take a look." The boy obliged and Eddie winced at what he saw. The poor kid's throat looked like raw hamburger. He put a hand on Harry's flushed cheeks. He'd guess a fever of over a hundred, easily. Harry whimpered a little as Eddie palpated his throat. The lymph nodes were swollen.

"It's probably the flu, but we'll need to check to make sure it isn't strep." Quickly he brushed Harry's throat with a cotton-tipped swab. He rolled the swab in the petri dish and then disposed of it.

"Do you brush your teeth twice a day, Harry?"

"Uh-huh."

Eddie fixed him with a mock-stern gaze. "Really?"

The boy smiled and looked away. "No."

"Well, I can tell, because your gums are bleeding just a little." He found a thermometer, shook it down, and placed it under Harry's tongue. While he waited, he turned to Mrs. Chee.

"Any other symptoms?"

"He's been complaining of a headache, and he hasn't been able to keep food down," she replied. "And he's so tired all the time. No energy." She smiled wanly. "He's normally my little troublemaker, but the last few day's he's been a perfect child." Her eyes told Eddie louder than words ever could how much she missed the troublemaker.

"Well, we'll see if we can't get him back to mischief soon." He removed the thermometer and his eyes widened slightly. A hundred and two. He reached for his prescription pad and began to write. "It's the flu, Mrs. Chee. His throat's too sore for pills, so I'm asking for the liquid form of this prescription. This should bring the fever down and help the pain. Make sure he drinks a lot of fluids—that fever is dehydrating him. Keep an eye on the fever. If it's not down by this time tomorrow, bring him back in. All right?"

"All right. Thank you, Dr. Rainsinger. Come on, sweet one." She helped her boy down. He really did looked wiped out—his eyelids were drooping, and he moved like a zombie.

"Next year, why don't you and Harry go by the Drake Free Clinic for a flu shot?"

She gave him an odd look. "But, Dr. Rainsinger, we did."

CHAPTER FOURTEEN

• • •

January 13, 1982
Turquoise Mesa
The Navajo Reservation

It was late when Cale finally joined Rita. She had gone to bed early, saying she was particularly tired. She had circles under her eyes and looked pale; Cale hoped she'd sleep. Rita had been having problems with insomnia recently.

She stirred as he slipped down beside her, reaching out with warm arms. He smiled to himself and gathered her close.

"I had the most wonderful dream," she murmured in his ear.

"Tell me about it," he whispered, stroking her cheek.

"I dreamed that this was all over . . . all the running, and the fear." Her voice was singsong; she was still half-asleep. "I dreamed that Alana calmed down."

Cale chuckled. Alana and her people—five young men—had been training with them for over two months now. Sometimes, after practice, she and he would talk for a while. Cale had agreed to let Alana learn what she wanted, and in return, he—how did the humans say it—"bent her ear" about the situation on Earth and back on Tyrus. Recently, it seemed to him that she was actually starting to listen. But calm down? He didn't think it likely, even if he did persuade her to give up her futile and dangerous fight against her government.

"That's how you knew it was a dream," Cale told Rita.

She giggled. "It was wonderful. You were at a meeting of the U.N., and everyone was listening. We had a baby boy, and he was beautiful, and everyone was going to work together and everything was going to be all right."

Cale closed his eyes. "*Kia-thamaa,* may your dream be a prophesy." But she was already asleep again, breathing softly and regularly in his arms.

She was still asleep when he gently disengaged himself a few hours later at dawn. He decide not to wake her. Her time was near, and she'd need her strength if—

He didn't want to think about that. Humans and Tyrusians were almost physically identical. So far, the pregnancy had progressed without undue strain. Surely, the birth would be no more difficult than most.

Rafe had prepared breakfast—a big pot of hot oatmeal, eggs, and coffee. Cale and the rest ate hungrily, wrapped in blankets to keep warm in the early-morning chill. They'd warm up soon enough, when they began their rigorous drills.

As he ate, Cale surveyed his people. They were in top shape. No one was shooting at less than a 95 percent accuracy rate, with any weapon. He himself had honed his skills, especially with the Exotar, beyond anything he had expected. But what was next?

"Good morning," came Alana's voice. She was alone today; the rest of the supporters of the Independent Navajo Nation movement wouldn't be able to be here until the afternoon. With her was her dog, Bisoodi. The black-and-white mongrel barked enthusiastically and bounded toward Cale. He adored the young ruler and was never happier than when Cale was paying attention to him. Cale grinned and patted his head.

"I've brought some bread," said Alana, digging into her backpack and coming up with two small bundles. "Any of the oatmeal left?"

"Plenty," said Rafe. "I—"

A scream from the cave cut him off in mid-sentence. Cale was up and running toward the sound at once. *Rita . . . !*

He skidded to a halt at the sight that met his gaze. Rita had propped herself up on her hands, her knees drawn up close to her torso beneath the fabric of the sleeping bag. She gasped and her face was red. "Cale . . ." She groaned deeply and clutched her belly.

The baby. It was coming. Damn it, they should have taken Shalli's offer and slept in the pod. . . .

"Rafe!" he cried. "It's the baby! We've got to get her in the pod!"

Several agonizing minutes later, they had placed Rita on top of the sleeping bag and were carrying her as quickly as possible to one of the escape pods. Rita went deathly pale and dug her fingernails into Cale's hand. Five little half-moons appeared on his flesh and began to bleed. He barely noticed.

"Rita, talk to me," he pleaded.

"Hurts . . . I think there's something wrong . . . oh, God. . . ." She writhed on the makeshift stretcher. For the first time, Cale desperately wished she were Tyrusian. There were ways for pair-bonded couples to link minds, so that the pain of childbirth could be shared and thus halved. But Rita was utterly human, and Cale had never been able to touch her mind— though he had never needed to before. She had always given so freely of her thoughts, her love, it hadn't been necessary.

He wondered if he could reach the child. It couldn't understand language, of course, but he had touched minds with the unborn infant before to sense the most basic of its needs—hunger, discomfort, sleep. As Rafe, Shalli, and Baris gently laid Rita on one of the fold-down beds of the pod, he sprinted back for the Exotar. When he returned, Rafe was using the diagnostic tool from the medikit on Rita, and his face was grave.

Cale placed his Exotar-clad fingers on Rita's enormous belly.

And staggered back to stumble against the wall as if felled by a punch from a mammoth fist.

The baby was in agony. Something was very definitely wrong. Cale trembled and fought to shake off the overwhelming fear that had been transmitted through the mental link. The thought crossed his mind that this child had very powerful skills. He only hoped that she or he would be around to use them.

"Something's wrong," said Cale, blinking and shuddering. Rafe had gotten out another medical tool and was punching data into it. An image appeared on the screen. The Tyrusians watching groaned. Rita's birth canal was too narrow for the infant to emerge in the proper position—sideways, head touching toe. But that was how the baby was positioned inside. The amniosac that cocooned the child also was adding to the bulk. Rita's hips, unlike those of Tyrusian women, were not opening sufficiently. Nor could she "speak" with the baby, as Tyrusian mothers did, and coax it to shift.

"She's not wide enough," said Shalli softly. "Damn it."

"Human babies come out headfirst," said Alana, who had followed them and was watching intently. "Their skulls are soft to withstand the pressure of going through such a narrow birth canal. I take it Tyrusian babies are born differently?"

"Very differently," said Rafe. In Tyrusian he said for Cale's ears only: "She's dying, Cale. I'm sorry. There's nothing I can do."

"No!" cried Cale. "She can't die!"

"Her blood pressure's plummeting, and the baby's attempt to come through the proper way is ripping her apart. We don't have the knowledge of human anatomy to help her. She can't communicate with the baby, and you don't have a strong enough link."

"Cale," whimpered Rita. "Something's . . . wrong, isn't it?"

He couldn't lie to her. She could tell. Tears filled his eyes and ran down his cheeks. He was unashamed and made no move to wipe them away. "Yes, *Kia*. But we're working on it."

Her hand gripped his tightly. "Save the baby. Don't worry about me."

"No!" His eyes bored into hers. "I will not sacrifice one for the other. Never. You'll both survive, *Kia*. I promise."

A smile stretched her mouth. "You always keep your promises."

"Cale," Rafe again spoke in Tyrusian, "it's not possible. I grieve with you. But Rita is right. If we perform the surgery now, we may be able to save the child. I know of no other option."

He felt someone squeeze his arm. Shalli was there, her heart in her face. He recalled Jaran, dying in his arms. If anyone knew what he was going through, it was this small, brave woman. "We won't lose her," said Shalli intently. "Not without a fight, Cale." Her voice caught. "We've lost too many already."

"She needs to be in a human hospital," Cale told Rafe in English. Rafe raised his eyebrows.

"You might as well put an ad in the paper! There's no way we can pass this off as a natural, human birth."

"I will not permit Rita and my child to die!"

"I know someone who might help," Alana said unexpectedly. Everyone turned to look at her. "I have— an old friend who's a doctor. He'll come if I bring him."

Rafe looked doubtful. Cale felt hope brush him, as

sweet as an unexpected ray of light in a dark place. "Do you trust him?"

Alana hesitated. "I think I do. We've had our problems, but he has a good heart. I think he'll keep your secret. I know he'll want to save a life—two lives," she amended.

"Then go." Rafe knew better than to protest. "And Alana—"

"Yes?"

"I thank you. From the depths of my soul and heart, I thank you."

She seemed surprised, then smiled. It wasn't the hard, cynical smile he had grown so used to seeing on her face before. This was sweet, surprised—genuine. He had been right about her. He could reach her, he knew it. She turned and ran out of the pod, and a moment later he heard the grinding sound of her pickup.

On the bed, Rita moaned and shivered. Cale braced himself, then placed his hand again on her belly. He couldn't help Rita, but he could help their child. He spread his fingers on the rounded flesh of his wife's stomach and sent a message of calm to the tiny being housed within.

Hurry, Alana. Please, please hurry.

Eddie slammed the file on Bill Tsosie's desk. Bill jumped. "A hundred and eighty cases since December 19. A hundred and eighty, Bill, out of a total of five hundred and seven who received the shots to date. And those are only the ones *I've* treated. Good God, is Drake *giving* these people the flu?"

Bill looked startled. "I had no idea. I mean, I've treated some, but it never occurred to me. . . ." He flipped open the file. Eddie controlled his outrage and paced the little office, clenching and unclenching his hands while Bill perused the records Eddie had been keeping ever since he saw little Harry Chee on December 19.

"My God," breathed Bill. "These statistics are dreadful. I don't know what's going on."

"Dr. Drake's Fabulous Flu Fighter is too damn potent, that's what's going on. It's a bad strain, too. These people are really sick. And these are the ones who are able to come in to see me. God knows what's going on in the hogans on the farside of Broken Rock. Listen—you've got to get me Drake's file on this."

"No can do."

"Why not? I'm administering these shots. I'm a licensed doctor. I have every right—"

"I agree, and I'm curious as hell, too, now. But Drake won't let anybody back in his offices. I've never even been in—only caught a glimpse now and then."

"Then we break in."

"Damn it, Eddie, calm down!" He glanced back down the hall to the waiting room.

"Don't bother. It's too early for patients, and Susie just called in. Sick. With the *flu*. I hope to God you didn't—oh, no, don't tell me."

Bill gave him a rueful smile. "Come to think of it, I have been feeling a little sluggish lately."

Eddie swore. "At the very least, I'm taking a few vials of the stuff over to Flagstaff. I can analyze it in the lab there. I've never trusted the guy, and I'm mad as hell that his overzealousness is making people sick."

He stormed off toward the supply room and found the vials of flu shots. He took three, the better to run a variety of tests on them. He should have trusted his gut. But the shots had always been so effective in previous years. . . .

He paused, straining to listen. No, it couldn't be. It was. Alana.

"Morning, Bill. Is Eddie here? I checked at the hospital, and they told me he was volunteering at the clinic this morning."

"Sure is. Right down the hall, second door on your left."

Quick, light footsteps, and then she was there, framed in the doorway. "Eddie," she said, stepping inside and closing the door. "I need your help."

"What is it?"

She licked her lips. Her hair was disheveled. It had begun to snow outside, and her sheepskin jacket had a mantle of white. The eagle feather was sodden. "Someone's in trouble. A woman. There's a problem with the birth."

"Birth? Why isn't she in a hospital?"

"You'll understand when you get there. Please, Eddie, I think she's dying."

He had already grabbed a medical bag and was heading for the supply room. "Damn it, we have a perfectly good hospital. Okay, let's go."

He didn't say anything as they jounced along in her ancient pickup. She had insisted on driving. The snow was falling more heavily now, and the wipers labored to keep the windshield clean. Eddie's mind was racing. He hadn't participated at many births, but he knew well enough what to do. Alana had refused to answer questions about the mystery woman, merely repeating that Eddie would "understand when they got there."

"Turquoise Mesa?" he asked in surprise when Alana killed the engine. "I didn't know there was anyone out here."

"Good," said Alana cryptically. "Come on. She's up there." She pointed toward the mesa itself. Eddie raised an eyebrow but grabbed his bag and followed. It was not an easy climb, especially with one hand hampered by the bag, but he kept up with her. He expected to see a hogan or two nestled in the flat area, but what he saw when they cleared the rise was totally unexpected.

He swore loudly, in shock, and froze as he took it

in for a moment. It looked like a military base—a really small, desperate military base. There was camping equipment, and weapons, and—

—people with guns—

"My God," he breathed, "you *are* involved in the Independent Navajo Nation movement. I didn't believe it, but—"

"Keep moving, Rainsinger, someone's dying," Alana reminded him. He nodded, still shocked, and followed her down to the camp like an automaton. Alana broke into a run as they reached the flat area. She seemed to be heading for an empty space.

"Alana, what—"

A head appeared, floating in midair. Eddie stumbled and nearly fell. The rest of the body appeared out of nowhere. "Come on," said the young woman, waving them toward her, "hurry!"

And then Eddie was close enough so that he could glimpse inside—inside a thing that wasn't there. Alana ran in and Eddie followed. They were inside some sort of vessel, he guessed, and there were people—

He saw the woman on the strange metallic bed and suddenly the whole bizarre situation cleared for him. She was writhing in agony, her knees up under a blanket, and everything coalesced into this one thing: someone was hurting, and he could help. There would be time for explanations later, and by God, Alana was going to provide them.

He glanced around, looking for someone to talk to. A tall, dark-haired young man stood beside the woman's bed, holding her hand and looking almost as racked and drawn as she. The father, Eddie assumed.

"Anyone want to tell me the situation?" he asked, and was shocked at how calm he sounded.

"The baby's in the wrong position," said the father. "You've got to turn it around."

Eddie nodded. This, he understood. He opened the bag and brought out scrubbing soap. Hot water was brought to him—someone here knew something, at least—and he plunged his hands in, working up a lather. "Breech?" he asked.

"Sideways," replied the man.

Eddie gaped and felt a chill. That was bad—almost unheard of. "I'll do what I can," he assured the man. He moved the blanket and got yet another shock on this day of stunning revelations.

The woman's water had broken—and it was a thick, green substance that stained the bed and the blanket. "What the—"

"That's normal," said the father.

"Like hell it is!"

"It is normal," insisted the man, "for my people. You will encounter a thick membranous sac around the baby. That is also normal. Rita's hips are too narrow for the baby to come through in this position. Turn it around and—"

"But—"

"She's dying!" the man exploded. "Didn't you take an oath?"

Startled by the outburst, Eddie nodded. He glanced over at Alana. *What the hell is going on?*

"Please," said Alana. "Bring the baby out before it's too late. Don't waste time on questions."

Eddie swallowed, took a deep breath, and began.

The father was right. Reaching inside Rita, his gloved fingers found a thick swath around the infant. It was indeed turned sideways. Without his intervention both of them would have died. Gently, Eddie manipulated the tiny being. The task was complicated by the thick sac, but he managed—straightening a tiny limb here, pushing back the head ever so gently, turning the little torso this way and that. Fear kept hammering at his consciousness, a terror of the unknown. But his training kicked in and kept him calm through the ordeal.

Finally, he thought the baby was in the correct position. He lifted his head up and said to the girl—Rita—"Okay, we need your help, Rita. Push!"

She did. And screamed. The baby moved ever so slightly.

"Come on, that's it. Again!" It slid farther along the tunnel toward the waiting world. "Again!" Rita gasped, whimpered, and continued pushing. Eddie found that the weird sac actually came in handy—he could grasp it and pull the baby forth without risking potentially dangerous manipulation of the delicate limbs.

"Almost there . . . again!"

Rita took a deep breath and pushed for all she was worth. In a rush of green, thick fluid, the leathery cocoon that housed her baby slid into the world.

Eddie stared at the little bundle, looking around wildly. He had no idea what to do next. The father of the baby was there. "Get a sharp implement. You must cut it off." Eddie reached for his bag, but Alana had already fished through it and handed him a scalpel. The father held the infant, which was ominously still, as Eddie carefully sliced it free of the sac.

It was beautiful. No ugly, red, wrinkled, placenta-smeared being this. He—for it was a boy—was almost moon-pale, with fuzzy black hair and wide, blue eyes. He was still motionless. There was no sign of life. The boy might as well have been a wax figure. Quickly Eddie and the father worked to free the child of the sack. Then the father cradled the boy and stared deeply into his eyes.

As Eddie watched, the father's pupil dilated. In the black depths, Eddie saw flecks of white, swirling light. He uttered a low sound of shock. The baby's eyes blinked, and then the infant returned the gesture. His tiny, newborn pupil swelled and revealed the same doppled field.

The small chest heaved with breath. He began to coo, and his little hands moved.

A cheer went up. The dark-haired girl began to cry. Others clapped the father on the back. He smiled, then moved quickly to the drained woman on the bed.

She was clearly exhausted, but her face was radiant. "David," she breathed, faintly, cuddling the baby to her, "my little David. I've waited so long to see you." She turned her face up to the man beside her and he gave her a lingering, sweet kiss. "Oh, Cale. Cale, he's beautiful."

Eddie began to tremble with delayed reaction. "Now," he said in a voice that shook, "who the hell *are* you people?"

January 14, 1982
The Drake Free Clinic

Dr. Elliott Drake arrived early, as was his wont. Susie Benally was still out sick, and he was certain she wouldn't be back. He went into his office and seated himself behind his desk.

He pushed a button under the desk, and a hidden door opened with a soft whir. Inside were several glowing lights and a crystal orb about the size of a baseball. He pressed the blinking blue light and a small display monitor unfolded itself.

Drake ate his breakfast, a cup of yogurt and a banana, while the tape played. There were hidden video cameras positioned in every room of the Drake Free Clinic, and every morning, Drake viewed them all. Part of keeping on top of things. At a touch, the tape would fast-forward over empty rooms.

He watched Dr. Tsosie come in and set up, then leaned forward as Dr. Rainsinger entered. Rainsinger slammed a file down on Tsosie's desk.

"A hundred and eighty cases since December 19. A hundred and eighty, Bill, out of a total of five hundred and seven who received the shots to date. And those are only the ones *I've* treated. Good God, is Drake *giving* these people the flu?"

Drake felt a cold fury descend upon him. He listened to the rest of the conversation between the two friends, his breakfast forgotten. When it was over, he picked up the phone and dialed.

"O'Connell."

"Agent O'Connell. I believe we may have a problem."

CHAPTER
FIFTEEN

• • •

January 13, 1982
Northern Arizona University
Medical Research Center
Flagstaff, Arizona

It was after hours, and Eddie had the lab to himself. He'd called in a favor from a friend after returning from his unexpected and revelation-filled visit to Turquoise Mesa, and had gotten access to the university's research lab. Everything he needed to analyze the sample he'd brought from the clinic was here.

He set about preparing the sample for analysis. It had been a while since he'd done this sort of thing, but the habits were ingrained in him. He'd done this hundreds of times during the year and a half he'd spent with the Epidemic Intelligence Service.

He opened one of the small bottles of flu vaccine and poured the contents into a flask about the size of his thumb, which fitted easily into the microscope. Scooting his chair around, he peered through the binocular eyepieces of the microscope.

"Good God," he breathed. How many surprises was he in for today? He adjusted the resolution and double checked.

There were cells in there. He couldn't tell without further testing what kind—probably either human or monkey. There weren't a lot of them, but there weren't supposed to be *any* in the standard flu vaccine.

"What were you doing, Drake?" he asked aloud. Injecting cells into human patients—that was the kind of stuff mad scientists did. Mad scientists and aliens in one day. Hoo-boy.

And these weren't normal cells, either. They seemed swollen and puffy. And there were tiny dots on them that shouldn't be present on normal, healthy cells. They appeared oddly reflective, as well, as if there were crystals embedded in the tiny specks. These cells were sick, no question about it.

Eddie's skin began to crawl. He was afraid for a moment to take the next step, afraid of where it might lead. A doctor was taking standard, government-issued flu vaccine and placing sick animal or human cells in it, and then injecting people with it.

His mind went back to something Alana had said, long ago before he'd left the Rez with stars in his eyes. During one of her rants, she'd mentioned that several million Indians had died in the last few centuries of smallpox, a vicious "gift" brought by the Europeans into a population that had never known it. Eddie had listened, because this was a disease—something that interested him. Alana had told him that in the late 1700s, right before the American Revolutionary War, a British commander had suggested deliberately distributing smallpox-laden blankets among the Indians with the hopes of decreasing their numbers. No one ever knew if this plan was actually carried out, but smallpox had decimated the indigenous population.

Was Drake a racist? Eddie didn't like the man, but he'd never seen any hints that Drake particularly disliked Indians. He seemed to dislike everybody in an egalitarian fashion. But did he have a warped mind that wanted to see the Navajo suffer with a violent bout of flu, a strain so bad it might actually kill people?

Eddie shuddered again. This investigation into which he'd so blithely entered was turning into a nightmare. He forced himself to take a deep breath and move to the second step—"putting the cells in a beam," as the jargon went, examining the mystery cells beneath an electron microscope.

He was grateful for the gloves as he placed the tube in a centrifuge machine and spun it around. A small kernel of gray-brown matter collected at the bottom, tinier than the period at the end of a sentence. This kernel was the dead cells. Working carefully, Eddie lifted out the small cell nugget with a wooden stick, embedded it in resin to preserve it, and then waited for it to dry. His mind drifted back to the incidents of earlier that afternoon.

Aliens. On the Navajo Rez. Something he'd have thought preposterous if he hadn't seen them with his own eyes, touched them with his hands. If he lived to be a hundred, he knew he would never forget the slightly rough texture of the amniosac beneath his gloved fingers, the sight of Cale's pupil dilating and provoking such a dramatic response in the infant.

He'd sat for hours and listened to a tale that might have come right out of *Star Trek* or something: of another world, an alien civil war, plans for, heaven help us, invading America. In the end, it wasn't Cale's calm, reasoned discourse or Rafe's gruffness that persuaded Eddie. It was Rita's normalcy, whose mind seemed to belong completely to her, thank you, and who clearly adored her husband and new child, little David. And it was also Alana. Alana's thinly veiled annoyance at the restriction Cale had placed on her "tutelage" in weapons did more than any declarations of noble intent. Cale wasn't going to give a militia group weapons. It was that simple—and that convincing.

Eddie shook his head, still marveling. He thought of a show he had loved as a kid, where a benevolent alien with retractable antennae was passed off as someone's "Uncle Martin." "My Favorite Tyrusian," he said, chuckling a little. He checked his watch; the resin had had sufficient time to dry.

He took the ring of keys his friend had given him and began searching for the diamond knife. It was certain to be locked safely away. A diamond knife was a beautiful and valuable thing. About the size of an eraser, it had a diamond edge. It was easily damaged and could easily *do* damage, as it was sharp enough to split a cell. After a few minutes of rummaging, Eddie found it. He maneuvered the tiny plug of golden resin that encased the dead cells onto a small wooden stick and took it and the diamond knife next door into the cutting room. Fitting the knife into the cutting machine with extreme care, he then positioned the little ball of resin in place. He took a quick glance through the eyepieces of the microscope attached to the cutting machine and nodded.

He found the switch and the machine began to do its job. The little ball of resin-and-cell matter slid against the blade and tiny slices fell into a droplet of water. They didn't break the surface tension, floating serenely on top.

Eddie used a pair of tweezers to maneuver a small copper grid through the droplet of water and up under a slice of cell-and-resin. He captured one and then placed the metal grid in a small box. He permitted himself to let out the breath he was holding.

He wasn't sure where the electron microscope was in this place; he hadn't expected to need it. Carrying the little box, he opened the door and peered out into the hallway. It was dark and empty. He went across the hall and tried that door. No electron microscope. It would logically be located here, convenient to the labs—ah, there it was. The door was even conveniently labeled ELECTRON MICROSCOPE LAB.

Eddie unlocked the door and closed it quietly behind him. He flicked on one of the several lights, just enough to see by. In the center of the room, taller than Eddie, stood a tower of metal—the electron microscope. Using his tweezers, Eddie placed the copper grid into the sample holder and slid the metal sample holder into the microscope until it locked into place with a clanking sound.

Eddie switched off the lights and sat down at the viewing console. Soft green light bathed his face as he peered down. He always was awestruck by the complexity of the cellular world, its tiny marvels and hidden secrets. He was gazing now at the corner of a single cell, but it had a terrain as vast and complicated as any that could be viewed from an airplane. He was prepared for a long night. At this magnification, a cell was a big canvas indeed.

Eddie found one of the peculiar reflective specks and zoomed in. He frowned. What the—

There was something definitely not organic attached to the cell. It looked like . . . like *metal* of some sort. He had thought it a crystal, but he'd been wrong. His breathing became short. He zoomed in closer on the metallic thing. It was a perfect octagon, and there were lines of some sort on it . . . closer still, and his heart almost quit beating.

The lines looked like writing.

Eddie swore, softly, deeply. Attached to the cell was a miniature machine. He was no James Bond, but he was willing to bet his career that no scientist in the world had technology this advanced. No human scientist.

"Cale," he breathed. Had the young king of a lost throne somehow intercepted the flu vaccines? But somehow that didn't ring true. It had to be alien technology. Drake couldn't have—

Eddie's palms grew suddenly damp. He wiped them on his jeans. Drake. The high temples, which Eddie had always dismissed as a receding hairline. The slanted, almost violet eyes.

Dr. Elliott Drake, of the Drake Free Clinic, was a Tyrusian.

He swallowed hard. Could those little machines be responsible for making people so sick? He wanted to run screaming from the room, but that wouldn't do any good. He forced himself to stay calm. Evidence. He needed evidence. Quickly Eddie began to take photographs of the little metal machines attached so snugly to the dead cells. Several negatives came out of the microscope. While he was here, he would continue searching for more evidence. Who knew what he would find on these cells?

He continued searching the cell's landscape, hoping to find another machine. He didn't, but he did find a large cluster of something crystalline—presumably organic—and zoomed in on it.

"No," he breathed, staring through the eyepieces. "Dear God, please, not this, not here. . . ."

Before him lay what looked like a big bowl of spaghetti that had been dumped on the floor. Masses of ropes twined about one another. Some were long and thin, looping around into a shepherd's crook at the end. Others were circular, like Cheerios. Words sprang to Eddie's mind, all of them evil. *Snakes. Worms. The head of Medusa.*

Eddie Rainsinger was staring at a cell crammed full of filovirus.

During his time with the EIS, Eddie had only a few times been privileged—if that was the word—to enter a Level Four zone. Level Four was where scientists and doctors worked with the most dangerous diseases known to man. Clad in a light blue Chemturion suit that made him feel like an astronaut, sucking air from a tube, he had peered through electron microscopes just like this one and seen the tiny killers. Hantavirus. Lassa fever. And the three dark siblings of the filovirus family—Marburg, Ebola Sudan, and Ebola Zaire.

They were unmistakable; they looked like no other virus on earth, with their distinctive loops and curls.

So very little was known about these viruses. One thing was certain. Even at their most benign, the least violent of them, Marburg, claimed one in four of those who got infected. Ebola Zaire, the most virulent, killed nine out of ten. Eddie had done a lot of research on Marburg; he'd been fascinated by the filovirus. It had come out of nowhere in 1967 to claim seven lives in Marburg, Germany. The Behring Works factory produced vaccines using the kidney cells from vervet monkeys, which they imported from Uganda. The virus first killed the monkeys, then "jumped" species into humans. A WHO team went into the jungles of Uganda to investigate. They never found the natural host of the virus, and it disappeared as abruptly as it had come.

Rumor had it that the monkey trader had knowingly been selling infected monkeys, had in fact owned a secret "Island of Plagues" in Lake Victoria, where the ill monkeys were allowed to breed. The symptoms were—

"Headaches," whispered Eddie as the full horror began to settle upon him. "High fever. Sore throat. Bleeding, especially from the gums. . . ." Tears of impotent rage sprang to his eyes as he suddenly, vividly recalled little Harry Chee, Susie Benally, and all the others he had seen. The half-closed lids were also typical of filoviruses. The virus attacked the connective tissue, and the result was that sometimes victims' faces looked as if they were hanging off the bone. The symptoms got worse from there. The effect of the virus was similar to nuclear radiation. Marburg seemed particularly fond of attacking the internal organs. Hemorrhaging occurred from all orifices. And the brain, too, was affected—

The innocent-seeming vials of "flu vaccine" were hot with deadly virus, hot as hell. And he'd been carrying them around in his medical bag all day. The fragile glass had been knocking around against hard metal. It was a miracle one of them hadn't broken.

He stumbled backward, knocking over the chair. Panic had its claws into him, and he couldn't think. None of the filoviruses was airborne—but who the hell knew what Drake and his puppet masters had done? What was the function of the little machine? To regulate the dosage? To mutate the virus at will?

He ran his gloved hands through his thick black hair. "Okay," he said aloud, to hear the sound of his own voice. "Evidence. First, gotta get the evidence."

He righted the chair and resumed his position, taking shot after shot of the beautiful, deadly curls of filovirus while his hands trembled. Mentally, he was going over everything he'd done since that awful day when the clinic had begun giving flu shots. Had he spilled any of the "vaccine" on a hand that had been cut or scraped? Stuck himself with a needle? He didn't think so, but how could he be sure?

He couldn't. And with that realization came a sudden calming clarity. Eddie knew what he had to do. He finished his photographs, gathered up the negatives, and took them to the adjoining darkroom to develop them. Somehow, the pitch-darkness was comforting, and Eddie began to think.

The ropy strands certainly looked like Marburg, the virus he had studied and knew best. But the presence of the small machines boded ill. He was reminded of the book *The Andromeda Strain,* in which a virus from space came perilously close to obliterating the human race. Perhaps this wasn't Marburg or an Earth-born filovirus at all. Perhaps the Tyrusians had brought it with them. But it was close, too close. Wouldn't an alien strain be almost unrecognizable?

Eddie realized now why Drake hadn't wanted to hire him. His credentials had revealed the level of his expertise on dangerous viruses. Eddie Rainsinger would, quite literally, be the last person Drake would want at the Drake Free Clinic, where he was injecting the Navajo people with one of the world's deadliest viruses—

"They trusted you!" he exploded, surprising himself with the violence of the outburst. The *Dineh* had trusted Drake, had lined up to receive the deadly shots. The violation of the Hippocratic oath made Eddie sick to his stomach. But then again, it was doubtful that Drake had ever really taken that oath.

The irony of it all. He'd left the CDC, left a path that would have led to his becoming an Epidemic Intelligence Agent, to return to the Rez. The EIS was originally founded for the specific purpose of hunting down possible biological weapons. They were to be the "secret agents" of germ warfare. It became evident that humans were probably too smart to start biological wars and the CDC gradually settled into your basic disease-fighting organization. But here it was—not at the CDC, but right here where Eddie had grown up. Germ warfare. Except it was perpetrated not by one group of humans on another, but by aliens on what they must regard as an inferior species.

The pictures were completed. Eddie examined them and nodded. Clear—and damning. They'd get the son of a bitch. He hung them up to dry, went back into the main lab, and picked up the phone.

"Center for Disease Control, how may I help you?"

"My name is Dr. Edward Rainsinger. I need to speak with someone in Special Pathogens. It's an emergency. I believe we have an outbreak of Marburg or possibly Ebola on the Navajo reservation."

He was transferred immediately and relayed as much as he felt he safely could to the concerned EIS agent. For the moment, he didn't directly implicate

Drake, nor did he mention the machines he had found attached to the cells. He agreed to send samples of the tainted flu vaccine and gave his home number, the number at the IHS hospital, and the Drake clinic. Yes, he was familiar with how to safely pack hot samples and would follow every procedure properly.

Next, he dialed Bill. He recalled that Bill had taken one of the damned shots and went cold inside.

" 'Lo?" Bill's voice was thick with sleep and exhaustion. He sounded weak.

"Bill? Eddie. Listen, I found something you're not going to believe. Drake's up to something. I've got the evidence. The flu shots were tainted."

"Eddie? It's past midnight—"

"Bill, are you listening? Drake deliberately contaminated the flu shot! He's making people sick."

Silence. "What's he done?"

Eddie closed his eyes and clutched the phone hard. Bill believed him, sight unseen. He took a deep breath. "I can't be certain until the CDC does an ELISA test on it, but . . . Bill, I'm so sorry, but it looks like Marburg."

A long pause. "Oh, my God."

"Listen, I've got to clean up here, but I'll be heading back to the Rez shortly. Meet me at the junction of Route 4 and Little Bear Road in about three hours."

"Okay." Bill's voice was weak.

"Bill—listen. I could be wrong about this. It might not be Marburg."

A faint chuckle. "The James Bond of the medical profession. Mr. Epidemic Intelligence Service himself. No, Eddie, I don't think you're wrong. I think I've been a gullible fool."

Eddie winced. His heart ached for his friend. "We've found him out now, and we can stop it. You and me, old friend. See you in a few hours."

He hung up the phone and began the extensive task of sanitizing the hot lab.

*   *   *

Katie Benally, aged twelve, stared helplessly at her mother. Susie Benally lay on the earth floor of their hogan. She had stopped speaking a few days ago and yesterday had been unable to eat or drink anything. The snow had started coming two days ago. Frightened, Katie had tried to drive her mother's ancient vehicle to the Drake Free Clinic. Katie hadn't been given a single driving lesson and all she'd done was run the car into a ditch. The Benallys had no phone, and the nearest neighbor was too far away to reach on foot.

Katie curled in on herself, tears leaking from her eyes. Her mother had fallen ill two weeks ago. It had been bad then, but had progressed into something that would haunt Katie's nightmares for the rest of her life. The sore throat had progressed until it nearly closed off her mother's throat. Her mouth and eyes had begun bleeding. Her body raged with a fever that showed no signs of abating and, worst of all, bright, cheerful Momma had grown sullen and angry. She sometimes didn't even seem to recognize Katie.

This wasn't supposed to happen. Katie and her mother had taken Dr. Drake's flu shots for the past two years and had enjoyed healthy winters. Now, her mother was desperately ill, and Katie was starting to feel feverish and weak herself.

Suddenly her mother began to flail. Katie leaped to her mother, to try to hold her down, help her preserve what little remained of her strength. Her mother turned her head and began vomiting—not food, for she hadn't eaten, but bright red blood. Katie shrieked and drew backward, terrified.

Then her mother lay still.

For a moment, Katie wept, frozen in place with horror. Then she got to her feet and grabbed her coat.

She had to get out of here. Her mother had died, died in a horrible, painful fashion. Even in a peaceful death, a dark spirit lingered in the corpse until banished by a Ghostway sing. What was trapped inside the body of Susie Benally was certainly angry and evil.

Better to risk the snow than stay in the hogan. Coughing, swaying with weakness, Katie Benally stumbled forward into the foot-deep snow.

CHAPTER SIXTEEN

• • •

January 14, 1982
The Navajo Reservation

"You were right, Dr. Drake. Rainsinger called, just like you said he would."

"Was it taken care of?"

"Of course. We transferred him to one of our agents. Officially, the CDC never received the call."

"Outstanding. Thank you, Doctor."

"Hail to the Dragit!"

"Hail to the Dragit," replied Drake, placing down the receiver with a faint smile on his face. All might yet be well. Eddie Rainsinger, though annoying, was only one man, after all. One Earth man.

Eddie hoped he'd be able to see Bill's car in this weather. The snow was falling thick and fast. He was glad of his four-wheel drive and the fact that the Ford F-150 was new. He only hoped he wouldn't drive right past Bill's car.

He was approaching the intersection of Route 4 and Little Bear Road. He slowed down, peering through the onslaught of white flakes. Up ahead—there he was. The images of what Marburg did to its victims flitted through Eddie's mind and he shook with anger at the thought of his friend dying in such a fashion. Damn Drake. They'd get the son of a bitch.

He pulled over, keeping his lights on and setting the emergency blinkers. He grabbed his bag, found the flashlight in the glove compartment, and braced himself for the cold. Snow stung his face as he slammed the door. The wind was fierce, but it wasn't howling. In fact, it was very quiet, and Eddie heard another door slam and saw Bill—poor, infected Bill—stumbling through the snow toward him.

Eddie hurried, clasped his friend around the shoulder, and steered them back toward Bill's car. It would provide some kind of break against the wind and snow—enough for him to show Bill the photographs.

"I feel like hell, Eddie," Bill confessed as he leaned against the car door. "Survival for Marburg is a three out of four shot, though, right?" He laughed feebly.

If it is Marburg, thought Eddie miserably. "Right, Bill. You'll make it. Here—I wanted to show you this." He'd dropped the bag and now bent over to open it. Once Bill saw the pictures—

Even as Eddie bent down, a shot cracked in the silence. Above him, he heard Bill utter a muffled *uhhng* and topple backward. Something wet and warm pattered on Eddie's jacket and the back of his neck as Bill hit the snow.

"Bill!" screamed Eddie. The narrow white beam of the flashlight illuminated Bill's chest. Something black and liquid was creeping across his buttoned-up coat, and his face had gone slack, the eyes open and staring.

Eddie turned and raced for his car. Another shot cracked, hurting his ears, and he heard it ping against the truck. He flung open the door, sprang inside, and gunned the engine. A third shot shattered the windshield, missing Eddie by inches. He practically stood on the pedal and wrenched the truck up and over, heading offroad. He didn't really think he'd get away.

*   *   *

Agent Tom Alexander stood alone, sheltered by the twining limbs of an ancient piñon tree. He was warm enough in a parka and boots, and was glad he'd thought to stash them in the car before he left. He had followed his quarry to this site and then driven past where they'd pulled off, hiding his own vehicle as best he could in a small copse of weather-beaten trees. Alexander had watched everything unfold. He'd seen the first car arrive, and then the second. The two men got out of their respective vehicles. Alexander took careful aim.

The camera clicked. He continued shooting.

Agent O'Connell's car was a light color and almost disappeared in the snowstorm. Drake had suggested using one of the Tyrusian HCUs, but Kelly had turned her nose up at it. "All that technology creeps me out," she'd said. "Give me a gun and a clear shot and I'm happy." It was cold in the car, and Drake blew on his hands to keep them warm.

Since the first day he'd begun work at the Drake Free Clinic, Bill Tsosie's phone had been tapped. Every call he made or received had been monitored, and when Rainsinger had phoned him a few hours ago it had been ease itself to set up an ambush. The two had watched in silence as first Tsosie's car had pulled up, then Rainsinger's. Leaning out of the window, Agent O'Connell had taken careful aim, waited for a clear shot, and fired.

Except Eddie Rainsinger had chosen that moment to stoop and open his medical bag. Tsosie died immediately. That wasn't the problem; they had planned to eliminate Tsosie as well—he knew far too much—but they'd missed Rainsinger. She fired again, as he sprinted for the truck, and a third time as he frantically pulled the truck over into the snow.

"I thought you had to practice with that thing," snarled Drake.

She gave him an angry look and started her own car. They'd get him. There was, really, no place Eddie Rainsinger could run.

Alexander swore softly. An innocent man was down. With everything he knew about Agent Kelly O'Connell, he supposed he ought to have expected this. Grimly he reached for his gun and trained it on O'Connell's car.

The tire blowing sounded like a gunshot. O'Connell and Drake lurched forward. O'Connell swore, slammed the wheel with the palm of her hand, and swore again in pain. She leaned out the window and emptied the chamber in the direction of the fleeing truck. Then the taillights faded from her view.

"Oh, bravo," Drake said in a dry voice.

She glared at him. "I've got a backup plan," she said, reaching for the radio. "Broken Rock Police."

The crackling of static filled the car. Then, "Police. State your name."

"This is FBI Agent Kelly O'Connell. I want to report a homicide. The Navajo Tribal Police need to put out an APB on one Dr. Edward Rainsinger. He shot Dr. William Tsosie. I'm a witness."

"Understood, Agent O'Connell. Your location?"

"At the intersection of Route 4 and Little Bear Road. And tell one of the officers to get a car out here. We're stranded, and it's damn cold."

January 14, 1982
Charles Air Force Base
The Utah Desert

"We've found him, sir." Harrison's voice was full of barely contained pride. "Saris has been tracked to the Navajo reservation, in the vicinity of the town of Broken Rock."

"Outstanding," approved Konrad. He kept his voice calm. Inwardly, though, he was practically jumping with delight. He couldn't believe his luck. On the Navajo reservation! He turned to his console, placed a hand on the com orb, and concentrated.

The globe shimmered for an instant, then cleared.

"Well?" said the Dragit.

"I have news of Saris Krai, sir. He's on the Navajo reservation." The Dragit's expression remained blank. "That's where we're conducting Operation Hamstring," Konrad reminded his master.

The Dragit's brows drew together, and a dark cloud of fury settled on his face. "Operation Hamstring is the most delicate part of the invasion!" he bellowed.

Konrad put on his best expression of chagrined concern. "I know, sir. Has Krai been advised of its importance?"

"Krai doesn't even know about it. Curse it!" The Dagit fell silent, brooding.

Konrad waited patiently. Finally he ventured, "Krai's accomplishments on this particular mission have not lived up to his record, sir. Might I suggest calling him back?"

The Dragit smiled, but there was no humor in the expression. "Don't you think I know that you two have been at each other's throats for years? Nothing would please you more, would it, than for me to take him off this assignment."

Konrad shrugged. "The decision is yours, of course."

"Of course. Well, then, *my* decision is that you contact Krai and tell him that I want him to report to me with his latest findings. He is to depart the area of Operation Hamstring immediately."

Konrad placed a hand on his chest and bowed. "As my lord commands," he purred.

*   *   *

"You can't be serious," said Saris.

Konrad's face, slightly distorted by the curving surface of the orb, twisted into a smirk. "Oh, but I am. The Dragit's orders. You've been a disappointment, Krai. Just as I always knew you to be."

Saris nearly choked on the angry words that crowded into his throat. It couldn't be—but then again, Konrad wouldn't say something like this, something that could easily be verified, if it weren't the truth. Saris wondered what lies the bastard had fed the Dragit.

His thoughts raced. He had arrived only a month ago to find that his fondest hopes had been realized. Cale, Rafe, and several other Tyrusian "jumpers" were here. The elusive Rita Carter was here as well, her belly swollen with the Oosha's offspring. He was biding his time, waiting for the perfect moment to descend and capture all of them. It would be the ultimate coup—the sweeping gesture that would assure his place in the Dragit's affections for the rest of his life. To bring back Cale, Rafe, and the Oosha's child— what wouldn't the Dragit give for that!

For a wild moment, he considered letting Konrad in on the secret. Perhaps they could work together. But that thought vanished like mist before the sunlight as he examined the smirk on his old enemy's face. Konrad would merely sweep in and claim the victory for his own.

Krai made his decision. "*Yecktik tasik,* Konrad." And he slammed his hand down on the orb.

Konrad reeled backward as if he had been physically struck. The insult burned in his ears and turned his face hot with embarrassment and anger. "So be it, Krai. You're going to get what you deserve."

Krai had a chance to retire with dignity. He had refused a direct order from his Dragit. Such a refusal branded the spidery man as a traitor, and by all the powers, Konrad knew how to deal with traitors.

A smile curved his lips. This was what he had been waiting for. His only regret was that he would be unable to deliver the killing blow himself.

Pretending not to listen, Harrison was standing rigidly at attention. "Harrison, put a dampening field over a hundred-mile radius of the area in which Krai's com orb signals were generated. Then send in your best men. Time to clean this mess up."

"Sir! Yes, sir!"

January 14, 1982
The Navajo Reservation

The dream woke Hosteen Yazzie. He opened his eyes, calm, refreshed, as if he had had his full seven hours of sleep. Alana was sound asleep on the other side of the hogan.

He rose and began to build a fire. The guest who would be arriving soon would be glad of the warmth, and to be honest, Hosteen Yazzie was glad of the cheerful flames. They banished the last of the dark shadows of the dream. He let his eyes grow soft and unfocused and watched the smoke as it curled up and outward. Shapes, warnings, images of the dark things and hostile forces that were at work on the reservation. He was too old to take an active part in the conflict that was to erupt shortly, but he could provide warmth and food and comfort to those who would fight the battle against darkness, against that which threatened the harmony the *Dineh* craved. He had spoken to Alana about the bad medicine of her Independent Navajo Nation, but that was as nothing compared to the darkness that was approaching.

By the time Yazzie heard the approach of the truck, the breakfast was ready. The smell of sizzling bacon filled the hogan, and even Alana, who slept so deeply, rolled over and sniffed appreciatively.

"The nights seem to get shorter all the time," she murmured.

"This one is," said Yazzie. "It's barely three o'clock."

"What the—" Alana fell silent as, from outside, she and Yazzie heard the exaggeratedly loud sound of a door opening, and then closing.

Yazzie rose and went outside. He shivered in the cold. A few yards away, barely visible in the snow, was a dark-colored pickup truck. Beside it, its driver paced, his hands thrust under his armpits for warmth.

Hosteen Yazzie nodded his approval. Eddie Rainsinger might have been away from the People for a long time, but he had not forgotten his manners. The *Dineh* always waited for the resident of a hogan to approach them, not the other way around.

He trudged through the snow toward the youth. Eddie glanced up at his advance. He looked cold and scared.

"*Ya'eh t'eeh,* Edward Rainsinger. Come inside and warm yourself. I was expecting you."

Confusion flitted over the young man's handsome face, then a wry smile of resignation. He hastened to follow Yazzie back to the warmth inside the hogan.

Alana had just finished dressing and turned at their entrance. "Alana," Eddie said, "I'm sorry to bust in on you like this—but I'm in trouble. I need your help."

"You can talk while you eat," said Yazzie, handing Eddie a steaming bowl.

While the three of them downed the oatmeal, Eddie told them a tale that made Yazzie sorrowful, but did not surprise him—not with what he had dreamed this night. Dr. Elliott Drake of the Drake Free Clinic was infecting his flu shots with a deadly virus. Eddie paused in mid-sentence and glanced over at Yazzie. Alana smiled, then nodded to Eddie.

"My father is a *haatalii*. He deals with things that surprise me all the time," she said. "It's time we surprised him for a change."

So Eddie and Alana took turns telling a tale so fabulous Hosteen Yazzie might not have believed it, had he not known the things he knew. He listened as they spoke of people from another world and their war among themselves; of a young king striving to regain his throne and the evil usurper who had stolen it; of an alien doctor experimenting on the People for reasons yet unknown; of the coldhearted murder of a good man.

"Hmmm," was all he said as he slowly spooned cooling oatmeal into his mouth. They stared at him, and inwardly he chuckled. He was as shocked as they could have imagined, but he wasn't about to let them know it. They could continue to think that there was nothing that could surprise Hosteen Delbert Yazzie.

"I have to get to the base," said Eddie. "I need to know what that artificial construct on the cells is. Cale might know, and their technology might help me figure out some kind of cure for this thing."

"I thought you said Marburg has no cure," said Alana.

"I *think* it's Marburg. I don't know. For all I know it could be some weird space strain. Ebola Tyrus," he said with a feeble attempt at humor. "Cale might know that, too. They're looking for me—I can't take this to a hospital."

"We've got to hide your truck. We'll take mine."

Relief was plain on Eddie's face. "Thank you, Alana. Hosteen Yazzie—I'm sorry to put you and your daughter in danger. They might track me to you."

"It sounds as if we are all in danger. You two go to your friends and see if they can help. I will stay here and throw the FBI dogs off your scent." He picked up their bowls.

"Hosteen . . . how did you know I was coming?" Eddie asked.

Yazzie arched a white eyebrow. "A little bird told me."

The snow was still falling thick and fast, and for that Eddie was grateful. It would help hide the trail he'd left to Yazzie's hogan. He drove the truck a mile down a side road and parked it in some trees, leaving it pointing in the opposite direction of the hogan. Then he hopped into Alana's truck and they headed for Turquoise Mesa.

For a long time they were silent, staring ahead into the darkness and the white swirl of snowflakes. Finally, Alana spoke.

"Eddie . . ."

"Yeah?"

"Why did you come back?"

Eddie squeezed his eyes shut. "I don't want to talk about it."

Another long pause. Then, "I'm frightened."

Eddie snorted. "Alana, you've never been frightened of anything in your life."

"I know. But I'm frightened now. This is all—so big." She waved a hand in an expansive gesture. "There are whole other worlds out there with people on them. And some of those people are trying to kill us. Not just you, or me, but hundreds of people—maybe everyone on the planet. If this virus is as bad as you say it is, then we're at risk. Especially you."

She took her eyes off the road briefly to gaze at him. Despite everything that had happened—his friend's murder, the revelation of the virus, the gut-wrenching panic—Eddie's heart sped up at the sight of her dark eyes and sculpted face. Who was he kidding? He was still in love with her, and he hadn't ever not been.

"I want to know why you came back to the reservation. It's important that I know." She turned her attention to the road again and he gazed at her sharp, strong profile.

Eddie was surprised to hear his own voice. He had never told anyone about this before, and he was terrified by what Alana would think, but the words spilled out as if of their own accord. "It was during my fellowship at the CDC. They believe in on-the-job training; they like to send you out to the places where outbreaks are occurring. I was over in Gallup on an assignment. One of my colleagues had a patient he wanted me to see, a little Navajo kid. He was about six years old. The mother was at work, and the grandmother brought him in. Neither of them spoke English. So they brought him in to see me. I'm Navajo, I must be able to speak the language, right?"

He realized that his voice was raw with anger and pain. Alana stayed silent, her eyes on the road, letting him talk. He rubbed his right eye with the heel of his palm, sighed, and continued. "I couldn't understand a damn thing either of them was saying. So I did what any other doctor would do—made a diagnosis on the symptoms. Fever, headache, stiff neck, and a rash that spread almost as I watched it. Meningococcal meningitis—a bacterial infection of the brain. The rash meant that it had spread to his bloodstream."

He paused, waited for Alana to comment. She didn't.

"I had to administer antibiotics immediately or the kid was going to die." He turned his head, stared out the window at the white, blowing snow. "I couldn't talk to them. I couldn't ask about any allergies, and there was no time to find someone who could speak Navajo. So I ordered that he receive intravenous ceftriaxone, a type of antibiotic. Next thing you know his blood vessels dilated, his blood pressure dropped through the floor, his lungs closed up—anaphylactic reaction. He was dead a few minutes later, even though we realized almost at once—"

"He was allergic to the antibiotic," said Alana softly.

Eddie couldn't look at her. He nodded, his throat thick and his eyes burning with tears. "He died from the antibiotic, not the meningitis. We later learned he'd had had a reaction to cefaclor—an antibiotic used for ear infections. Cefaclor and ceftriaxone are in the same family of antibiotics; if you're allergic to one, you're usually allergic to all of them. If I'd been able to talk to him—if I could have remembered my Navajo—I'd have found that out. There were other antibiotics that would have done the trick, and he'd be alive today. But I had to guess. I had to guess because I'd forgotten my Navajo, put it away with my high-school yearbooks and never once thought about it."

He took a deep breath and waited for the inevitable. The explosion, the accusations, the scolding. *If you'd remembered who you are, that boy would be alive! You killed him, Eddie!* She couldn't tell him anything that he hadn't already told himself.

Alana said, her voice soft, "I can help you relearn Navajo if you'd like."

He stared at her. "You're not going to . . ."

"Yell at you? Accuse you? What good would that do? I know you, Eddie, and I know you'd do everything in your power to bring that boy back if you could. You did the best you could with what you had. It's not your fault."

Then, to his amazement, she slipped a gloved hand over to his and squeezed it tightly. He clutched it like a lifeline.

*   *   *

"The situation's turned bad," said Tom Alexander to his boss. "O'Connell's just killed a man, and she's framed a local doctor for the murder."

"Damn it! Are you certain?"

"I have the photos. I saw it all—helped the poor bastard get away before she got him, too. She was with someone—a Dr. Elliott Drake. Can you get me everything we know about him?"

"Can do."

"Listen—up till now you've told me to observe and record. But we didn't count on this. She's committed murder. I should take action—she might do it again."

"Negative. Do nothing out of the ordinary until further notice."

"It's time to bring a team in. Something's going down or she wouldn't have set up the ambush."

"Agreed. But for the moment, we need you to keep a low profile."

Tom Alexander smiled, a sharp, almost feral grin that would have stunned any of his colleagues and acquaintances if they had seen it.

"Don't I always?"

CHAPTER SEVENTEEN

● ● ●

January 14, 1982
Turquoise Mesa
The Navajo Reservation

Cale could not believe what Eddie was telling him. Or, more accurately, he wished he could not believe that his own people were using humans as guinea pigs. He clenched his teeth in an effort to control his rage. By the time Eddie was finished and had passed around the damning photographs, Cale's jaw ached, testimony to what his restraint had cost him.

"Do you recognize those metal things attached to the cells?" Eddie asked.

Rafe nodded, his face angry. "I dismantled a larger version of one of these that someone had planted in a temple piece. It's Tyrusian, all right—a tracking device. Drake clearly wanted to make sure no one left the reservation without his knowing about it."

Cale glanced up from the photographs as he realized he no longer needed artificial light by which to see. Dawn had come and the snowfall was slowing. His gaze fell on Eddie—tired, looking much older than he had just yesterday, when he had saved the life of the Ooshala and the infant heir.

Cale's gaze fell on Eddie's jacket. In the early-morning light, he saw that something had spilled on it. Eddie turned his head this way and that, trying to ease the tension that had built up in his neck. Something brownish-red that had once been wet had dried on his neck.

"Eddie," Cale said, keeping his voice calm. "What is that stain on your jacket?"

Eddie craned his neck to see. The color drained from his dark face as dawning horror spread over his drawn features. He bolted up and wrestled with the jacket, tearing it off as if it were burning him.

"God! God!" he cried, finally breaking under the tremendous strain. "It's Bill's blood. It's hot. Oh, God, nobody touch me . . . !"

"Hot?" asked Rafe.

"He means highly infectious," said Alana. She, too, had gone pale. "Eddie, I'm sorry. . . ."

Eddie swung around and stared at Cale. "I know you didn't do this," he said in a voice that cracked. "But Drake did, and he's one of you. You've got to help me—help all of us!"

"Eddie, I will do everything I can, I swear," promised Cale. Inwardly, he grieved for this good man who was, most likely, infected with this abominable "hot virus." He rose and went to him. Eddie backed away, raising his hands as if to fend off the young king.

"Don't touch me. I don't know what this thing'll do to you!"

"Tyrusians are highly resistant to disease," Cale reassured him. "Come. I will take you to one of the pods. We have a great deal of diagnostic equipment inside. At the very least, we should be able to determine if this virus is known to us."

Eddie nodded and ran a hand through his hair. "Okay. Makes sense. Let's do it. But first, do you have any bleach?" He gestured feebly at his neck.

"I believe so. Let me check the supply area." As Cale went toward the small second cave that they used to house such items as bleach, soaps, and the pots and pans, Rita emerged from one of the pods. She carried David, who snuggled against her drowsily.

"Rita, you shouldn't be up," Cale chided gently.

She smiled wanly. "I heard all the excitement. What's going on?"

Cale had moved forward as if to embrace her, but now he stopped in mid-stride. The filovirus, as Eddie had called it, was clearly dangerous to humans. Rita was human. His son was half-human.

"Cale? What is it?"

"Stay in the pod," he said, more harshly than he had intended. "When I can, I will come and speak with you. Do not, under any circumstances, let Eddie or Alana in here. Do you understand?"

"Sir, yes sir!" she said, snapping a salute. Her eyes flashed anger.

"I'm sorry," he said. "I should not have been brusque. It is my fear that is speaking, *Kia*. Eddie brings news of another attack by my people on yours—more evil, if possible, than an out-and-out invasion. They are planting a sickness that is highly lethal to humans, no doubt in an attempt to deplete their numbers before the final invasion fleet arrives. Eddie is probably contagious, and we do not know how easily this illness is passed. Please—stay here. Stay safe."

Her eyes had widened as he spoke, and now she nodded her comprehension. She cradled David closer, as if she could protect him, and retreated to the pod. The door irised closed.

Cale, Rafe, and Eddie worked together for several hours. Somewhat to his surprise, Eddie found that he was able to put aside his awe at the shockingly advanced and complicated technology and simply concentrate on harnessing it. Cale and Rafe translated for him, and helped him conduct a battery of tests. The results came much faster than anything Eddie could have hoped to accomplish even in the most advanced medical research lab, and for the first time since he had spied the beautiful, deadly loops and curls of the filovirus he suspected was Marburg, he began to feel a cautious sense of hope.

Rafe explained that the pods were emergency escape vessels from larger ships. They were equipped with everything that those fleeing a destroyed ship might need—food and water, medical supplies, and diagnostic equipment, even a computer. For who knew where such a pod might land?

The computer kept insisting that it "did not recognize" the virus. "Which means," said Cale, "that it is either of Earth or of a planet unknown to Tyrusian scientists. I think it is safe to assume the former."

"Believe it or not," said Eddie, rubbing his temples, "that makes me feel better. Better the devil you know, right?"

Cale was staring at him. "Does your head hurt?"

Eddie's stomach roiled. "Yes. Damn it, yes. One of the first symptoms. Marburg kills fast. I better—wait a minute." He frowned to himself. "I didn't start seeing patients with symptoms until around mid to late November. The shots were given out starting in mid-September. That's a two-month time frame before the symptoms got bad enough for anyone to think of seeing a doctor. Damn!" He slammed his fist down on his knee.

"What?" Cale asked.

"He's messed with it. Altered it, somehow. Victims of a filovirus begin manifesting symptoms within seven to ten days. That's why it's so rare—at least until the jet age, people died before they could spread the disease to any neighboring areas. If he's altered the incubation period, he could also have altered its virulence." He turned wide brown eyes to Cale's purple-blue ones. "This thing could be a hundred percent fatal."

"How is it transmitted?"

"Normally, you have to have penetration or ingestion. It's got to enter the bloodstream in some fashion.

But now—hell, Cale, I don't *know* what Drake's done to it. It could even be airborne. No, wait a minute . . . if that was the case, then he wouldn't have just left it lying around like a regular flu vaccine." Eddie's mind was racing now. He tried hard to remember how Drake had behaved around the little bottles of death. He'd been very casual—had grabbed two or three at a time, just like Eddie and Bill had.

Bill. Damn it, I'm so sorry. . . .

He certainly hadn't given any hint that it was a hot virus. Which could mean—

"Cale. You said that Tyrusians are highly resistant to disease."

"Correct."

"And this is an Earth virus. We know what it can do to humans. But maybe Tyrusians are immune to it. If I had a small sample of blood, I could run some—"

Two arms, one slender and strong, one beefy and knotted with muscle, were thrust down toward him. Eddie had to smile. These guys were all right. If only all Tyrusians were like them.

Shalli stuck her head in. "Sorry to interrupt, but there's something you need to know, Your Majesty. All Tyrusian signals that we've been monitoring have suddenly gone dead."

"Do we know why?" asked Cale.

Shalli shook her head. "Negative, sir."

"Go to second-level alert," he told her. "Until we know why, we must be prepared for anything. It's possible, though unlikely, that we might have been found, and they're attempting to prevent us from summoning allies." He gave a wry smile. "As if we had allies we could contact."

"There's more. Eddie," Shalli said, and her voice and face were grim, "Earth transmissions haven't been interrupted. We've just learned that they suspect you of your friend's murder. There's a warrant for your arrest, and the Navajo Tribal Police are out searching for you."

Eddie took a deep breath. "I see."

"We will keep you safe," Cale told him.

"Thank you, Cale. If it's not a problem, I need to keep working—for all our sakes. I'm betting Drake was behind Bill's—Bill's murder. I think they meant to get me. I was getting too close, and if I can prove what he was doing, I can clear my name and perhaps save some lives."

"Continue. If we need the computer, we will let you know."

He decided to draw blood from Rafe because the warrior's veins were closer to the surface. All the tools in his medical bag had been sterilized with a bleach solution upon his arrival at Cale's encampment. He didn't think they'd been contaminated, but he didn't want to take any risks. Now he strapped a rubber tourniquet on Rafe's arm and drew a single vial of blood. If all went as he'd hoped, he'd need more of Rafe's blood later.

Quickly he introduced some of Rafe's pure Tyrusian blood to the lethal virus. Using some of the pod's equipment, he was able to speed up the experiment.

The results unfolded as they watched.

The virus didn't stand a chance.

"It's a miracle," he breathed. "Your white blood cells are like tanks, Rafe. No antigen can get past them. No wonder you have such a resistance to disease and heal so quickly. The white blood cells have obliterated the virus. Your people are completely immune to it. I could shoot you full of this stuff, and you wouldn't even know it."

"I don't understand," said Cale. "I am certainly pleased that none of my people are at risk, but why are you so happy?"

Eddie turned to him, grinning like a madman. "I can separate out the serum from Tyrusian blood and inject it into humans. Theoretically, anyone who receives this will also develop an immunity. We're looking at a possible cure right here," he said, holding up the small vial of Rafe's blood. "Now, what I have to do is go back to the Drake Clinic, get my list of people who were injected with Drake's flu shots, and prepare a serum."

"Back to the clinic?" Rafe repeated. "The police are looking for you."

"Rafe, I have to go. I can't remember everybody who got a flu shot. I don't have the equipment here to draw enough blood to develop a sufficient amount of serum, and I've used up my last vial of evidence. I'll wait till tonight and try to break in."

"I will go with you," Cale said, quite unexpectedly.

"Majesty, we're on a second-level alert—"

"Rafe, you will stay here and be in charge. You know what you're doing—you don't need me. But these Navajo are dying because of what Tyrusian technology has done to them. Eddie saved two lives yesterday—Rita's and David's. I owe it to him to help him and his people where I can. Besides"—his eyes twinkled despite the grimness of the situation—"you will recall that the Exotar comes in very handy for picking locks."

They emerged and called a general gathering. Eddie told them what he had found and what he needed to do. "I'm coming, too," said Alana.

"Alana, I don't want—"

"Eddie, I'm probably already exposed to this thing. I'm the daughter of a *haatalii*. I have to do something."

"What about I.N.N.?" he replied. "You weren't too interested in helping people that long ago."

Her dark eyes flashed, but she curbed her anger. "I have always wanted to help my people. I thought that by opposing the government, I could do that. Now, to hell with the U.S. government. There's a bunch of alien killers out there bent on the destruction of *all* of us—Anglo, Indian, Oriental, black—and race doesn't mean a damn thing to me anymore. The only race that matters now is the *human* race, and keeping it alive!"

"Alana," said Cale, his voice warm with affection, "I knew that one day you would see with opened eyes."

I love you, Eddie wanted to say, but contented himself with, "I'd be glad to have you along."

It had been, without a doubt, the worst day in Saris Krai's long life. Only a few hours ago, he could practically taste victory. Cale, Rafe, and Cale's infant heir were within his grasp. Then had come the brief com orb conversation with Konrad, and suddenly everything was shattered.

He had been returning from a reconnaissance mission at Turquoise Mesa, patiently waiting for a *ga'lim* vessel to pick him up, when Konrad had contacted him with the bitter news that the Dragit himself had requested that Saris's mission be terminated. He had burned his bridges with Konrad with the searing insult and had terminated the conversation immediately. An instant later, Saris had tried to summon his private ship, located several miles to the east and crewed with men loyal to no one but him. No response. Konrad had clearly set up a dampening field about the area, ensuring that Krai couldn't contact the Dragit and explain the situation. It also cut off his escape route.

He didn't dare wait for the *ga'lim* vessels. They would have received the recall order and be well on their way to obeying it—if they hadn't been instructed to wait for Saris and then murder him on sight, which, knowing Konrad, was entirely possible.

There was no choice. He was on his own, now. He had one chance if he were to survive Konrad's dogs— find proof of Cale's existence and get through to the Dragit on Tyrus. An idea was already forming in his mind, but first, he needed transportation and shelter from the snowstorm.

He slogged through the knee-deep snow, grateful for the skin-thin layer beneath his outer clothes that constantly regulated his body temperature. It took him several hours, but he made it to the main road that passed through the area. Panting from exertion, he stumbled on, following the indentation in the snow that marked where the road was.

Not too far away, if he recalled correctly, was a small grouping of the houses the Navajos called hogans. Surely, one of them would have a vehicle he could steal.

After nightfall, his luck changed. Up ahead, he saw two bright lights shining through the falling snow. He could also see other lights—flashing red and blue. Impossibly, a car was coming along here. He pulled his headcovering down and lowered his face. Stepping forward into the path of the oncoming car, he waved his arms.

"Help!" he cried, in both Navajo and English. "Please stop!"

The car, which wasn't going very fast anyway, slowed even further. Krai realized that his luck was improving—it was a Navajo Tribal Police vehicle. The two dark-skinned officers rolled down their window as he hurried up to them.

"Thank goodness you stopped, officers!" he gasped, clutching his chest and feigning exhaustion. "My car broke down and—"

"What were you doing out in—what the hell. . . ." One of them had gotten a good look at Saris's features and gaped at him in shock.

He didn't bother with a witty retort, merely lifted his arbus and efficiently blasted both of them. He hauled the bodies out of the car and eased into the still-warm driver's seat. Saris had learned how to operate a car early on during his Earth assignment, and was glad of the preparation. Chatter filled his ears from the radio in the car and he listened absently as he carefully maneuvered the car around and headed back in the direction from which he had come.

He had one chance, one hope of recovering his standing in the eyes of the Dragit, and that chance waited for him at Turquoise Mesa.

Alana drove. It was a tight fit with her, Cale, and Eddie, but they managed. The snow, after stopping for a brief time, had started up again and vision was limited. They pulled over before they reached the clinic. Cale got out; climbed nimbly onto the cab of the truck, and using a pair of night-sensitive Tyrusian binoculars peered in the direction of the Drake clinic.

"I see no vehicles, nor any lights on at the clinic" he called down to Alana and Eddie. "I think it is safe to approach."

Slowly, they moved forward, Alana's truck protesting but obeying. They pulled into the parking lot and leaped out. Cale was the first to reach the door. He wore the strange glove he called the Exotar, and as Eddie and Alana watched he placed his fingertips lightly on the door. The doorknob turned, and the door eased open.

"Freeze," said a voice.

CHAPTER EIGHTEEN

● ● ●

January 14, 1982
The Drake Free Clinic
The Navajo Reservation

They froze.

From behind a corner a figure approached, clad in a dark green parka and leveling a gun at them. Relief washed over Eddie when he recognized, not Drake's patrician features beneath the fur-fringed hood, but the bland, almost forgettable face of FBI Agent Tom Alexander.

They had met a few times before at the Broken Rock Trading Post. Agent Alexander had always struck Eddie as a genial sort. There was nothing genial about the ice-hard eyes and thin lips of the man who stood before them now, and Eddie's relief wavered a bit.

"Thank God it's you, Alexander," he said.

Alexander's cold eyes flickered over Eddie and Alana and came to rest on Cale. The eyes narrowed. "Who are you?"

"He's a friend of mine," said Alana, too quickly. Alexander favored her with a quick glance.

"What are you doing here?"

"Hey," said Eddie, "I volunteer here."

"You're wanted for murder in the first degree, Edward Rainsinger, and unless you start telling me something I want to hear, then you're all going in my car, handcuffed, for a nice visit to the Window Rock jail."

Eddie had recovered from his first shock and had started to put the pieces together. "You're here for Drake, aren't you?" Alexander did not reply, but neither did he move to arrest Eddie. "You are," repeated Eddie, "and I can help."

"What do you know about Drake?"

"I can't prove it, but I think he was the one who shot Bill Tsosie. We had agreed to meet, and I was about to show Bill what I'm going to show you," said Eddie, speaking distinctly. "Someone began shooting at us, and Bill was killed."

"I know," said Alexander, shocking Eddie. "I saw it all. What did you have on Drake?"

"He's been distributing free flu shots, right? Well, they're not vaccinations at all. They're loaded with a hot virus that I believe is Marburg—it's certainly a lethal filovirus of some sort. I think he's conducting some kind of sicko—"

"Experiment," finished Alexander in a cool, clipped tone of voice. "It's called Operation Hamstring, though I'm damned if I know what that means, and it's almost perfect. The Navajo reservation is fairly isolated, and the comings and goings of the populace can be monitored—especially if you've got the cooperation of an FBI agent like Kelly O'Connell."

"My God," breathed Eddie, thinking of the tiny machine attached to the cell. "It all makes perfect sense—"

Alexander snapped the fingers of his left hand. The right hand, still holding the gun, hadn't wavered an inch. "You have something to show me, Dr. Rainsinger?"

"Sure." He brought his bag forward, put it down, and opened it.

"Slowly."

"You got it," said Eddie fervently. He paused,

glancing down at the pictures. He didn't know what kind of trouble he would get in if the FBI caught him withholding evidence, but he wasn't about to betray Cale and the others. The disease that Drake was spreading was all Alexander needed to know about. Deliberately, he straightened, holding out to Agent Alexander only those photos in which the small machine was not clearly visible. If, later, they analyzed the "vaccine" itself, they would find the tracking devices on their own, but Eddie wasn't going to be the one to alert them to it.

Alexander took them and glanced at them briefly. "Those curly tendrils—that's the Marburg?"

"Yes," Eddie said.

"This will help the case, Dr. Rainsinger. Thank you. I'm going to have to lock this place down and ask you to come with me now. We've got a USAMRIID team coming in here, and nothing must be touched."

"No!" yelped Eddie. Alexander raised an eyebrow.

"That wasn't a request, Doctor," Alexander said softly.

"You don't understand. I've got to get in there—get some files."

Alexander smiled with little humor. "You've been shot at quite enough for one night, Dr. Rainsinger. I'd hate to be the one to shoot at you again."

"Listen to me! I've found a cure for this thing! I've got to get in there, get supplies and start cranking out serum. I need the complete list of everyone who was infected."

"If what you say is true," said Alexander, doubt in his voice, "then USAMRIID will want to consult with you on it. Don't worry, we won't let these people die."

"But they *are* dying—they're dying right now!" Of course, Eddie couldn't tell the United States Army Medical Research Institute of Infectious Diseases that the cure came from alien white blood cells. He had to do this on his own.

"Alexander," came Cale's soft voice, "You must let Dr. Rainsinger proceed. Lives—hundreds of lives—depend upon it."

"I was getting to you," said Alexander. "You're the one who picked the lock. If anybody's under arrest here, it should be you. What's your name?"

"My name," said Cale in that same soft voice of command, "is Cale-Oosha. And I am very sorry for what I have to do."

Before Alexander could react, Cale gestured with his Exotar hand. Alexander's gun sprang from his hand to land in Cale's. At the same moment, the FBI agent went hurtling backward to slam hard against Alana's truck. He fell to the earth, limp.

Eddie rushed to him and placed two fingers on Alexander's throat. The pulse was strong. Quickly he examined the agent's head. "He's going to have one hell of a headache, but he'll be all right. He won't be out for long, though. Let's go."

"Here," said Cale, handing Alexander's gun to Alana. "You are unarmed."

"Thanks," said Alana uncertainly, curling her fingers around the deadly weapon.

Eddie shined his flashlight about and they hurried into the office area. He stuck it in his mouth while he rifled through the manila file folders. There it was—the list of everyone who had come in and received a flu shot. It was long—over seven hundred people. He desperately hoped he was in time to save them, but feared the worst. He put the file folder in his bag and hurried to the supply room. Carefully, knowing full well what danger they housed, he gathered up a handful of the vials of flu vaccine and placed them in an unbreakable container used for mailing samples. He then seized as many needles and vials as he could. He'd have to take a lot of blood, from a lot of Tyrusians, to make the serum.

"Eddie! Come here!" called Alana. Cale had managed to get into Drake's private office, and he and Alana had pulled out several folders which were now strewn on the desk.

"Operation Hamstring," said Cale grimly, reading from one of the folders. "A three-stage covert operation, under the auspices of Dr. Elliott Drake. It is part of the overall invasion plan, as I suspected." In the narrow beam of the flashlight, his face was distorted with anger. "The Navajo reservation was a perfect lab to test the virus. It is Marburg, Eddie, except—"

"Except unlike the naturally occurring Marburg, this strain is 99.92 percent fatal to humans," came a smug voice. They wheeled to find themselves staring at Elliott Drake and Agent Kelly O'Connell.

Eddie heard the click as O'Connell cocked the gun.

"You should still be in bed," Rafe grumbled as Rita sank down beside him at the eleven o'clock change of shift.

Rita shook her head. "I'm all right, and I was going nuts in that little pod. Shalli's stationed in the pod, and she can hear David if he cries. He's been fed and changed, so he should sleep for the next four hours. I don't know if it's typical of Tyrusian children, but he's a very easy child. I haven't even heard him cry."

"I wouldn't know," said Rafe.

"No, I guess you wouldn't," agreed Rita. "Why are we on second-level alert? Nobody's told me yet."

"All signals from Tyrusian instruments have suddenly been interrupted. We've had nothing but silence for several hours. It could mean they've found us and are planning an attack."

"So—why aren't we evacuating?"

"Because it could have nothing to do with us, and if that's the case, we'd lose the camp and possibly reveal our location."

"Oh." Rita was silent and adjusted the uncomfortable semiautomatic in her arms. She had lied, partially, to Rafe. She was indeed going crazy inside the pod, with no one to talk to and only little David to keep her company. Wonderful a thing as her child was, she craved adult conversation. Now that all the humans, with their potentially fatal diseases, had left the encampment, she wanted to do what she could to again belong to this little band. She was not quite well yet. Despite a combination of Eddie's drugs and Tyrusian painkillers, she felt a dull ache inside when she moved. But she wanted to be outside in the cold night air, feeling like she was doing something to help. The shift was only two hours, and then someone would relieve her. Surely she could last that long.

They had a tense minute when a police car approached in the distance, but it continued on and finally they lost sight of it. Other than that, nothing broke the night's silence. Rafe, of course, was not about to make idle chitchat.

Midnight came and went. The gun grew cold and heavy in her arms. She thought longingly of the soft bed in the pod, and her baby curled up. They smelled so good, babies; their soft—

She tensed.

"Rita? What is it?"

"I'm not sure. I hope I'm wrong." She rose and sprinted for the pod.

Saris didn't know if Cale's encampment posted sentries or not, but he decided to take no chances. He drove past Turquoise Mesa in full view, lights on, and then hid the car in a curve of the road past the mesa. From this angle, even he, who knew they were there, could see nothing. He put on his temple piece and concentrated. At this distance, he couldn't hope for much, but if they had seen him, their collective fear would be detectable.

Nothing. Just the cold night air and the sting of drifting flakes on his face. Excellent.

He moved forward. The snow was deeper now, but Saris pressed on. He began to climb, silent, grateful for the snow and the darkness that hid his presence. Finally, he could see the encampment, and he frowned to himself.

He had hoped to find them asleep. Instead, the camp was wide-awake. Sentries were stationed at various points, and the pods were clearly visible, prepared to lift off at a moment's notice. Still, Saris could only sense a taut alertness. No one knew of his presence here.

He closed his eyes and pressed against the cold stone. A few moments later he opened his eyes, smiling. He slipped like a shadow down into the encampment, moving softly toward the nearest pod. His salvation was inside, sleeping. Again, he tried to sense fear or anger; nothing.

Saris sidled up against the dark-colored, metallic pod and pressed long, thin fingers against it. He willed it to open to him, and it did, with only a soft hiss. Flattening himself against the metal, he waited for signs that the sound had been heard. Nothing.

Carefully, he moved inside. It was dark in this area, lit only by the small, colored lights of various instrument panels. He let his eyes grow accustomed to the dimness.

The little heir was lying on his stomach, covered by a blanket. His body rose and fell, and his eyes were shut. Sound asleep. Saris couldn't help himself. He bent closer and whispered, "Greetings, Your Royal Highness."

As gently as he could, he slipped his hands beneath the newborn's tiny body. The baby—David—stirred, and his eyes flew wide. He stared at Saris and a tiny squeak emerged from his toothless mouth. At once, Saris slipped a hand beneath David's head and sent a message of sleep. To his surprise, the infant fought him for a few seconds, then surrendered. His body went limp, and Saris turned to leave.

"Rita, is that—*hold it!*"

Saris whirled. Faster than the dark-haired woman pointing the arbus at him could react, he lifted a hand, concentrated hard, and sent her sprawling with the power of his thoughts. She hit the bulkhead hard, but surprised him by managing to get to her hands and knees. He narrowed his eyes and focused all his energy into the command. The woman groaned. Her eyes rolled up in her head, and she crumpled to the floor.

Saris staggered back, gasping. He felt exhausted by the effort, but rallied himself. The Oosha and his people were not fools. Sooner or later—probably sooner—they would miss their prince, then whatever lead he had on them would not be sufficient.

He turned and fled, clutching the baby close.

Fear spurted through Rita as she and Rafe hastened up to the pod. Rafe, his temple piece securely on his head, pressed the controls, and the door irised open.

Rita's knees buckled. Shalli lay sprawled on the floor, still clutching her arbus. The bed where David had been was empty. She tried to breathe, found she couldn't, and leaned up against the bulkhead.

David. Cale's child. Her child. Gone.

Rafe had gone to Shalli and was shaking her. She moaned, clutching her head, but sat up. "He took David . . ." she said. "I tried to stop him. . . ."

"Was it anyone we know?" Rafe demanded.

"No. Couldn't pass for a human—"

"Oh, God," breathed Rita. Suddenly she was back in her old apartment, staring down the barrel of a gun at an alien man who smirked at her even as he raised his hands in compliance. "It's him. He's found us again."

Rafe knew what she meant, and his face hardened

even further. "Shalli, listen to me. Prepare for evacuation. Now. Get our people out of here before this—this intruder has a chance to come back with reinforcements. I'm going after David."

"But what about Cale—"

"We'll wait for him. We found you once, we'll contact you again. The main thing is that you get to safety. Rita, you go with Shalli."

She found the strength to shake her head. "No. He's my son. I'm going after him."

Rafe's brows drew together in a frown. "You just had a baby. You're in no condition—"

But the strength in her was growing, flowing through her like a volcano about to erupt. Weakness disappeared. She straightened and marched to the weapons cabinet and began seizing ammunition, arbuses and her own small, familiar handgun. "Some bastard took my child," she said in a deep, angry voice. "I'm going to find him."

"Rita—"

"Rafe, that's enough!" She whirled on him, the anger pulsing through her body. She wondered if she was glowing with it. "You swore fealty to me, damn it, and you will not question the orders of your Ooshala. Come on. We know he didn't arrive by ship—we'd have spotted him. He must have used a car or a truck. We might still be able to catch him." She turned and marched down the ramp, seizing her parka and shrugging into it. Her hair was wild and starting to get damp from snowflakes.

Rafe did not follow. She turned and impaled him with her gaze. "Are you coming or do I go without you?"

"On my way," growled Rafe. *"Majesty."*

"Three birds with one stone," said Agent Kelly O'Connell. "Dr. Rainsinger, Agent Alexander, and the ringleader of the Independent Navajo Nation movement. I'd call it a good night."

Eddie stared at her and wondered how he'd ever thought her beautiful. Her small stature seemed squat instead of petite, as if it housed something too large and malevolent to be comfortably contained in so small a place. Her beauty was an obscenity, the full lips twisted in a sneer.

"You," she said, addressing Cale, "are the one thing in this equation that I can't figure out."

"It's easy," said Drake. "He's Tyrusian. One of the jumpers the Dragit mentioned."

"You're right," said O'Connell. "I'll be damned."

"I am not just any Tyrusian," said Cale, drawing himself up to his full height. "I am your rightful king, Elliott Drake. I survived the treachery planned against me, and I will not stand by and permit you to murder innocents!"

"Save it," snarled O'Connell, and swiveled the gun toward Cale. A shot rang out. Eddie and Alana screamed.

A large red stain appeared in the front of O'Connell's blouse. The gun fell from nerveless fingers as she stared, shocked, at the spreading redness on her chest. She crumpled to the floor, like a marionette whose strings had been cut. In the doorway, leaning heavily on the frame for support, stood Agent Tom Alexander.

Drake spun around, his arbus pointed at Alexander, but Cale was faster. He lifted his Exotar-clad hand and the arbus began to melt in Drake's grasp. The Tyrusian doctor shrieked in agony as the hot metal fused to his skin. Then Alana was there, leaping over the desk and uttering a war cry in Navajo. She spun and kicked Drake on the side of his head and punched him as he went down. He landed hard. She lifted a booted foot and was about to bring it down on his neck when Cale's cry stopped her.

"Alana, no! You'll be just like them!"

She stumbled a little, turning to stare at him. Her eyes flashed righteous anger and her chest heaved with emotion. "He tried to massacre hundreds of my people, Cale!" she wailed. "Would you have me spare him?"

"He has nowhere to go," said Cale, speaking gently and moving slowly toward her. "Eddie has pulled his teeth. Your people will recover, and he will pay for his crimes. Agent Alexander will see to that."

"You bet I will," croaked Alexander.

Tears of anger sprang to Alana's beautiful eyes. She said something harsh and biting in Navajo, then spit on the limp form and stepped away.

Alexander moved forward as if to pick up Drake's body. Alana tripped him and brought her interlaced fingers down on the back of his head. Again, the agent went unconscious.

Cale and Eddie stared at her. "He wouldn't let us take anything," she explained, "not even now."

They tied Drake's arms and legs with telephone cord and left him sprawled next to the FBI agent with whom he had allied. Alana picked up O'Connell's gun, hesitating only a little at taking the weapon from the dead fingers. She also retrieved Alexander's second gun. The man had come prepared. Cale volunteered to sit in the back of the truck so that they could transport the unconscious Alexander inside the cab.

"Time to pay the piper," said Eddie, as they sped off into the snowy night.

Drake opened his eyes and stared into the dead face of Kelly O'Connell. He gasped and tried to bolt upright, only to find himself hampered by something tied around his legs and wrists. His hand hurt terribly. Through a red haze of pain, he recalled what had happened. He had to get out of here, contact a rescue ship. He had to get to his office. They hadn't removed his temple piece—in too much of a hurry, the fools—and now he tried to calm his fear and concentrate on freeing himself.

Drake was not used to failure—especially not failure on so spectacular a scale. One curious human had ruined Operation Hamstring. They would have to move the whole facility now and start all over again. Perhaps in one of the small African villages he had visited in earlier years.

The phone cord snapped and he was free. He sat up slowly. Pain. He was not used to pain. First the headache and nausea, and now the pain of an attack. Pain was why he and O'Connell had even come to the clinic tonight. Drake had started getting headaches yesterday, followed by fever and nausea.

He never got sick.

He hoped it was something he had eaten. Certainly, the vile stuff humans choked down as "food" left much to be desired by the Tyrusian palate. Or, it could be a human disease such as the flu or the ubiquitous "cold." But he had to make sure.

What it definitely was not was the modified Marburg virus. Hundreds of tests and many years had gone into making certain that there was no possible way for Tyrusians to become infected with the virus. He himself had overseen these tests.

Wincing with pain, he limped into his office and flicked on a switch. The light seemed to slice through his head like a blade. He blinked, getting used to it, and pressed a button underneath his desk. The hidden door opened, and he placed his hand on the com orb. He had to notify the Dragit of the breach in security. They were all at risk now, and—

Drake frowned. The com orb just sat there, like an ordinary piece of crystal. Something was blocking his transmission. He swore angrily, then closed the door. He'd try again later. His fingers found and pressed a second button. The left wall of his office slid away, revealing a small but effective lab recessed into a false wall.

Drake eased himself into the chair and drew a sample of his blood. It was awkward, as his right hand was a useless amalgamation of charred flesh and metal. He placed the blood in the small cup that served as a sample holder for the small, complex machine that was the Tyrusian microscope. Deftly, Drake added a drop of a fluid, then peered into the microscope.

Before him, he saw his own cells, a landscape of hills and valleys. "Zoom in," he instructed, and the microscope did. "Search for anything unusual." He experienced a brief, startling bout of vertigo as the scope moved swiftly over the cell's landscape, then paused.

Before him, twining languorously, was something that reminded him of a fishhook—or the tendrils of the aquatic *thiji* plant.

Marburg.

"No," he breathed. "It's not possible. . . ." Frantically, he located a second cell. This one was crowded with the virus that had become so familiar to him since he first encountered it in 1967. A third cell was caked with crystals, chock-full of disease.

The virus had mutated, and Drake was infected.

A peculiar calm descended on him. He knew what he had to do.

Over the next few hours, Drake worked with an energy he had not known he possessed, despite the increasing lethargy and keen pain he was experiencing. First, he tried to reach the Dragit again, and this time when he failed to get through he didn't swear. He whimpered. He methodically scrubbed down every inch of the clinic, going through all of the bleach containers on site. He gathered all the files that pertained to the operation—hundreds of them—and took them into his office. He went to his car and siphoned the gas from the fuel tank into the coffeepot. Finally, he dragged the body of Kelly O'Connell into the room with him.

He took the coat rack that stood by the door, hefted it to test the weight, and nodded. He began by smashing his computer, the com orb, and all hints of Tyrusian technology. Satisfied with his handiwork, Drake turned toward the final stage of this particular operation. He carefully doused the body, the papers, and what remained of the telltale Tyrusian equipment with the gasoline, saving some to sprinkle on himself.

"For Tyrus," he whispered, and struck a match.

CHAPTER NINETEEN

• • •

January 14, 1982
The Navajo Reservation

The Tyrusian kidnapper had at least several minutes' lead on them, but the snow was kind—it made certain that Rita and Rafe had a clear trail to follow. They had another advantage. The kidnapper was driving a police car, while they had a truck with four-wheel drive.

Rita drove like a madwoman. Snow sprayed up and hit the windshield as they bounced along, following the trail of the stolen Navajo police vehicle that stayed just beyond their field of vision. Rafe wore his temple piece and rolled down the passenger-side window. He leaned out, an arbus in each hand, ignoring the snow that tried to blind him.

"What are you doing?" demanded Rita.

"What's it look like? Trying to get a clear shot the minute I can see it!" he yelled back.

"David's in there!" she cried, frightened.

"I know what I'm doing," he answered. "I'm aiming for the tires. They're not going to crash into anything—the snow will protect the car. Wait a minute—I can see it now!" he yelled back to Rita.

She didn't reply, concentrating on driving. She didn't care about her personal safety, or that of Rafe, but if their truck overturned, they'd lose their quarry. And that was unacceptable.

David. My little boy.

He had been named for her dead father; a way of somehow keeping Dad alive through his grandson. But that grandson was in danger. God knew what the kidnapper had planned for him. Unbidden, an image of the tiny infant's bright eyes fastened intently on her face surfaced in Rita's mind. She banished it, for the image brought tears to her eyes. And if she wept, she couldn't see the road clearly.

Rafe began firing. The light from the arbus blast lit up the snowy road, and for an instant even Rita could see the car up ahead. The driver didn't return fire. He just kept going.

That bothered Rita. Why wasn't he attacking them, or at least trying to defend himself? Perhaps because he had his hands full with trying to drive and manage a newborn.

"Where does he think he can go?" she yelled to Rafe. He'd tossed the arbus back into the car and was using a semiautomatic.

"I've no—" Rafe fell silent.

Rita saw it, too. It came to life like an awakening monster. First, there was nothing to see, and then slowly the image began to form, a solid darkness against the night gray sky. Lights flickered on, and, even as she watched, a ladder of light descended from the ship that had only seconds before been hidden from them. This was where the kidnapper was headed—back to his ship.

With David.

"No!" screamed Rita, and stepped on the pedal. The truck surged forward. Rafe lost his balance and almost fell out of the window. The truck began to fishtail, and slid to a halt, embedded in a thick bank of snow.

Rita was out almost before they came to a stop. She

didn't feel the cold. Dimly, she was aware of a deep pain in her abdomen, but she ignored it. She slogged through the snow, cursing its depth, her awkwardness, her heart crying silently *David!* In front of her, the police car had also madly skidded to a halt. Its flashing colored lights played eerily over the snow as the driver got out.

Time seemed to slow as he turned to look at them. Rita was plunged back in time to that awful moment where she had leveled the gun in the intruder's face. Their eyes locked then and did again. The look of malevolent triumph on that nonhuman face made her sob aloud. In his arms, he clutched a small bundle. David.

The Tyrusian turned and began to scramble up the light-ramp. Without thinking, Rita tore off after him. Rafe ran beside her. He made no attempt to halt her, wasting precious moments in argument, and for that she was grateful.

The ship was beginning to lift off. The light ladder slid slowly up into the vessel's belly. Crying incoherently, Rita launched herself at the disappearing ladder and felt something tear inside her.

She caught the last rung of the light-ramp. It felt cool to the touch, but distinctly unlike metal. She couldn't hold on. Her hands were slippery with sweat and yet her fingers were numb at the same time. Desperately she struggled to reach upward, grab the second rung—

—and felt Rafe behind her, pushing her up so that she seized the fifth rung and found footing as well. Rita scrambled upward as fast as she could, the weapons slung about her shoulders impeding her progress. Behind her, she heard Rafe grunting as he, too, attempted to climb.

Craning her neck, she saw figures silhouetted against the light coming from inside the vessel. Anger gave her strength. Why didn't they just pick her and

Rafe off right now? Because they were toying with her. She heard orders given in Tyrusian and wished desperately she knew the language.

Grimly, she kept moving upward. If this was the way she would die, then so be it. Better than having to tell Cale and watch his face, knowing she had not done everything she could to rescue her child.

Suddenly she heard a high, searing noise, and the ship rocked violently. Rita fell, holding on by a single hand, and flailed until she again was securely on the light-ramp. What the hell—

The sound came again, and again the ship rolled and heaved, but this time Rita was prepared for it and clung for dear life. The ladder was almost up to the top. She risked a glance up and saw that the shadowy figures had disappeared. Bright, multicolored lights danced about her. She couldn't help it—she turned her head to see what was going on.

Above the Tyrusian's ship hovered two smaller vessels. Rita recognized them—they were the Tyrusian escape pods that had become so familiar to her. They were firing furiously, in an effort to keep the ship from lifting off.

Shalli had disobeyed orders.

Renewed by the loyalty of her friends, Rita pressed upward and flung herself onto the metal floor. She turned and reached for Rafe, who barely made it to safety before the hatch irised shut.

"Damn her," he growled. "I told Shalli to evacuate!"

Rita stumbled to her feet, angry with her body for its trembling, its injured weakness. She feared it might let her down. The lighting was dim here, only a trail of blue dots to illuminate where curving black metal wall met flat black metal floor.

Pain surged through her and, unwittingly, she clutched her abdomen. Something warm and wet was seeping between her legs. Dimly, Rita acknowledged that she was hemorrhaging, but that wasn't important now.

"Where's David? Can you sense him?"

"No," replied Rafe, gasping for breath. "But it's my guess this man wants him alive. Probably as a hostage to lure Cale into surrendering."

Rita mentally called the Tyrusian several scathing names as she caught her own breath. The blood was soaking through her jeans now, but she ignored it. Time enough to rest and heal when they had David back—and if they failed, then Rita wasn't sure she even wanted to live.

She turned to look at Rafe. "Do you know the layout of—" She didn't finish the sentence. Instead, she lifted the barrel of a semiautomatic and fired several rounds right above Rafe's head. Rafe didn't question—he just dived, tucked, and rolled, and came up shooting.

Six armed *ga'lim*, wearing black uniforms instead of their more familiar trappings of trench coats, fedoras, and sunglasses, fell beneath Rafe and Rita's combined gunfire. She didn't think of them as people. She couldn't.

When they lay still, Rafe glanced over at Rita. She saw surprise and appreciation on his face. "Thanks," he said roughly.

She flashed him a grin. "Come on."

They hastened through the corridors, but now whoever commanded the ship had been alerted to their presence. Alarms whooped, jangling Rita's nerves further. At one point Rita lost her footing and fell hard when there came a deep *boom* and the ship rolled. Wordlessly Rafe pulled her to her feet, almost yanking her arm out of the socket. She was grateful for the sharpness of the pain; it chased away the dull ache of her insides that was threatening to wear her down.

"Someone's coming," said Rafe. He pushed them both hard against the curving wall of the corridor and

fired shots in the direction of the sound of running
feet. Rita glanced back down the way they had come
and saw shadows. Up came the semiautomatic and she
began firing. Screams and grunts told her she'd hit her
targets. There was silence. Then again the ship rolled,
like an injured whale flailing from a harpoon, and Rita
bit her lip as she tried to keep her footing.

She pushed past Rafe and kept going. The corridor
began to slope upward, and her hopes rose with each
step. Again and again, guards tried to surprise them,
but luck—and skill—were with them. Rita's small size
also helped, making her a harder target to hit.

The corridor dead-ended. Rita leaned against the wall,
gasping. She unzipped her parka and tore it off. Sweat
poured from her. Behind her, Rafe came to a halt and
glanced around. "Up there," he said. She scarcely had
time to grab a weapon—her small, familiar handgun—
before he had hoisted her up toward a narrow tube.
A light-ladder provided the only illumination.

"Keep going. If I'm right, this should take you to
the bridge. He's probably there."

"Aren't you—" Rita's voice sounded thin and tinny
in the enclosed space.

Rafe didn't answer. She heard gunfire and the
shriek of arbuses. He was cornered. She blinked back
angry tears. Rafe. He'd be slaughtered, caught like
that—

No. If anyone could defend himself in a tight spot,
it was Rafe. He'd follow her if he got a chance, she
knew it. She sucked in a breath and began to climb,
hand over hand, up into the dimness.

She heard voices, all speaking in Tyrusian. One of
them rang clear and commanding. Rita recognized it
as that of the man who had kidnapped her child. Her
torn shoulder screamed in protest, her abdomen ached
as the hemorrhaging continued, but she began to climb
even faster.

And then a sound issued forth that sliced her heart.

A high, frightened wail, the sound of an infant in pain and terror. *David!*

He was only a day old, but in that time, he had never cried. He'd never had to. A few unhappy grunts and the adult Tyrusians would sense immediately what he needed and tend to it. Rita, too, had developed a sixth sense regarding her baby, and it had been that that had alerted her to his disappearance. What she was hearing now was David's first taste of pain and fear.

"David," she whispered, her stomach twisting into a cold knot of empathy. What was he doing to David?

She didn't think to hide in the tube's entrance, survey her surroundings. She burst forth like an avenging angel, hurtling from the mouth of the tube to crouch on the deck in full sight of seven men.

Rafe had been right. Rita was now on the bridge of the ship. Out of the corner of her eye she saw an enormous view screen that comprised most of an entire wall. Smaller screens showed different images. Some of the people on the bridge completely ignored her, far too engrossed in defending themselves against Shalli and her people to worry about a lone *Erdlufa* trespassing on their vessel. But others whirled, training their weapons on her. In the center stood the kidnapper, and in his hands, his face beet red and open-mouthed, was David. There was an arbus an inch away from David's small face.

"Put him down!" demanded Rita. Her voice was hoarse, and her own weapon pointed right at the kidnapper's ugly face.

The man raised an eyebrow and began to laugh. "Rita Carter," he said, "so we meet again. Allow me to introduce myself. I am Saris Krai, personal valet to the ruler of Tyrus. I owe you a debt, for bringing this brat into the world. He will buy me high favor in the Dragit's eyes. Imagine, the heir of Cale-Oosha! Hush, little one."

Absently he juggled the baby in his arms, but David was having none of it. Saris Krai clearly terrified him. With each cry, Rita's heart broke a little more.

She heard movement in the tunnel. Either it was Rafe, coming to her aid, or it was more of Saris's men. She stared at him, the hate coursing through her veins.

"Careful, my dear," said Saris. "Put your weapon down and surrender. You're not quite the superb bargaining chip that your husband is, but perhaps you'll help me trap the Oosha."

Rita choked on her words. The gun never wavered in her grasp.

"If you don't cooperate"—the mellifluous voice turned harsh—"then I will kill the boy. I need him as proof of Cale's existence, and a few simple tests from tissue samples will suffice. He's just as good to me dead as alive."

The horror of it crashed over her in a cold wave. He was serious. He *didn't* need David alive. And the arbus was pressed to her baby's soft flesh—the flesh that until now had only known softness and tenderness—

Logic struggled to override terror. She knew a little about how the arbuses worked. Cale and Rafe had had to reconfigure the weapons so that Rita, who didn't have the mental powers of a Tyrusian, could operate them.

It would take a mental command for Saris to be able to fire on David. That meant at least a split second of thought. She narrowed her eyes. David's cries of pain and fear kept assaulting her ears.

"You made him *cry,* you bastard," she snarled, and pulled the trigger.

Saris's head exploded, and the body began to topple. All around Rita, people sprang into action. She heard Tyrusian war cries, and shrieks of pain, and the explosion of guns and arbuses. But it was as if her head was wrapped in cotton. The sounds were faint and muffled, and meant nothing at all to her. Out of the corner of her eye she saw Rafe leap out of the tunnel, firing. An arbus blast whizzed past her, singeing her back with white-hot agony.

She moved, and it was as if she were running through molasses. Her legs covered the distance to the falling body of Saris Kari, valet to the Dragit, and her arms reached out to her baby as he hurtled through the air—

She caught him and pulled him close to her breasts, sheltering him as best she could, as she crashed into a control panel. Sparks flew, she felt a hot burning sensation, then she knew no more.

CHAPTER TWENTY

• • •

January 15, 1982
Turquoise Mesa

"Welcome back, *Kia*."

Slowly Rita opened her eyes. She smiled tiredly at the sight of her husband's face. He bent and kissed her forehead.

"How do you feel?"

"Like I've been run over by a truck." She wasn't exaggerating. She was exhausted, utterly drained. There was an ache in her arm, and it was an effort for her to move her head and see that she was hooked up to a slowly dripping IV. Rita frowned. Why was she so tried? She—

"David!" she shrieked, bolting upright.

"He's fine, he's fine, he's right here," soothed Cale. Rafe stepped forward and handed the small bundle to Rita. Sobbing, she reached out for him. Pulling away the blanket, she saw the large dark eyes and rosebud mouth of her infant.

"He took him," she said, choking on the words. She lifted tear-filled eyes to her husband. "He took him and he made him cry, he scared him so badly. . . ."

"And you saved him," said Cale, pride in his voice. "Rafe told me all about it." Then, gently, "Rafe has not left your side for a moment since you became unconscious."

"Rafe?" The dreadful fear started to subside as the baby began to squirm in her arms. "Thank you, Rafe." She reached out a hand to him. To her astonishment, he clasped it in both of his and went down on one knee.

"I must beg your forgiveness," Rafe said. "My foolishness put us all in danger."

She frowned. "I don't understand. . . ."

"My lady, I underestimated you. From the very beginning until last night, when it was almost too late. I feared you would put Cale at risk, somehow hurt his chances for reclaiming the throne. I thought that if the time came for action, that you would not be ready—or willing—to do what was necessary. Last night, you proved me wrong. You saved David's life—and mine, and you never hesitated to do what you had to do. When you and Cale wed, I did my duty and swore fealty to my Ooshala. Now, I swear it to Rita Carter. You are a devoted mother, a worthy wife and a noble queen—and one hell of a good shot," he added, lightening the solemnity of his statement. Then he sobered. "I hope that if you grant your forgiveness, I may in the future prove more worthy of your trust."

"Rafe," and she squeezed his hand, "there's nothing to forgive. I don't blame you. If you hadn't been with me last night, David would be halfway to Tyrus by now, and we'd all probably be dead. Now, tell me what's happened."

"Shalli and the others kept Krai's ship from departing long enough for us to board and find David," said Rafe. "After you killed Krai, his men panicked. Many died fighting, but others fled in small escape vessels. Kari's ship is now ours."

Shalli entered the pod. "Cale, we're about ready—Rita! You're awake!" Shalli hastened to Rita's side, smiling broadly. "I'm so glad you're going to be all right. We're all so proud of you!"

"You disobeyed orders," said Rita. "Thanks."

Shalli squeezed her hand, straightened, and turned to Cale. "The ships are ready to depart."

"Wait a minute," said Rita, "what's going on?"

"Shalli and the others are taking Krai's ship and one of the pods and heading back to Tyrusian space," said Cale. "I am hopeful that we will be able to rally others to our cause. I can do little from here, and it's too risky for me to go myself until we know for certain there is support. You, Rafe, and I will go—" He paused, looking uncertain. "Somewhere. We can no longer stay here."

"Massachusetts," said Rita slowly. "I have a house in Glenport, Massachusetts. My mother left it to me. There's also several acres on an uninhabited island called . . ." She racked her brain. Thoughts were coming sluggishly today. "Maple Island. That's it."

"Is Massachusetts far from here?" asked Cale. "The more distance we can put between ourselves and Charles Air Force Base, the safer we will be."

"It's almost as far away as you can get and still be in the country," said Rita. David cooed and squirmed, and she gave him her index finger to suck on. "You've only seen our deserts, Cale. I think you'll love the ocean."

"Very well, then. Shalli, when you return, look for us in Massachusetts." His smiled faded, and he hugged her tightly. He said something in Tyrusian, and she looked surprised.

"You honor him, Majesty. Rita, may I hold the heir for a moment?" Puzzled, Rita nodded and gave the precious bundle to her friend. Gently, Shalli pulled back the blanket and gazed deeply into David's eyes. Her pupil dilated, and David's responded immediately. Their eyes locked for a long moment, then Shalli handed the child back to his mother. Her own eyes were bright with tears.

"What did you do?" asked Rita.

Shalli wiped at her face and smiled, though her lips quivered. "Cale wanted me to give David a memory of Jaran, so that one day David would know of the man who gave his life for his father." She swallowed hard. "I had better leave. Farewell, Rafe, Rita. We will meet again."

The excitement and emotion was tiring Rita. She lay back on the pillow, cradling David. "What a lucky baby. So many people love you."

"You should rest, *Kia*," said Cale, pulling the blanket around her and gently taking David. She didn't argue. Her eyelids were heavy.

"What happened with you and Eddie and Alana?" she asked sleepily.

"I will tell you the whole story later. For now, I will say that we returned after Rafe brought you back last night. Eddie treated you, then took blood samples from all of us. I do not know for certain, but I believe the danger is over. Now rest, my love. Rest."

Eddie was bone-weary. He'd only been able to snatch a couple of hours of sleep over the last two days, and it was starting to show. The adrenaline that had propelled him was beginning to ebb, and not even Hosteen Yazzie's mule-kick-strong coffee was doing the trick anymore.

They had returned just before dawn with an armload of vials filled with Tyrusian blood. He was still wanted for the murder of Bill Tsosie, so he had been forced to separate the golden serum from the red blood cells the old-fashioned way—he'd put the samples in the freezer and waited for them to separate. Alana and Hosteen Yazzie were quick learners, and he soon had them helping. Now, they were just about ready to go. The sheet that Eddie had managed to seize at the clinic had the addresses of all the patients who had received the deadly shots. Eddie and Alana would simply make house calls. They had to—Eddie couldn't operate from a hospital until his name was cleared.

They were carefully packing the vials of life-giving serum when they heard the car approach. They tensed. Yazzie rose. "I will see who it is. Eddie—stay here."

As if he had a choice. The hogan was practically bare. There was, literally, no place to hide. Eddie sat on the bed, his heart pounding. "I can't go to jail," he whispered. "I've got to give those people the shots."

"I know," Alana whispered back. She reached for Agent O'Connell's gun with one hand and Eddie's shoulder with the other. "Don't worry. I won't let anyone take you."

"Alana—!"

"Shhh," she hissed. "Listen."

Someone was talking to Hosteen Yazzie. Eddie strained to listen and his heart sank. Agent Alexander. He closed his eyes in misery.

"I know he's here. Look, I have some good news for him. Please let me talk to him—and to Alana."

"My daughter is out tending the sheep, and—"

Alexander opened the door. Alana cocked the gun and aimed it straight at his chest. Alexander slowly raised his arms.

"Oh, good. You did pick it up. I'll need the gun, Alana. It will help prove Eddie's innocence." He glanced at Eddie and smiled a little. "Tending the sheep, huh?"

"Baaaaaa," said Eddie. Alana didn't budge. Alexander sighed.

"I have photographs that clearly show that Eddie couldn't have killed Tsosie," he said. "Plus, if I have O'Connell's gun, I can prove that it was the one used in committing the crime."

She hesitated, then rose and handed it to him.

"Thanks," he said, taking it with a handkerchief. "And mine, too, please?" Silently, she reached beneath the pillow and handed the agent his own gun. "Both of them?" Frowning, Alana yielded the third and final weapon. "Your prints on O'Connell's gun will be hard to explain, but we can get rid of those."

"Destroying evidence?" asked Eddie.

"Only the evidence that might confuse people," said Alexander. "My pardon for barging in, Hosteen Yazzie. But I can help all of you if you'll listen to me and do what I say."

"You want some coffee?" As usual, nothing seemed to unsettle the venerable *haatalii*.

"No, thanks. All right," said Alexander, sitting cross-legged on the floor. "Let me bring you up to speed. Last night, the Drake Clinic was burned to the ground. The bodies of two people we believe to be O'Connell and Drake were found. We'll need to wait for a positive ID of course, but I'm pretty sure it's them." His bright eyes darted from Eddie to Alana. "I've canceled the USAMRIID team. All the evidence was destroyed in the fire, and the threat is gone. Isn't it, Dr. Rainsinger?"

"Yes indeed," said Eddie, catching on. "There's no need for USAMRIID to get involved in this." He sat on the bed with a boxful of serum vials—vials that were not in the least hidden from Agent Alexander's view.

"That's what I thought. You're merely going to quietly notify those who received the flu vaccinations that the batch was ineffective and give them a second shot. Correct?"

"Absolutely." Eddie was getting into this.

"Now, wait a minute," interrupted Alana. "Drake deliberately shot seven hundred people full of a deadly virus! You can't just pretend—"

"Yes, I can. And so will you, if you don't want to spend the next few years behind bars along with every other member of the Independent Navajo Nation. I can connect I.N.N. with several deaths."

"But—That's not true! We never hurt anyone!" protested Alana. "This is blackmail!"

"Yes, it is. But I'll do what I have to." Alexander's eyes were cold and hard. "Dr. Rainsinger has developed a cure. The bodies of those who have already died, and thank God there are only a handful, will be . . . taken care of. Drake is dead and his lab destroyed. There's no need for a scandal or a panic."

"It's a lie!"

"Sometimes," said Alexander in perfect Navajo, "lies are necessary." Alana stared at him in utter shock. Eddie smothered a grin. "I think we finally understand each other," said Alexander, and rose.

"By the way," he said to Eddie, "is it possible to have hallucinations from a blow to the head?"

"Short-term memory loss isn't uncommon," said Eddie. That much was the truth. "What do you mean?"

"I thought, when your friend Cale attacked me, that I saw—and later, Drake's gun—no, it couldn't be."

"I'm sure your mind is simply trying to fill in the gaps with your imagination," lied Eddie. "You really shouldn't be out of the hospital this soon, you know."

Alexander grinned and went to the door. "Go ahead and distribute the vaccinations, Eddie. Everything will be straightened out by the time you're done."

"Wait a minute," said Eddie, the hairs on the back of his neck prickling. "How is that possible? I'm not a suspect, but I am a witness. Surely I'll have to go to the police and give a statement or something."

"No." Alexander shook his blond head, a slight smile curving his lips. "That won't be necessary."

Another chill. "You're not really with the FBI, are you?" asked Eddie.

The smile widened. "Let's put it this way, Dr. Rain-

singer. I *am* one of the good guys. And that's all you
need to know."

January 18, 1982
Turquoise Mesa

"Are you certain Agent Alexander does not suspect?" asked Cale as Eddie helped him load the truck.

"Suspect? Oh, yeah. Know? No, he's got no proof.
The evidence of the tracking devices was destroyed in
the fire, and I think he bought my story about the
hallucinations."

"Regardless, it becomes increasingly clear that our
decision to leave was the correct one," said Cale.
"Though we will miss you—and you, Alana."

"Where will you go?" asked Alana. She was carrying David, and the infant seemed fascinated by the
eagle feather plaited into her long black hair. Rita
watched, grinning. She thought that Alana looked just
a little uncomfortable with the idea of motherhood.

"I think it's best that you don't know," said Rafe,
swinging a large tarp over the bed of the truck. "The
less you know, the safer you'll be."

"I am sick to death of this," snarled Alana. David
hiccoughed unhappily at the tension he was sensing
from the Navajo woman, and Rita smoothly stepped
in to take her child. "Being told what's best for me."

"Alexander was right, though he did not realize just
how right," said Cale. "Operation Hamstring was a
failure for the Dragit. He is a clever man and a patient
one. He will not try something like this again soon,
and he will most certainly not attempt it twice on the
Dineh. Now, he believes no one knows—that the virus
simply was not as virulent as he was told. In that lies
the safety of your people. If you spoke up—revealed
that you knew about this—it would alert him. You'd

be a threat. You and your people would be brutally silenced. As it is, you are safe."

Alana frowned and kicked at a stone with her boot. "When you put it that way, I guess I have to agree with you."

"We're ready, Cale," said Rafe. The young king nodded.

"Eddie, Alana—I have a present for you," he said. From his pocket he produced a smooth crystal sphere that Rita recognized. She was confused. What was Cale doing giving them that? They weren't Tyrusians, they couldn't use it. "We call this a com orb," he explained, reaching for Eddie's hand. "Tyrusians have advanced mental capabilities. With a thought, we can communicate with others at any distance through this orb." He took Alana's hand and folded it over the crystal, so that both of them were holding it.

"You and the rest of your people who were injected with the Tyrusian serum now have our blood inside you. Perhaps this will mean nothing; perhaps much. It could be that someday, your children will be able to use this orb."

Rita hid a smile in David's soft hair as the two Navajos exchanged shy, uncomfortable glances. It was clear they cared for each other. She only hoped they'd eventually realize it themselves.

"Thank you, Cale," said Alana. "We will take good care of this." She removed her hand and reached to touch her hair. "Rita, I have something for you."

"For me?" Rita was surprised. They'd come a long way, she and Alana, from their first meeting, when Alana had pressed a cold knife to Rita's throat.

"The eagle feather. It is a warrior's badge. Here." Her face was solemn. "You earned it when you faced the kidnapper to rescue your son."

"Oh, Alana," said Rita, deeply moved. "Thank you, but I can't take it. I'm not an Indian. It's not legal for me to have an eagle feather."

"Besides," said Cale, taking the feather and affectionately rebraiding it into Alana's hair, "you still need this. You are a warrior, though your enemy is different now. Someday, perhaps many years from now, I or my son may need your help in fighting those who would destroy your world. We will need the courage of a warrior. And," he added, turning to shake Eddie's hand, "the wisdom of a healer."

Alana's eyes were bright. She swallowed hard. "The Navajo word for human being translates literally into English as 'the one that has five fingers.'" She held up her own hand, splaying her five fingers. Cale hesitated, then placed his hand on hers. Their ten fingers intertwined—the dark, rich hue of Alana's strong fingers with the moon-pale ones of Cale-Oosha. It was a sign of unity between peoples that made tears spring to Rita's eyes.

Then, abruptly, Alana freed her hand, turned, and marched back to her truck. Eddie followed, turning and waving good-bye. There was the sound of slamming doors, then the revving of the ignition.

"We had best be on our way, too," said Rafe. Rita nodded. The single remaining pod, piloted by the dour Baris, had already gone ahead to scout out Maple Island. If all went well, they would establish a smaller base underground, disguised by a vacation house—shack, probably—where they would "fish."

It was time to go. Rita felt a tug of sorrow. David was born here; they had fought a brave fight here against Tyrusian evil—and won. She'd finally gotten used to the cave and the pods and thought of this place as "home."

She wondered how many more times they would be forced to run—she, Cale, Rafe, and little David. If they would live their lives in fear of discovery. If they would ever truly find peace.

"Rita?" Cale had stepped beside her, and now

slipped an arm around her shoulders. Rita's apprehension fled before the joy that always filled her in his presence. She smiled up at him through her tears. He touched her cheek.

"I will not leave you. I shall not fail you," he whispered, finally putting into words the promise that Rita had sensed all along. Her throat closed up.

Fail her? Never. But leave her? Who could say? If Shalli came back into their lives one day with the word that a fleet stood ready for him to lead them, she knew Cale would not bring his wife and child into the conflict. He would have to leave, or else they would have failed. The Dragit would have won, and Earth would be destroyed.

She reached and clutched his hand, hard.

"*Kia?* What is it?"

"Show it to me again," she asked.

He chuckled, and obliged. Lifting a finger, he pointed to a single star amidst the billions that swirled in the night sky. "There it is. That's the sun Tyrus circles. You really should learn to find it on your own, *Kia.*"

"I know." She lifted David up, bringing him as close to the heavens as her limited reach could take him. "There it is, David! There's your other home. There's where your father came from, and where someday you will rule as you were born to do!"

David's face was bathed in moonlight and starlight. He kicked and squealed happily. To the uninitiated, he looked like every other human baby, but Rita saw the Tyrusian traits emerging daily in her son. She loved him so much, this living symbol of human and Tyrusian, of all that one day could be if her dream ever came true.

"Let's go," she said, turning to the truck. Cale opened the door for her.

The snow gleamed white before them. Ahead lay

Glenport, Massachusetts—a new chapter in their lives together. Someday, she knew, Cale would leave.

But until then, he belonged utterly to her and David, and they to him. It would suffice.

The adventure was just beginning.

ABOUT THE
AUTHOR

• • •

Christie Golden is the author of ten novels and over
a dozen short stories. Her credits include the noveliza-
tion of *Invasion America*, three *Star Trek: Voyager*
novels, *The Murdered Sun Marooned*, and *Seven of
Nine* as well as two original fantasy novels, *Instrument
of Fate* and *King's Man & Thief*.

Golden lives in Colorado with her husband and two
cats. Readers are invited to visit her web site at:
www.sff.net/people/Christie.Golden.